Dead

Cow in

Aisle

Three

H. Mel Malton

D1487309

RendezVous
Crime

Dead

Cow in

Aisle

Three

H. Mel Malton

RENDEZVOUS
PRESS
Toronto, Ontario, Canada

Text © 2001 by H. Mel Malton

Cover art: Christopher Chuckry

Le Conseil des Arts du Canada depuis 1957 | The Canada Council for the Arts since 1957

We gratefully acknowledge the support of the Canada Council for the Arts for our publishing program.

Napoleon Publishing/RendezVous Press
Toronto, Ontario, Canada

Printed in Canada

05 04 03 02 01   5 4 3 2 1

National Library of Canada Cataloguing in Publication Data

H. Mel Malton, date—
    Dead cow in aisle three: a Polly Deacon murder mystery

ISBN 0-929141-82-2

I. Title.

PS8576.A5362D42 2001   C813'.54   C2001-901969-6
PR9199.3.M3462D42 2001

Acknowledgements

This book is dedicated to my dear aunt, Mary Elizabeth Tanton, who died in 2000. She would have liked this one the best and would have laughed like a drain at the LSJ bits.

Many kind thanks to Teri Souter and Cate Elliot for sage advice and to Pat Misek, Lynn Uzans and Kareen Burns for moral support and a firecracker up the wahzoo at appropriate moments. I am indebted to my publisher, Sylvia McConnell, for her patience and steadfast confidence in Polly, and to my editor, Allister Thompson, who has more backbone than Becker does.

This is a work of fiction. There are no intentional references to real people, events, places or things. If some things seem familiar to those living in the Muskoka area, well that's just coincidental, eh?

One

There's bargains here for everyone—
At Kountry Pantree, saving's fun!
—An advertisement in the *Laingford Gazette*

You're a traitor, and you should be shot," Aunt
Susan said. She was sitting in the guest chair at my kitchen
table, shelling peanuts and swigging beer out of a bottle.

"I'm just doing a job, Susan," I said. "The store would go
ahead anyway, whether I'm involved or not. I have to eat, you
know." I was at my drawing board, preparing some sketches
for the Kountry Pantree PR committee. They'd hired me to
design and build a mascot costume for their new grocery
superstore in Laingford.

"Just doing a job—that's my point," Susan said, tossing a
couple of unshelled peanuts to my dogs, who sat begging
shamelessly at her feet. Crunch, crunch. "This thing is all
about money. No matter what one's principles might be,
everyone has their price—even my own niece."

"I'm sorry I can't afford to take a political stand with you
right now," I said. "I'll support you behind the scenes if I can,
though."

Susan snorted. "Maybe you'd be so good as to build a
mascot for the League of Social Justice, then. A pit bull would
be nice. Or an enraged bear. We're going to fight the Kountry

1

Pantree to the death, you know." She placed a peanut on the table and brought her fist down on it, hard.

Secretly, I thought that Susan's newly-formed lobby group would be better represented by a valiantly squeaking mouse. You can't halt progress when a bunch of fat-cat developers starts throwing money at Town Council.

"The League is meeting down at George's tonight, isn't it?" I said.

"Yes, and I came by to make sure that you'll be there," Susan said. "You have inside information about those sharks that will be very useful."

"I refuse to be a mole," I said. Okay, maybe I'm going overboard with the animal imagery, but that's the way it is with town planning issues. They bring out the beast in everybody. Survival of the fittest, dog eat dog, nature red in tooth and claw and all that. Grrrr.

"We won't ask you to divulge any company secrets," Susan said. "We just need names and dates and that sort of thing. We don't want to tip our hand just yet, and we decided it was better to get it from you than from the *Gazette*."

"The guy at the paper probably knows way more than I do," I said. "He's the one following the story."

Back in May, the *Laingford Gazette* had appeared on the stands with a big headline, "Council okays new Superstore." Local reaction was swift and frantic. The new store, into its third month of construction where the main road into Laingford meets the highway, was going to be huge. It wasn't so much a store as it was a shopping complex. Acres of state-of-the-art convenience, offering groceries, fresh flowers, a photo processing lab, a pharmacy, a video rental outlet, a fast food joint and, as they say, much, much more. The downtown business people were horrified.

2

"It'll kill the downtown core," they said in angry letters to the paper.

"It'll create jobs and boost the economy," its proponents countered. The arguments were academic anyway. After a dozen weeks of round-the-clock construction, the huge building was almost finished, growing like a toadstool in the muggy July air.

The publisher of the *Laingford Gazette*, Hans Whiteside, had stirred up the small town very handily with inflammatory editorials and a public poll. "What do you think of the new superstore? Fill out this ballot and drop it off at the *Gazette*." It was rumoured that Whiteside had a financial interest in the project, but he had kept the fire burning under the issue, presumably in order to make sure that everybody, for or against, kept on buying his paper. He had put his star reporter, young Calvin Grigsby, on the story, then sat back and watched the fur fly.

"Town divided on Superstore issue," the headlines went. "Kountry Pantree: Jobs, Jobs, Jobs," said one, and "Is downtown doomed?" said another.

The League for Social Justice (LSJ) was hastily formed in the weeks following the announcement. Its members, the owners of businesses threatened by the development, included a grocer, a pharmacist, a florist, a photo shop owner, a video store owner and the guy who owns the downtown pizza place.

The League was my Aunt Susan's idea. She owns a feed store in Laingford. Not that the Superstore proposed to sell agricultural supplies; Susan had been burned already by a big American farm supply company, the Agri-Am, opening up near her place on the other side of town. It had undercut her prices, poached her customers and crushed her like a potato bug. Her store was now up for sale, and her reasons for establishing the LSJ were revenge-based. As she said in a letter to the editor, "Corporate greed can devastate small business. I know first-hand. We need to join together to prevent it from happening again."

"Why don't you invite Calvin Grigsby to your meeting?" I said. "He can give you the low-down, and at the same time, you'll get some publicity."

"We don't want publicity, at least not yet," Susan said. "When we make our presentation at the next council meeting, we want it to be a surprise."

"Want what to be a surprise?" I said.

"You'll see. In the meantime, I'm relying on you to come down to the house tonight. You don't have to stay for the whole thing. In fact, I'd rather you weren't in on the strategy session. I know how good you are at keeping secrets from the authorities."

"Thanks a lot, Susan," I said. I guessed she was referring to my relationship with one of Laingford's policemen, Mark Becker. A couple of times in the past, I'd been involved in some messy situations that had required police investigation. It seemed I was always saying the wrong thing to the cops, which usually led to them arresting the wrong person. "You're not planning to do anything illegal, are you?"

"Never you mind," Susan said and drained her Kuskawa Cream Ale, depositing the empty bottle on the table with a decisive thunk. "Just be there tonight, if you please." She stood up to leave, brushing peanut shells off her green work pants. "Your puppy has just defecated under the table," she said.

"Oh, Rosie!" I said, picking up Rosencrantz and carrying her to the door. Rosie was a three-month-old yellow lab who had experienced a certain amount of stress in her first few weeks on the planet. I'd inherited her from a screwed-up actress at the end of an ill-fated puppet show I'd been working on in May. Her mistress had treated her like a human baby, carrying her everywhere wrapped in blankets. No attempt had been made to housetrain her, and she was still unclear on the concept. My other dog, Lug-nut, was doing his best to be a mentor, but he wasn't exactly police-dog material either.

"I don't know what on earth induced you to take in that creature," Susan said, as I carried Rosie to the poop-place next to the composter.

"Compassion, Susan. Your feeding her all those peanuts probably didn't help."

"Nonsense. It's fibre. Very good for dogs."

"Precisely my point," I said. Lug-nut, seizing the opportunity to provide a little canine instruction to his young housemate, watered a nearby fern, and Rosie followed suit. I administered lavish praise.

"You can bring them too, if you come," Susan said.

"Since when did I need your permission to bring my dogs to George's house?" I snapped. Susan had recently moved in with George Hoito, my farmer-landlord and good friend and, incidentally, her lover. She and her teenaged ward, Eddie Schreier, had kind of taken over his life, and I resented it.

"Touchy, touchy," Susan said. "See you at eight." She set off down the path through the woods to George's place. I watched her go, inwardly fuming. Susan had brought me up after my parents died in a car accident. We were very fond of one another, really, but this new domestic proximity wasn't working very well.

Before Susan and Eddie had moved in, I was the official farm hand, helping to take care of George's herd of dairy goats, milking them, assisting at births and doing chores around the farm. Now my position had been usurped. Eddie did most of the chores I used to do, and Susan was filling George's head with all sorts of newfangled ideas. She'd bought him a computer and was setting up a bunch of goat-husbandry programs. I knew that automatic milkers weren't very far away, and I wanted no part of it.

I'm a puppet maker by trade and don't make much money at it. The arrangement, pre-Susan, had been that I did the chores in lieu of rent. Now that my job had effectively been taken over by Eddie (who is seventeen and as strong as a horse), I felt I had to pay George something for the privilege of living in his homestead cabin. The log cabin, set on a hill overlooking the farm, is primitive, with no running water (there's a hand pump at the well), no hydro and no plumbing (outhouses are very low-maintenance). It's heated by a small wood stove, and it's perfect for someone like me, a slob who needs a lot of space. George had so far refused payment, but I didn't think he'd refuse forever. Milking machinery is expensive, and I knew perfectly well that Susan thought I shouldn't be living there for free. She was the one who had arranged for me to move into the cabin in the first place, four years ago, when I had been suffering from a bad case of city burn-out. It was supposed to be temporary, until I could find an apartment in town, but frankly, I had never bothered to look. George's place was my dream home. Perhaps Susan still believed I would one day return to the Big Smoke. It was decidedly awkward.

Now she was holding subversive political meetings in George's old farmhouse in the valley and was planning some sort of revolutionary tactic that would probably get her into trouble.

When I'd taken the Kountry Pantree job, I had thought it would signal a new, calmer period in my life. In the previous year, I'd been involved in, well, a couple of murders. That's how I'd met Becker, the cop Susan thought I couldn't keep secrets from. We'd had a sort of on-again, off-again flirtation going, and after the last mess in May (involving the theatre company I was working for) we had both worked hard to repair the damage. Now it was late July, and we were actually "seeing each other", as the saying goes.

Trust Susan to wreck it. She'd never liked Becker, and I could just imagine the triumphant look she'd give me as he was forced to haul her away from some sit-in protest in the Kountry Pantree parking lot.

"Stay, Rosie, Luggy," I said, using the hand-signal I'd learned from reading *Your Perfect Puppy*. I wanted to go clean up Rosencrantz's poop, and the book said you're not supposed to let them see you do it, or they'll treat you as a housemaid. The dogs stared at me for a moment, then bounded up the stairs ahead of me. By the time I'd gathered up paper towels, disinfectant and a spatula, the poop was gone and Luggy was licking his lips.

Fighting nausea, I went back to the drawing board.

TWO

Everything is at steak!
At Kountry Pantree, our meat's the freshest in town.
Let our experts help make your family barbecue sizzle!
This coupon entitles you to three free steaks!
—A flyer distributed with every new gas
  barbecue at the Laingford Canadian Tire

In the District of Kuskawa, true summer is a
fleeting thing. Most of June's a write-off, because the blackflies
and mosquitoes gather in thick clouds that block the sun and
drive all but the insane indoors. Before you know it, you're in
the last week of August, and you can see your breath in the
mornings again. Blammo, it's fall. The trees put on a
spectacular show of colour, delighting the tourists and
reminding the locals that there's another nine-month winter
just around the corner.

July had been unusually hot and sunny—the kind of
picture postcard weather that people around here regard with
deep suspicion.

"Another gorgeous day," we whispered to each other, as if
saying it too loudly might make it disappear. Day after day the
sun rose unencumbered, magnificent in an azure sky. We trod
the baking pavement in a daze, dodging the crowds. Summer
visitors swarmed over everything, thick as ants on a dropped

ice cream. Downtown traffic was solid from eleven in the morning until dusk, and local retailers developed goofy, banner-year grins.

The Laingford Library was an oasis in all this. Tourists tend to purchase their reading matter from bookstores and checkout displays, believing perhaps that using the library in a strange town is as unthinkable as using a stranger's toothbrush.

"Nice and quiet in here today," I said to Evan Price, the head librarian, a gaunt, melancholy man with thoughtful hair who ruled his territory with the threat of incipient tears.

"Quiet for now," Evan said. His voice sounded as if it were coming from some distance away, down a long tube. "We've got a children's entertainer coming in at four to do a concert in the boardroom. Audience participation. Lots of hand-clapping and shrieking. It'll be chaos in here in about half an hour."

"Awful for you," I said. "I won't stay long, then." I was headed for the children's area, where I was hoping to find some good source material for my drawings.

My preliminary sketches for the Kountry Pantree mascot were expected on Saturday, when the PR committee would discuss them and choose one. They wanted me to come up with a couple of different designs based on the ideas thrown around at the first meeting, a brainstorming session where its members had tossed suggestions at me for more than an hour. They'd called it a focus group and served Colombian coffee and danishes.

"I think we should have a giant moose, wearing an apron," one member had said.

"It's been done," the chair of the meeting said.

"How about a cow in an apron? We could call it Kountry Kow." (I could just hear the K in Kow—a hard, commercial, who-gives-a-crap-about-spelling kind of sound.)

"No, a beaver. A beaver in a chef's hat."

"We need a mascot that will make our customers think 'fresh' and 'healthy'. Beavers are disgusting animals that live in stagnant ponds," said the chairman, David Kane, the frontman for the new superstore. Kane was a young executive type from the city who had moved permanently into his parents' monster summer home near Laingford. He stank of money, and his teeth were too perfect to be natural. The committee had finally decided on three options; a cow, a Canada goose or a gopher.

I love the kiddie corner of the Laingford library. It's an airy, sunny space with wide gaps between the aisles, mats and cushions strewn about for serious floor-readers (a posture frowned upon in the stuffy, grown-up section) and a great collection of material.

A boy of about eight was seated on a fat red cushion on the floor right next to the "Wide World of Animals" shelf. "What are you doing in here?" he said belligerently.

"Same thing you are," I said.

He looked down at the dinosaur picture book in his lap, then back up at me. "You can't have this one," he said.

"I don't want that one," I said.

"I need this because I can't find a good Tyrannosaurus rex on the Internet, and I need one for my website," he explained, suddenly chummy. "I can scan this into the computer and then use my animation program to make its mouth move."

"Ah," I said.

"What's on your website?" he said.

"I, ummm, don't have a website," I said.

He reached into the pocket of his shorts and produced a grubby business card, which he handed to me. "I can design one for you, if you want," he said. "I don't charge much."

"I don't have a computer, either," I said, taking the card. He looked at me like I was one of the creatures in his picture book.

"How do you do e-mail, then?" he said.

"I write letters," I said. My face burned. He smiled very sweetly, shook his head and stood up. The top of his head came up to my chest.

"You need a computer if you want to be competitive," he said. "Call me when you get one, and I can help you do your website. It's not hard." He walked away, heading for the circulation desk. I looked down at the card in my hand.

"Webmaster Bryan," the card said. "For all your Internet needs." Sometimes the universe likes to remind Luddites like me that the rocket ship left a long time ago, and most of the world was on it. I sighed, pocketed the little Webmaster's card and took his place on the red cushion. I pulled *The Big Book of Animals* off the shelf and started looking for gopher pictures.

When I got back to the truck, where I'd left Luggy and Rosie in the cab (It's okay—I'd parked in the shade with the windows down), there was a note on the windshield, under the wiper.

"Polly," it said, "when are you going to get a phone? Call me at home. M.B." Detective Constable Mark Becker really hated that I didn't have a telephone. I'd explained that if people were truly eager to get in touch with me, they could leave a message at George's house, or they could come and find me. Being phone-free meant that I was saved the hassle of bill collectors and telemarketers, but he said I was just in denial.

It surprised me that he'd said to call him at home, because summer is an awfully busy time of year for the local police force. The population quadruples, and the streets fill up with city drivers who can't leave their road-rage at home. Every season, a fresh gaggle of underage drinkers descends on the bars, camp

11

counsellors on day passes and sophisticated urbanites who may only be sixteen but look thirty. Cottage break-ins, loud parties, out-of-control campfires and downtown vandalism are all part of the policeman's summer lot. The cop shop's usually short-handed from June to September, and everyone works double shifts. I figured Becker had noticed my truck (it's George's really) on the way to arrest some mid-afternoon mischief-makers, and it was nice that he'd left me a note, even if it was terse and completely devoid of affectionate terms. "Dear Polly" would have been nice, or "Darling...", but it wouldn't have been his style, and I would've known at once it was a fake. I scurried back into the library and called from the payphone in the lobby, but I just got his machine.

"Hey, Becker," I said. "Polly, returning your call. I'll try again when I get back to the farm." If it had been urgent, he could have come into the library and found me. Maybe cops are allergic to libraries. He was probably still out arresting people.

I had a couple of stops to make before heading home. I don't go into town much in the summer if I can help it. The traffic jams are frustrating, and the line-ups are wretched. Still, Laingford is the only place you can get a case of beer within a ten-kilometre radius of Cedar Falls, our rural village address.

It was a Friday afternoon, and I'd avoided the northbound highway and taken a back route into town. The stream of cars, campers and mini-vans peeling off the highway onto Laingford's main street made it look like Highway 401 in rush hour. I waited in the beer store line-up for an eternity, got my two-four of Kuskawa Cream Ale (a local brew, and therefore much healthier than the conglomerate brands), then braved the downtown gridlock so I could drop off a classified ad at the *Gazette*. Along with my Kountry Pantree gig, I was also preparing for a small exhibition of artwork in an empty downtown storefront. Two artist friends and I had decided to take advantage of the tourist boom to stage a "Weird Kuskawa Art" show. We'd rented the storefront for next to nothing from a retailer who'd gone belly-up the previous summer. It was my job to do the advertising; hence my visit to the local paper.

I was standing at the front counter filling in a classified order form for our ad when a beefy man with a very red face stormed into the building.

"Where's that Grigsby?" he shouted. "Where's that slimy little two-bit reporter who can't get his facts straight? Where is he? I want to see him right now!" I froze, and the receptionist, who had been talking quietly to someone on the phone, muttered something into the receiver and rose slowly to her full height, which must have been close to six feet.

"Archie Watson," she said, in a cold voice, "that ain't the right way to behave in a newspaper office. Have some respect."

"It's Grigsby who oughta have some respect, Bonnie," the man called Archie Watson said. "You see what he wrote about me in this week's rag?" He looked vaguely familiar—I knew I'd met him somewhere before, or maybe I'd just seen his picture in the paper.

"I never read the *Gazette*," Bonnie said, primly. "Too much to do around here to waste my time reading. Now if you sit nice and quiet over there, I'll see if Cal is in and if he's free, though I don't see why he'd want to talk to you when you're acting like such a maniac."

"He wanted to talk to me bad enough last week," Watson said. "Begged me to return his calls. So I talk to him and then he twists everything around and makes me look like an eejit." Bonnie gave him the kind of look that suggested that an idiot was exactly what he was. She picked up the phone, punched out a number and kept her eye on Watson, who had not obeyed her instructions to sit down.

"Cal? Archie Watson's here to see you and he's loaded for bear, dear. Shall I tell him to get lost?" Bonnie listened to the response, nodded to herself and placed the receiver gently back in its cradle. Then she turned to me with a smile.

"How's that ad comin', sweetheart? You got your words figured out?"

"Well?" Archie Watson said, leaning over my shoulder.

"You wait your turn," Bonnie said.

"I'm a busy man," Watson said.

"I'm sure this here young lady is a busy person, too, Archie. Didn't Selma teach you no manners at all?" Watson let out an exasperated breath right behind me, and I resisted the urge to wipe my neck.

"I, uh, I'm not quite finished," I said. Bonnie, determined to torture the man, flicked the form around to her side so she could read it.

"Weird Art of Kuskawa, eh? I like that. Got any nude paintings? Maybe you could get Archie here to pose for you. That'd be weird." She chuckled at her joke. I could feel Watson vibrating with frustration behind me. "Have a seat, Archie," she said. "Cal's on his way down." But he didn't have time to sit because the door marked "Editorial/Sales" opened, and a young man stepped into the reception area.

"Archie," he said, striding towards the big man, who was one stage away from hyperventilation. "Good to see you." The young man, Calvin Grigsby, I assumed, held out his hand in such a natural manner that Watson shook it automatically before thinking better of it and snatching his away.

"I have a bone to pick with you," Watson growled.

"Of course you do. Everybody does, sooner or later," Grigsby said. "Come on back, and we'll talk about it." Grigsby's easy manner put Watson completely off his stride. I've never seen anyone turn the other cheek quite so effectively before. It was impressive. Watson followed the young newspaperman meekly and even turned to close the door behind him.

"Wow," I said.

"Cal's a people person," Bonnie said with pride. "The sales people call him in if a client's getting into a tizzy about a mistake or something. He's like human Valium."

"Useful trait in the business you're in, I guess. What was that guy so upset about, anyway?"

"Oh, Archie's hopping mad about that new store going in," Bonnie said. "His family has run Watson's General Store since the town was born, and he thinks he's going to lose all his customers. Cal probably quoted something stupid he said." Watson's General Store was up at the top of Main Street, a handsome brick building with the original wood and glass counters in the front—a big tourist attraction. The front of the store featured hand-scooped ice cream and candy displayed in big glass jars. It also sold groceries, bread and fresh produce and had an excellent meat counter at the back.

I remembered where I'd seen him before, wearing a big white apron and smiling cheerfully as he handed over a slab of steak wrapped in butcher's paper. Watson's wasn't cheap, but it was family-run, and the service was great. Remembering the array of cleavers and knives behind Archie's counter, I thought privately that having him mad at you could be dangerous. Better Calvin Grigsby than me, I thought. Fortunately, the work I was doing for the Kountry Pantree was behind the scenes. Nobody ever looks at a person dressed as a cow and wonders who designed the costume. In the mind of the average Joe, store mascots just are; they're a given, a fact of life, like those little plastic forks you get with Kentucky Fried

Chicken. There was no point in worrying about Watson coming at me from behind his meat counter, waving a chopper and calling me a slimy little two-bit puppet maker.

I paid for the art show ad and grabbed a copy of the *Gazette* on my way out. If I was working for the Kountry Pantree people, it would probably be a good idea to keep abreast of the situation. I had a nasty feeling that this mascot-gig was going to turn out to be trouble.

Three

Why waste your money at a flower shop?
Kountry Pantree's prices won't make you drop!
Make our Bouquet Boutique your fresh flower stop!
—A full-colour ad in the *Laingford*
   Gazette summer supplement

The midsummer evening light had ripened into that particular golden colour which makes everything touched by it impossibly beautiful. From the top of the hill leading down into George's valley, the big old brick farm house, weathered barn and outbuildings looked like they'd had warm honey poured over them. Curve after gentle curve of meadow, in diminishing shades of tender green and bronze, receded into a horizon wreathed in mist. Near the house, I could see the stooped figure of George, in a bright red shirt and straw hat, tending his vegetable garden, watched over by a scarecrow that looked more than a little like him. I'd made the scarecrow that spring, borrowing an old barn coat and hat from the mud room and using a mop head for the hair. Poe, George's tame raven, perched on the scarecrow's shoulder. (Nothing scared Poe except thunderstorms.)

Off in the distance, in the apple orchard, George's goats were snacking on windfalls and grass, and could easily be mistaken for a herd of deer, if you didn't know better. There was no sign of Susan or Eddie, but I figured they were probably in the barn, preparing for the evening milking.

I drove slowly down the driveway, savouring the scene. After the bustle of Laingford, this profound peace was reassuring. There really are some quiet places left in the world, I reminded myself, then wondered (as I often do) how on earth I had managed to live in Toronto for so long without going completely bonkers.

George straightened up and came over to greet me as I clambered out of the old Ford pickup. Luggy and Rosencrantz met him halfway, Luggy sniffing politely at his boots and Rosie trying as usual to climb up his body so she could lie like an infant in his arms.

"Off, Rosie," I said in my best "I mean business" voice. She ignored me. George crouched to her level, gently squeezed her paws and placed them on the ground, then patted her head as she settled down.

"She is learning," he said in his soft Finnish voice.

"Huh. Faster than a speeding pile of frozen molasses. How's the veggie garden?"

"It has been a good growing season," George said. "Too good. There is too much, almost. Tomatoes, zucchini—the zucchini is taking over. I should not have planted it so close to the onions."

"The zucchini was Susan's idea, wasn't it?"

George looked at me a bit sadly. "Yes, it was her idea. A good one, Polly. I just put in too many seeds, that's all." What he meant was "stop being so critical of your aunt," and he was right, but somehow I couldn't help it. Once you start down the blame road, it's hard to stop.

"Well, you'll have lots of zucchini bread and frozen zucchini for the winter, anyway," I said.

"Do you need any tomatoes? Let me give you some."

"That would be great," I said, and we spent a pleasant few minutes wandering in the jungle of George's garden, filling a basket with warm tomatoes, ripe almost a month before their usual time, a couple of fat ears of corn and some green beans. I had spent a few frustrating seasons trying to make a vegetable garden of my own up at the cabin, but finally gave up after the deer, rabbits and groundhogs made it clear that anything planted so close to the forest belonged to them, not me.

"I'll come down on the weekend and do a little weeding in here," I said. Wild vines, the bane of every Kuskawa garden, were starting to get a stranglehold on the corn and beans.

"No need," George said. "Eddie and his girlfriend are going to do that on Sunday."

"Oh." I should have been glad that Eddie was making such an effort to be useful, what with doing the barn chores and all, but I couldn't help feeling redundant. The veggie basket on my arm grew a little heavier—yet another favour I wouldn't be allowed to return.

I borrowed George's little red wagon to haul my beer, a few other purchases and the veggies up to the cabin. I had a couple of hours to kill before Susan's Social Justice meeting, and I didn't want to stick around at the farm long enough to be invited for dinner. I wanted to sulk, and that's best done alone.

When I got home, I cracked a Kuskawa Cream and rolled a small joint, smoking it on the porch and watching the tendrils of blue smoke curl up in a spiral overhead. I'm not a heavy dope-smoker, you understand. Just the occasional puff for recreational purposes. The previous year, when I'd met Mark Becker, and we'd given in to a ferocious mutual chemical attraction, I'd ruined it by offering him a post-coital joint. Not the brightest move in the world, considering that he's a policeman who takes his job seriously. He'd gone ballistic, threatened to arrest me, and it had taken a long time to patch it up. Now we worked according to that U.S. military dictum: Don't ask, don't tell. I never smoke around him, and I confine my indulgence to the times when I'm certain not to be seeing him. He still looks steadily into my eyes whenever we meet, though, to see if I'm under the influence of narcotic substances. Not a very comfortable state of affairs, but it was the best we could do.

As usual, the dope lubricated the creative cogs, and I went back inside to do some more work on the Kountry Pantree sketches. Rosencrantz was asleep on her favourite chair, curled up into a unbearably cute ball of fuzzy puppyness, her tail wrapped around her nose. I wanted to gather her up and nuzzle her, but it wouldn't have been fair to wake her up unless I was willing to put in some dog-time. One must let sleeping puppies lie.

I am a firm believer in developing tactile relationships with companion animals. I regularly get close up and sniff the various composite parts of Lug-nut and Rosie to make sure they're clean and healthy. (This is not as disgusting as you might imagine, folks.) They let me examine their teeth and ears, massage their fuzzy necks, bellies and paws, clip their nails and do all those rather intimate things that responsible dog owners must do for their pets from time to time, and I like to think that their tolerance of such behaviour is because they're used to it. Mother/Alpha dog and all that. They like to lick my legs after I have a bath, too, but that's probably way more information than you need. It grosses Becker out, which is not surprising. Not only do I avoid smoking dope around him, I also try to remember not to stick my schnozz into Luggy's ears when he's around. I don't doubt I'll end up one of those eccentric old hermits who leaves all her worldly possessions to her dogs.

I pulled the library books out of my "I Brake For Frogs" book bag and turned to the top-quality chapter on cows I'd found in *Farm Animals Explained*. Not that I really needed to know about the four stomachs of a bovine ruminant, but if you're going to build a costume that looks like a cow, you have to have some idea of how the common cow is put together. Goats I knew back to front and sideways, but my experience with cows was limited.

An hour or so later, I had a fairly respectable sketch of Kountry Kow, complete with apron, udder and a cunning tail that, if the cow mascot made the final cut, would swish, thanks to a secret wire inside.

I slugged back a cup of elderly coffee, washed my face in a basin of rainwater and headed down to be grilled by Susan and her Social Justice League.

George's driveway was crowded with vehicles, several of them bearing store logos. A purple mini-van announced that "Emma's Posies (45 Main Street E.) are Bloomin' Lovely." A boxy, boat-shaped sedan had "Downtown Drugs: Your Family Drugstore" written on the door, and I guessed that the yellow Camry belonged to the owner of the Laingford photo shop, because it had a huge plastic camera mounted on its roof.

As soon as I arrived, I realized I'd neglected one of the first rules of etiquette which govern rural meetings at somebody's home. You're supposed to bring food. I came in the back door leading into the kitchen, to find Susan bustling around making coffee, surrounded by plastic-wrapped plates of goodies. There was a platter of small cakes, a mound of little triangular sandwiches, some miniature pizzas and a box of After Eight mints with a gift bow on the top.

"Somebody having a birthday party?" I said to hide my embarrassment. I should have whipped up a batch of granola bars or something, I thought to myself, except for the fact that it was too warm for me to have the woodstove going, which would have been the only way to bake them. Luggy, smelling food, threw himself to the floor and grovelled at Susan's feet. Rosie, who generally copied everything he did, followed suit.

"I'd forgotten that people always come with offerings," Susan said. "We'll never get through this lot. You'll have to take some back with you, Polly." She halved one of the sandwiches, made the dogs sit, then handed the pieces over. I'd finally given up asking my aunt not to spoil them. I wasn't about to give her grand-nieces or nephews, after all. The dogs knew better than to try the begging routine with me.

"Maybe I should have a meeting of my own," I said. "I'd never have to buy groceries again."

"If you want to live on sugar-laden squares and white-bread sandwiches, go for it," she said. "You go in and introduce yourself. We're still waiting for a couple of people. I'll be there in a moment. Oh, wait. You can take this with you." She handed me a tray of coffee-things, which I manoeuvred through the door into George's living room. The dogs stayed in the kitchen with the goddess of food.

Sitting beside George on the sofa was Pete Somebody, who ran Pizza Madness, next door to the *Gazette* office. I'd bought a slice from him often enough to know who he was, though we didn't exactly run in the same social circles. I'd seen him coming out of Kelso's, Laingford's West End girlie-bar, enough times to figure him for a regular. He nodded at me, then turned back to George, whose ear he was obviously bending. George puffed on his pipe and slipped me a sly wink.

Two men were having an intense conversation by the

window, their backs to the room. One was pear-shaped, dressed in baggy jeans and a black T-shirt with "Shutterbug" printed on the back. The owner of the camera-car, I guessed. His hair was blonde, flat-topped in a crew cut, and he gestured wildly with a lit cigarette. The other guy just had to be the Downtown Drug guy—not hard to pick out, as he was wearing a white pharmacist's coat. Either he had come to the meeting directly from work, or he wore his badge of office all the time. I had a sudden, goofy mental picture of Mr. Drugstore climbing on top of his wife in bed, buck-naked under his white coat. Must have been the dope I'd smoked. He could have been a bachelor for all I knew, and the image wasn't the kind that you'd go looking for, if you know what I mean.

"Why, hello, Polly," a woman said as I put the coffee tray down on a side table. I turned to see a vision in pink bearing down on me from the hallway leading to the bathroom. She was about Susan's age, dressed in what appeared to be a frilly bathrobe—all flounces, set off by a rope of pearls the size of marbles. She hugged me.

"Umm…hi," I said. "How are you?"

"Who am I, you mean," the woman said and gave a whoop of laughter. "You don't know me from Adam, do you, dear? Never mind. I remember you when you were just a little thing. Your mother and I were great friends, and you used to come to my shop and play with the dried flowers while we had tea."

"Oh," I said, still completely at a loss. I was ten when my parents died, and I've managed to do some pretty heavy-duty forgetting since then.

"I'm Emma Tempest," the woman said, putting me out of my misery. "I run 'Emma's Posies.' Your mother was my 'Glad Lady'."

Another image rushed in on me like a freight train, me and

my Mom in her old Mazda crammed full of fresh gladiolas as tall as I was, pink and yellow and orange, an Eden on wheels. We'd deliver them to the flower place where a nice smelling lady gave me little sugar cakes and sweet, milky nursery tea while Mom conducted business. "Well, if it isn't the Glad Lady and her little flower girl," she'd say.

"You're Miss Tempest," I said. "I haven't thought about that in a long time."

"Call me Emma," she said. "It's nice to see you grown up, dear. Now I hope you'll follow in your mother's footsteps and help us nail these development rascals to the wall." Follow in my mother's footsteps and become a fanatical religious do-gooder who never talks to her daughter and ends up getting creamed by a drunk driver on a Kuskawa back road? Not likely.

Four

Free 8 x 10 colour print with every film developed at the Kountry Pantree state-of-the-art photo lab. Why settle for less?
—A flyer delivered to every mail box in Laingford

"Did you see the superstore article in this week's *Gazette*?" said Stan Herman, wrinkling his baby face in distaste. Herman was the pillowy blond person in the black T-shirt. I had been right—he was the owner of Shutterbug, the photo shop. The strategy meeting of the League for Social Justice had begun, all of us sitting in a circle in George's living room, balancing coffee cups and napkins full of genteel nibblies on our laps.

"I think we all read it, Stan," Aunt Susan said, "but don't forget that the publisher is one of the store's financial backers, at least so we've been told. We can't expect him to be entirely objective."

"It's not Whiteside that's the problem," Archie Watson said. He'd been the last to arrive, still red-faced and apoplectic after his chat with Cal Grigsby at the paper. "It's that little hack who's working for him. He talks a smooth line, but he's biased as hell." He glared around the room, challenging anyone to disagree with him. His gaze lighted on me and a dangerous spark flashed in his eye, identifying me perhaps as the witness to his show of temper in the *Gazette* office. I smiled blandly at him, and he looked away.

"I think Cal's very nice, Archie," Emma Tempest said. "Granted, he made you look foolish in his article, but if you will make inflammatory statements, you can't blame the boy for using them. He has a job to do, same as you."

I hadn't seen the article they were talking about. I'd meant to look at the *Gazette* before coming to the meeting, but I got distracted by Kountry Kow. Now I was itching to read it. I love a good bit of dirt in the local rag.

"I think we should all agree not to talk to the press individually," said Florence Levine, the small, birdlike woman who owned the Homerun Video Den. "If we have something to say about the development, we should issue press releases."

"That's a good idea," Susan said. "If we present a united front, we'll have more clout."

"I think this whole thing is a waste of time," said Mr. Drugstore, who had been introduced as Joseph Olszewski. He was an older man with a baggy, basset hound face and a voice like a foghorn. I still couldn't shake my mental image of him in bed in his white coat, except now, my wicked brain had added a long, wagging tail to the picture. Can't say why this was. I couldn't look at him without an inclination to snicker. "The Kountry Pantree is a done deal," Olszewski continued. "The building's almost finished, and if you look in the classifieds, you'll notice they're already advertising for staff. I don't see what we can possibly do to stop it now."

"We need to know who the proponents are," Susan said. "Polly can help us with that, I think."

"Why's she here, anyway?" said Pete Holicky, the Pizza man. "She's working for the enemy, isn't she?"

"She is?" Emma Tempest said, turning to me, her face sagging in disappointment.

"I'm doing a contract for them," I said. "And I don't really know why I'm here. Susan asked me."

"Polly's an independent freelancer," Susan said. "She's not a supporter, per se. Are you, Polly?" Ouch. On the spot. Time for my face to go red.

"Whether I support it or not is immaterial," I said, carefully. "I agree with Mr. Olszewski, though. I don't think there's much you can do at this point."

"Ah, but we have an ace in the hole," Emma said. "Does she know, Susan?"

"No, she doesn't, Emma," Susan said, "and it's best not to tell her. As you can see, she's an open book." This third-person "she" stuff really bugged me, and I didn't appreciate having my blushing mug pointed out to these people I hardly knew. Next she would be telling them that I was dating a cop and could be relied on to pass along everybody's dirty secrets to him. I blushed harder and glanced over at George, who wasn't saying anything. He was looking at Susan with an expression of mild amusement. You're laughing now, I thought at him. Just wait till she blabs to everybody that you sing opera in the shower, George, and see how you like it.

"You said I could help you, Susan," I said coldly. "Just how, exactly?"

"You met with one of their committees recently, didn't you?" she said, ignoring my tone.

"I did," I said.

"Well, who was there? That will give us some idea of who we're up against." I felt like I was in a bad spy movie. Kidnap the enemy. Feed her mini-pizzas and coffee, then make her spill the goods, boss. If she don't talk, make her eat a cupcake.

"You probably know already," I said. "It's no big secret. There was David Kane, of course. He's the front line man.

He's too young to be putting up all the cash himself, though. I think his parents may be helping him."

"That'd be the distillery Kanes in Toronto?" Holicky said.

"Yup. Big bucks there," Susan said. "Who else, Polly?"

"Well, this was just a focus group to come up with a mascot for the store. The others aren't necessarily backers, you know."

"A mascot?" Archie Watson said. "You mean like a logo or something?"

"No, a sort of mascot character, like the Zellers teddy bear."

"Huh. A big fat pig would be appropriate," Watson said. "A stinking, greedy…"

"Archie, let it go," Susan said. "So who was in the focus group, Polly?"

"I don't know if I should tell you," I said, feeling that at least a token resistance was called for. I was working for them, after all, and while they hadn't sworn me to secrecy or anything, I felt like I was ratting them out. It was obvious that the group was bent on taking some kind of action against them.

"You said yourself it's not top secret information, dear," Emma Tempest said, reading my mind.

"I know that. This just makes me uncomfortable," I said.

"Told you she was working for the enemy," Holicky said. "You watch. She'll go right back to them and say who was here and what went on tonight, and they'll get us back."

"This is not international espionage, Peter," Susan said. "There's no need to be melodramatic."

"This is how such things begin, though," Olszewski the druggist said. "Secret meetings, strategy, informers. Before you know it, there'll be a pogrom."

"Oh, please," I said. "If it means that much to you, the Elliots and Duke Pitblado were there too. Okay? Everybody happy now?"

"The Elliots. I might have known," said the photo shop guy, Herman. "They come to this town and take over a century-old inn and turn it into Disneyland. Of course they'd be behind it." Winston and Serena Elliot had bought the Mooseview Inn more than ten years ago. They'd upgraded the original building, built condos on the property and put in a golf course, but you could hardly call it Disneyland. If they hadn't bought the old place, which had been falling apart, it would have collapsed into the Kuskawa River.

"I knew Duke Pitblado negotiated the land deal, but I'm surprised that he's involved," Emma said. Duke was a local real estate broker. He lived in a palatial home in the East End, overlooking Settlers' Lake.

"I'd'a thought he was too busy making babies," Holicky said. Duke had married a woman half his age, who had been in a perpetual state of pregnancy since her wedding. It was sort of a town joke—not a very nice one.

"Well, there's local money behind it, just as I thought," Susan said, satisfied. "With the Elliots and Pitblado on board, David Kane wouldn't have had any trouble getting past any zoning restrictions at Town Hall."

"But the land belonged to the town to begin with, didn't it?" Florence Levine the video lady said.

"Yes, it did, but I think we'd better save that discussion for later," Susan said, casting a significant glance in my direction.

"Oh, I see," I said. "*Pas devant les domestiques*, is that it? Worried I might go scuttling off to the committee and tell them you're planning to sue them for corrupt practices?"

"What did she say? I don't speak Frog," Holicky said.

"*Pas devant les domestiques*—not in front of the servants," Susan said. "Polly, please don't be offended. It's just caution on our part, that's all."

"Well, you folks just carry on, then," I said, getting up and putting my empty cup on the floor. "You'll excuse me if I don't clear away the dishes. It's my night off, you know. I'll just go back to my sharecropper's shack and play the banjo for a while."

I flounced out.

In the kitchen, Luggy had his paws up on the table and was carefully licking the icing off the cupcakes. He'd knocked one off the plate and onto the floor for Rosie, who held it between her paws and nibbled at it delicately, like a lady. When Lug-nut saw me, he got down immediately and stood wagging his tail, looking only vaguely guilty. I didn't have the energy to scold him. The cupcakes were perfectly intact, except for being icing-free, and the League for Social Justice might not notice and eat them anyway, which gave me a curious sense of satisfaction.

"You'll be bouncing off the walls with all that sugar in you," I said. My eye caught the phone on the wall by the kitchen door, and I suddenly remembered that I was supposed to call Becker. Perfect timing, I thought. I'll get on the phone, and Susan will come in and assume that I'm calling someone about their stupid meeting. I dialled Becker's number, and a child answered.

"Becker residence."

"Umm, is Mark there, please?" I said.

"Sure. May I tell him who's calling?" the child asked, efficiently.

"It's Polly Deacon," I said.

"One moment and I'll see if he's free," the child said. "Dad! A lady called Polly Deacon on line one!" he called. Becker picked up.

"Don't tell me," I said. "You've hired an executive assistant from the child labour pool."

Becker chuckled. "It's my son," he said. "He wants to be a

30

business tycoon when he grows up. He's staying with me for a while."

Becker hadn't talked about his son or his ex-wife much, only enough to tell me that the boy lived with his mother and spent the occasional weekend with his dad. He'd kept me out of that part of his life, and I hadn't pushed it, not being terribly child-oriented. From what I gathered, his relationship with his ex was more or less amicable, and he never started a sentence with "my wife used to..." I had expected at some point to be introduced to the kid. I guessed that this was it.

"What are you doing tomorrow?" he said.

"I have a meeting at about six, but apart from that, it's just another lazy Saturday," I said.

"Want to go hiking? I'd like you to meet Bryan, and he's been asking about you."

"He has?"

"Yeah. He says things like, 'So, Dad. You seeing anybody? Got a girlfriend?' Stuff like that. I hope you don't mind."

"Mind? Of course not." Hooray, I thought. I've finally achieved girlfriend status.

"I was thinking we'd take the Oxblood Rapids trail—you know, the one with the falls? I'll bring the food," he said.

"You've actually got time off? How long?"

"A week."

"In the middle of the summer?"

"I booked it a while ago," he said. "Catherine's going on a training course in Calgary, so I'm doing the Dad thing." I was a little surprised that Becker hadn't bothered to mention it. A whole week off in the summer for a Kuskawa cop was a big thing. Maybe he thought I'd be jealous of his son or something. It's not as if we were living in each other's pockets. We went out for dinner or a movie about once every two weeks or so, that was all. In fact, I couldn't remember the last time I'd called his home number. He usually called from his cell phone or from the cop shop. "So you up for it?" he said.

"Of course. It sounds like fun," I said, although I had a sudden urge to run away, fast. Meet my kid. Engage. Yikes. What if the child hated me? What if he resented my relationship with his Dad and cast me in the role of the evil stepmother? What, oh God, what if he really liked me and wanted me to marry his Dad?

"Do you mind if I bring the dogs?"

"I was counting on it."

"Great. Can I bring anything else?"

"Nope. I got it covered. We'll come and get you around eleven-thirty, that sound okay?"

"I'll see you then," I said. As I had predicted, Susan came into the kitchen and stopped when she saw me on the phone. Becker had hung up, but I continued to speak into the mouthpiece. "…and I think they may be stockpiling weapons, Dave," I said. "Could be they're planning to blow up the building. I'd be calling the cops before it's too late. Right. See ya." I put the phone back, smiled sweetly at Aunt Susan and headed out into the night.

Five

We have everything you'll need
for dogs and cats— from treats to feed.
Your furry friends will wag their tails
to see our Kountry Pantree sales!
—A jingle on MEGA FM, Laingford's radio station

BUSINESSMAN CLAIMS NEW STORE ON BURIAL GROUND
by Calvin Grigsby, Staff reporter
Laingford businessman Archibald Watson believes that the
Kountry Pantree superstore, currently being constructed at the
corner of Main Street and Hwy 24, is desecrating an ancient
native burial ground.

Watson, who was born and grew up in the area, told the
Gazette last week that Indian artifacts had been found in the
meadow overlooking Lake Kimowan. The site, soon to open as
a $2.4 million shopping complex, is, according to Watson,
sacred land.

"My brother found a couple of bones there once, and I
found an Indian arrowhead," he said last week. "We should
get the Ministry of Indian Affairs or maybe the Heritage
people to look into it."

Watson, whose family immigrated to Canada from
England in 1867, said that the Indian contribution to early
life in Laingford should be recognized and preserved, not

desecrated with a shopping mall.

"I know we kicked them out and everything," he said, "but we could at least respect their cemeteries, eh?"

Contacted at the Mohawk reserve in Goose River, south of Sikwan, Chief Pauline Joseph said that her ancestors regarded the Laingford area as a canoe route only. The meadow site in Laingford would never have been used to bury their dead. "It would be like having a funeral for your mom at a highway rest stop," she said.

Watson is the owner of Watson's General Store, a grocery and butcher shop on Main Street.

"He said it was just a passing comment," Susan told me. "He thinks Grigsby was out to make him look bad." We were having coffee on the farm house porch as I waited for the arrival of Becker and his son.

"Well, the article certainly does that. Ancient burial grounds? Grasping at straws, wasn't he?"

"Archie has promised not to speak to the press again without consulting us first," Susan said. "And Grigsby did rather take Archie's words out of context. They were talking about the meadow, and how the children in the community used to play there."

"That's sad," I said. We sipped our coffee in silence, and I lit a cigarette—probably my last one of the day, as I didn't want to smoke in front of the kid.

"Polly, about last evening," Susan said.

"I wasn't really on the phone to David Kane," I said.

"I know. You were just making a point, and I understand why. I just wanted to apologize for pressuring you to come in the first place."

"That's okay. I should have said no, anyway. Next time I'll

declare a conflict of interest," I said. "You could have found out who was on the committee quite easily somewhere else. Or you could have asked me earlier. It was the public grilling I didn't like."

"Quite so. I got carried away, I think. Anyway, Emma said afterwards that she hopes you might drop in on her some time. She has something she wants to give you."

"Did you know she and Mom used to be friends?" I said.

"Well, business associates really, Polly. Your mother was very choosy about her friends."

"You mean she didn't have any," I said.

"Oh, she did, you know. Your father, for one."

"Right. And God. Very close friends with God, I seem to recall."

Susan nodded, gazing out across the fields. My parents had been what you might call "muscular Christians", my mother from a fervent Irish Catholic background and my Dad an evangelical Baptist. When I was born, he'd agreed to convert to Catholicism for my sake. That particular combination of religious traditions had seethed and boiled and coughed up a household that had been zealous in the extreme. God, as they say, ruled. Or at least my parents' interpretation of God did. After they died and Aunt Susan took me in, she told me that I could choose to attend church if I wanted to, but she wouldn't be coming along. I never returned.

Luggy, who had been splayed full length in the sun, catching some morning rays, suddenly sat up and wuffed. Rosie, ever his shadow, copied him. She was just learning to bark, little cartoon yips that were only endearing for the first couple of seconds. Moments later, Becker's black Jeep Cherokee crested the hill and started down the long driveway into George's valley.

"I'll see you later, Polly. Have fun," Susan said and left the scene, perhaps not wanting to be perceived as a chaperone.

You'd think that at age mid-thirty-something I would have moved past the sweaty palm stage in my dating career. After all, it was only a hike, and it wasn't as if Becker and I were strangers. I squinted at the approaching Jeep and made out a small head in the passenger seat: the boy, Bryan. I realized that my nervousness was linked to Mark Becker the father, a person whom I hadn't really met. There would be a triangular element to our outing that hadn't been there before. Neither Becker's son nor I would get his undivided attention, and we would not be able to give him ours. It would be a three-way thing, a dance, with each of us learning the steps for our respective roles of parent, child and romantically involved other adult. I'm a terrible dancer.

The Jeep parked and the dogs did a Hello frolic as the doors opened.

"Morning!" I called. The boy immediately got down to dog level and let Rosie climb all over him. "Dogs! A puppy! You've got a puppy!" he said. It was my little Webmaster of the day before, the fellow who had handed me his business card and offered to design a website for me. Becker, dressed in jeans and a plaid flannel shirt, walked around the front of the vehicle and gave me a hug.

"Hi there," he said. "I knew your dogs would break the ice a bit. How's it going?"

"Everything's great," I said, hugging him back.

"How's the mascot coming?"

"Still in the planning stages. Maybe Bryan can give me a little advice from a smaller person's perspective. We met yesterday, you know. At the library."

"I saw your truck there when I went to pick him up. That's

our meeting place. Catherine and I can do the handover while he's picking his books. It's sort of neutral there." I thought the term "handover" was a little peculiar, but what do I know about the language of divorce?

"He reads a lot, does he?"

"Well, he takes a lot of books out. I don't see him reading much, though. He spends most of his time glued to the computer."

"He offered to design me a website," I said.

"Did he tell you how much he charges?"

"It's a sliding scale, Dad," Bryan said, standing up, his arms full of Rosencrantz. "I only charged you that much because Mom said you could afford it. Is this a boy dog or a girl dog?"

"It's a girl," I said. "Her name is Rosie, and the other one's a male called Lug-nut."

"They're cool. Dad, I think she likes me. Can I get a dog?"

"I doubt it," Becker said. "Your Mom's probably allergic to them."

"I promise she's not," Bryan said. "Anyway, we could keep it at your place. I'd come over and feed it and walk it and stuff. There's lots of stuff about dogs on the Net. Pleeeze?" The boy's voice had taken on that wheedling tone that hits the ear in the same way Rosie's barking does. I think I winced.

"We'll talk about it later," Becker said. "Right now, let's just have fun with these ones."

"Here, Bryan," I said, handing him a tote bag filled with dog stuff, the puppy-mom's version of a diaper bag. "You can be officially in charge of their gear. There's biscuits, leashes, dog food and pooper scooper bags in there."

"Eeeew. Pooper scooper?"

"Yeah," I said. "When you take dogs to public places, you have to pick up their poop so people don't step in it."

"I don't have to do that, do I, Dad?"

Becker glanced at me and grinned. "We'll take turns," he said.

"We'll call it being on doodie-duty," I said.

"Gross," Bryan said, then gazed into Rosie's big brown eyes. "When I'm on doodie-duty, try not to poop, okay?" She licked his face, and he chuckled.

"Let's go," Becker said. "Dogs and boys in the back seat."

"Our kids seem to be hitting it off," I said, buckling myself into the passenger seat.

"They'll keep each other occupied, anyway," Becker said, pointedly, his expression suggesting that a little low-key fooling around might not be out of the question. This could turn out to be a good day.

Kuskawa is full of walking trails, criss-crossing the landscape like a vast recreational web. It wasn't always so—the thick forest which makes up ninety-five per cent of the surface area around here used to be untamed, but hiking and birding have enjoyed a vogue in recent years. Perhaps because of the ageing demographic (everybody with money retires here from the city), the local municipal governments all recognized that building trails would boost the tourism economy. Every time a new trail opens, there's a ribbon-cutting ceremony and a blurb in the paper, and another flock of fit, eager seniors bursts out of the starting gate, seeking the elusive fungus and the lesser spotted titwattle.

The Oxblood Rapids trail is one of the older ones, a natural path worn down by generations of locals and summer visitors seeking a good picnic spot by the falls. The Oxblood Falls aren't the biggest in Kuskawa, but they're pretty impressive, and there are picnic tables under the trees. The trail is easy to follow, carpeted in a thick layer of aromatic pine needles. The sun filters through the trees, dappling the trail with light, and there's plenty of room to walk side by side.

Becker and I linked hands as we walked, Bryan galloping on ahead with the dogs. We hadn't seen each other for a couple of weeks, and there was a lot to catch up on. Cottage break-ins were up that season, Becker said.

"More and more people are building summer homes up here and filling them with antiques," he said. "Used to be, you'd furnish your cottage with garage-sale junk and old appliances. Now, they put in state of the art entertainment systems and fully stocked bars and leave the places empty for weeks at a time."

"Pretty tempting," I said.

"Unfortunately. The monster cottages always seem to be built in areas where jobs are scarce and people are hurting. However, theft was still a crime last time I looked."

We chatted about the changing face of Laingford, and I found myself telling him about the League for Social Justice. I wasn't tattling, I swear. It just made a good story.

"What do you think this group is planning to do?" Becker said.

"Oh, I don't know. More letters to the editor, I guess. A delegation to council. Won't do any good. David Kane's on a roll."

"It'll be good to have another photo lab," he said. "I got a bunch of prints back from Shutterbug the other day, and half of them didn't turn out."

"That usually has more to do with the photographer than the processing," I said.

"What, me? A bad photographer? Not my fault I keep forgetting to take the lens cap off," he said.

"Don't give up your day job."

"Actually, I was planning to quit the force and become a fashion photographer," he said, pulling one of those disposable cameras out of his backpack. "Pose for me against that tree, would you? Good, good. Chin up. Now work with me, babe." Bryan rushed back down the trail, his face pale, the dogs behind him, barking excitedly.

"Dad! Dad! A guy just fell over the falls and he's floating in the water at the bottom and I think he's dead!"

Six

All set for camping? Forgotten something? Kountry Pantree has all your campsite food needs at "In-tents" prices! Fill your cooler at the Pantree!
—A billboard at the corner of Hwy 14 and the off-ramp to Laingford, 2 km. from Kuskawa Provincial Park

Becker immediately went into full alert mode. The camera disappeared, and, in two big strides, he was crouched at Bryan's level, looking him right in the eye. The terror on the kid's face was real. No way this was a little boy joke. "Where?" Becker said.

"Back there along the trail. In the shallow water," Bryan said. His face crumpled, and he fought back tears. Becker gave him a quick, powerful hug then ran down the path, the dogs following at his heels.

Bryan and I stared at each other for a moment, biting our lips, suspended in child/adult limbo. What was I supposed to do? Should I take him back to the Jeep? I tried to remember what it was like to be eight, although Bryan was more savvy than I'd been at twelve. He'd had a shock, certainly, but wouldn't it be worse not knowing the outcome? No way I was doing the nanny thing, I decided. Not my style.

"Let's go, Bryan," I said. "Your Dad may need help. Just stay back, okay?" He looked relieved. We ran together in the

41

direction his father had taken. Around a bend in the trail, the shallows of the falls lapped against a rocky shore. Becker was already in the water up to his armpits, hauling a motionless figure to the edge.

"Take care of this," I said to the boy, handing him the backpack that Becker had dropped before he ran. Bryan took it mutely, his eyes wide. "If it's too scary, you don't have to look," I said, then waded in to help. The guy in the water was very big.

"I don't think we've lost him yet," Becker said. "You know CPR?" I nodded. We laid him out and began, Becker doing the mouth-to-mouth yucky part and me doing the push-on-the-chest bit. We worked together as if we'd been doing it for years, like the guys on that seventies TV show, *Emergency*. The expression "Ringer's Lactate" popped into my head by itself, and I heard a snatch of the theme music. (The guys on the show were always plugging their rescued victims into an I.V. drip of Ringer's. It was kind of a catch word for those of us who watched it.) Funny where the mind goes when you're high on adrenaline. It only took a few moments of work before the man twitched, vomited all over Becker and started coughing.

Becker and I looked at each other for a long, joyful and triumphant moment. Since we'd known each other, our eyes had met over several lifeless bodies. Death had engineered the initial introduction and continued to check in on us from time to time to see how we were doing. There'd been my friend Francy, hanged in her kitchen; there'd been Francy's husband, shot in the chest; there'd been an anonymous drowned snowmobiler, a garotted actor and another I can't talk about. All very horrible, traumatic and gruesome. The emotional fallout had been brutal, and it wasn't as if we'd ever really sat down and discussed it. I'd never said "Hey Becker, how do you feel about all the dead bodies between us?" He had never asked me if I was troubled by ghosts. I was. I had nightmares sometimes.

For once, Death left the party early. Becker and I had just spent a few amazing and terrible minutes together in a place where the only thing that mattered was pumping life back into a soggy stranger, and we had done it. We had brought someone back. Oddly, this rescue utterly cancelled the other stuff out. I felt all those wispy, pathetic ghosts depart *en masse* like puffs of smoke, twisting in the air above us for a moment before being whisked away by the wind. I was soaked, and my heart was thumping so hard my ears were ringing, but I could feel the grin stretching my face muscles.

"Is he dead?" Bryan called timidly from his perch on the rock above us.

"I think he's going to be all right, son," Becker called back.

"You saved him?"

"I guess so," Becker said. The man was struggling to sit up now, still coughing, but obviously out of danger. Bryan cheered, his young voice sounding thin against the roar of the falls.

"Bring me that blanket in the knapsack, will you, Bryan?" Becker said. The boy did so, and Becker wrapped it around the man's shoulders.

"My camera? Where's my Leica?" the half-drowned man croaked.

"Take it easy, Vic," Becker said. "Don't try to talk for a bit. You had a close call there." Vic? Becker knew him?

"Where are the others?" the man said.

"The others?" I said, glancing around. There was nobody else to be seen.

"The Camera Club. We were all up there, getting shots of the falls," the man said, pointing above our heads to where the

Oxblood Falls cascaded down a steep incline, thundering over rocks and throwing up spray. How he had survived the descent without being battered beyond recognition, I couldn't imagine.

"Vic's a town councillor. Volunteer firefighter too, as well as a pretty good photographer," Becker said to me. "Vic, this is my friend, Polly Deacon."

Vic shook my hand. His was cold and wet. "I guess the Leica's in the drink," Vic said, grimacing. "Better it than me, I suppose."

"You remember what happened?" Becker said.

"Not really. One second I'm trying to get a close-up of the spray over one of those rocks, and the next second I'm ass over teakettle in the wash cycle," Vic said. His throat sounded raw, and he was shivering. "You know what? It's true what they say. Your life does flash before you."

"My son saw you fall," Becker said. Vic turned his head to look at Bryan, who had recovered a bit of his colour and was listening to the conversation with lively interest.

"You did, eh? Lucky for me. You didn't happen to see if I was pushed, did you?" Bryan blinked, and I felt Becker stiffen beside me.

"Pushed? Someone pushed you?" he said.

"Could be," Vic said. "It's kind of fuzzy, but I don't think I slipped. I'd remember that."

Becker gazed up at the falls, his expression doing a Polaroid transformation into grim cop-ness. "So how come the rest of your group hasn't noticed you're missing?" he said.

"We were fanned out all over the place," Vic said. "We were supposed to meet down here for lunch, actually. I guess I'm a little early."

As if on cue, a trio of retirement-age women appeared from behind a clump of bushes near the falls-side of the trail. When they saw us, they exclaimed loudly and hurried over. All three had cameras slung around their necks and camera bags over their shoulders.

"Land sakes, Victor, what happened to you?" the tallest one said. Her iron-grey hair stuck out like thatch from under her Tilley hat, and she had a comfortable, baggy face that spoke of years spent happily in the great outdoors.

"I fell in, Sophie. Detective Becker here and his friend rescued me. The breath of life, eh? Mark, I don't know how to thank you. Sorry about your shirt."

"We need to get you to Emerge and have you checked out, Vic," Becker said.

"No way," Vic said. "Hate hospitals. I'm fine. Besides, I don't want to miss the picnic."

"You almost drowned, buddy. You're in shock."

"Not half as shocked as I'll be if you drag me to Laingford Memorial. All I need is a couple of Sophie's lemon squares, and I'll be fighting fit in no time." The lady in the Tilley hat chortled.

"What makes you think I brought my squares, Victor?" she said.

"Saw them in your camera bag when you gave me that film," he said, then grimaced. "Lost my camera, though. At the bottom of the Oxblood, I guess."

"Oh, no, not your Leica?" Sophie said.

"Does he have any idea how close he came to dying?" I whispered to Becker as the three graces moved in to provide comfort, twittering like sparrows. Obviously, this crew considered the loss of a Leica far more traumatic than a mere near-drowning could ever be.

"It'll hit him later," Becker said. "He's stubborn, though, and right now there's no way he'll let himself be taken to hospital unless I arrest him."

45

"Can't you make him?"

"Victor Watson is not a man to be forced to do anything against his will," Becker said. "We should stick around, Polly. Do you mind very much? If he goes into delayed shock, we'll have to get him out of here."

The cosy picnic I'd envisioned melted quietly away. Instead, I realized, we'd have our lunch in the company of a bunch of photography nuts talking about f-stops and light-levels. Other members of the Camera Club had started arriving, and some of them gathered around Vic Watson, chattering excitedly about his accident. Someone was unpacking a huge hamper of food on a nearby picnic table, and things were already starting to take on a carnival atmosphere. "Of course, I don't mind," I said, trying my best to sound convincing. "What about Bryan?" We looked up and saw him grinning from ear to ear, posing with Rosencrantz and Lug-nut against a background of pine trees as several Camera Club members cooed and clicked.

"In his element. He's a born ham," Becker said, fondly.

"So's Rosie," I said, reminded suddenly of another picture of the puppy that had appeared on the front page of the weekend newspaper a few months before. Then, she had nestled in the arms of actress Amber Thackeray and actor Shane Pacey, three golden-haired beauties against a pretty Kuskawa background. The photo caption had been a sombre one, the circumstances tragic. I felt a prick of superstition and had a sudden urge to dash in and grab Rosie out of Bryan's arms before something bad happened to both of them. Becker, never one for recognizing omens, blatant or not, just smiled.

"You're soaked through," I said, noticing that Becker was standing in a puddle of river water.

"I've got a change of clothes in the Jeep," he said. "What about you? You're pretty wet too."

"I'll dry out. The sun's baking." It was, too. When we'd started out, it had been overcast, but as soon as we'd performed our emergency-team rescue—actually, at the moment that Vic had upchucked and returned to the land of the living—the sun had come out from behind a cloud. Lighting effects courtesy of God, maybe.

"Would you keep an eye on Bryan for a few minutes while I go and change?" Becker said.

"Sure. I was thinking of offering to be his agent, anyway," I said. The boy was red-haired, like his father, freckle-faced and wholesome-looking. He was totally at home in front of the camera, obligingly gazing with an impish seriousness at the cluster of photographers surrounding him. The Camera Club members had helped Vic to his feet and guided him over to one of the picnic tables, where he discarded his blanket and stretched out in the sun.

"How are you feeling?" I said to him. Sophie, the tall woman whose lemon squares he lusted after, settled companionably beside him.

"Not too bad, considering," he said. He unbuttoned his shirt and removed it unselfconsciously, wringing out the water and spreading it out on the table-top to dry. I reflected that if he'd been a woman, restored to life after being tossed in the river, and had stripped down to nakedness moments afterwards, she'd have been bundled off to the hospital no matter what. Watson looked familiar, not an unusual occurrence in a town the size of Laingford, where you'll meet everybody eventually if you hang around long enough. His muscular, barrel chest sported a thick mass of greying hair, not unattractive (I wasn't staring or anything) and his arms were like tree trunks. The powerful body twigged my memory, and I had a sudden image of Archie Watson, leaning over the counter at the *Laingford Gazette.*

"Watson. You're Victor Watson, right?" I said, inanely. "Any relation to Archie?"

"My little brother," Vic said. "You know him?"

"Not very well. I met him last night."

"He try to sell you one of his horse steaks?" Vic said, laughing in a way that was not exactly the epitome of brotherly love.

"Now Vic, that was uncalled for," Sophie said. "Your brother works very hard."

"Keeping up the family tradition," Vic said. "That's right. Never lets me forget it, neither. Never forgave me for ditching the grocery business and going to law school." He sneezed explosively and gave a great shiver like a draught horse caught in the rain.

Sophie produced a towel from her camera bag (which appeared to be bottomless, like Mary Poppins' carpetbag) and proceeded to rub him down. Vic didn't seem to mind, although I felt like I should maybe look away. There was something proprietary about the way Sophie wielded the towel, something decidedly intimate.

"You should try to be more careful," Sophie said to him. "That's the second time you've had an accident on one of our field trips. Remember last week?"

"What happened last week?" I said.

"It was just me being clumsy," Vic said.

"We were at the lookout tower taking bird's-eye shots of Laingford," Sophie said. "Vic was sitting on the railing like an idiot, leaning way out and he almost went over." Her face drained of colour at the memory. "I happened to be nearby and grabbed him just in time."

"She's a strong one," Vic said. "It was crowded up there, and I should have known better."

"You mean you were pushed?" I said, remembering Vic's remark about possibly being pushed at the top of the falls.

"I might have been jostled a bit," Vic said. "I forget. Moments like that, you don't remember much. I was lucky Sophie was there, though."

"You don't have any enemies in the Camera Club, do you?" I said, half-jokingly. Sophie shot him a warning look that I found very interesting indeed.

"Nope. We're all friends here," he said.

"Hey, Watson, get your damned shirt on. There are ladies present," came a loud voice from behind us. I turned to see David Kane, Kountry Pantree magnate, striding down the trail towards the picnic area.

Seven

"I didn't know you were a photographer," I said, when Kane got close enough. Like all the others, he carried a camera bag, which was leather and looked new. He wore designer hiking gear from top to toe, the kind that you can only get from the outrageously priced outfitting place next to the park. He had on a bright red sweatshirt and khaki trousers, and a khaki photographer's vest over that, its pockets bulging with what was probably a selection of expensive lenses and accessories. Tanned and fit, Kane looked like something you'd see in a glossy photography magazine, captioned "What the professionals are wearing." It was overkill, really. Everybody else was in scruffies.

"Oh, hello, Polly," Kane said. "Have you joined the Club too?" He seemed quite pleased, which was flattering, and I suddenly remembered Susan telling me that David Kane was a bachelor. Uh-oh.

"No, we just happened to be on the trail when Vic here needed a bit of help."

Kane looked Vic over. "Been swimming?" he said.

"Something like that," Vic said. I could feel Sophie bristling beside me.

"Most of us usually wear a bathing suit," Kane said.

"I'm not most of us," Vic said.

"Oh my God, Uncle Vic! What happened to you?" A heavy young woman of about seventeen bounded up to the picnic table and flopped down beside him, propping one bright red running shoe up on the seat to retie one of the laces.

"Hello, Arly," Vic said. He didn't sound all that thrilled to see her. "I'm surprised you're asking."

"Well, last time I saw you, you were dry, eh?" Arly said and laughed boisterously. I didn't have to ask her who her father was—she had Archie Watson's curly brown hair and the same wide face and serious nose. There was a slight weariness at the corner of her eyes, though, probably caused by too many people saying "you'd be very pretty if you'd only lose some weight." Rather than shrink into herself, as many large young women do, she had chosen instead to flaunt it. The result was impressive. She wore a tight T-shirt which showed off her generous bosom, and while her shorts were loose fitting and comfortable, they were brief, and her legs were smooth and tanned. Her fire-engine red sneakers bespoke a personality that was not going to be influenced by twenty-first century weight-ism. She looked terrific.

Vic shrugged and turned his back on her. For a brief second, Arly looked like she was going to clobber him, then the moment passed and she turned her head to bathe David Kane in a heart melting, come-hither glance that made even my heart beat faster. This girl had "it", whatever that is, and knew it.

At that moment, a large wasp buzzed in and landed on the picnic table next to Arly's shoe, attracted, perhaps by the strong pheromones that the girl was pumping into the air. Both Arly and David Kane reacted wildly.

"Ahhh!" Arly shrieked, backing away. "Arrrgh!" Kane shouted, lifted his foot and pulverized the insect with the sole of his hiking boot, twisting it this way and that, just to make sure.

"Geez," I said, "poor little wasp. It was just looking for some lunch, David." I hate it when people kill things for no reason.

"Poor little nothing," Kane said. He was pale, and his eyes shone. "They can be killers if they sting the wrong person." Arly had returned to watch Kane scraping the remains of the wasp off his shoe.

"My hero," she said, doing a *Perils of Pauline* thing and pretending to swoon. "You allergic, too?" She reached into a pocket of her knapsack and withdrew a thick tube, like a magic marker, and brandished it. "It's an epi-pen," she said. "I take it with me everywhere." I'd heard of those—the emergency hypodermic things that allergic people carry with them in case they get stung, or in case they eat peanut butter, or whatever. I'd never seen one before, but I suppressed the urge to ask if I could see it. Arly was getting enough attention as it was.

Kane grinned and patted a pocket of his own knapsack. "Don't leave home without it," he said.

"Some of us," Arly said, fixing me with a steely glare, "live in real fear of those little suckers. It doesn't mean we're bad people. See ya." She was off, bouncing with a kind of full-of-life energy that made it impossible not to watch her.

Kane's eyes met mine, and we exchanged a wordless comment. "Kids today", we silently said. Vic and Sophie, after watching the wasp episode, had retreated into a private chat, so Kane dismissed them both and focused on me. His eyes were very clear and dark, and I could see myself reflected in their depths.

"We?" he said. "You said 'we' were on the trail." At that moment, Rosie and Lug-nut came up to me, tails wagging. Being well brought up, I introduced the dogs to him, and he patted their heads. I couldn't help noticing his hands. They looked strong and well-kept. On one finger, he wore a manly signet ring, platinum, I think, with a green stone that I'll bet wasn't glass.

"What breed are these guys?" he said. I suspected that he came from a world where a dog wasn't a real dog unless it had the pedigree to prove it.

"Rosie's a purebred yellow Lab," I said, which was possibly true, although the only papers she had were the ones she occasionally peed on. "Lug-nut is a Kuskawa Retriever." I wasn't going to perjure myself by using the word pure in reference to Luggy.

"A Kuskawa Retriever? That's not a breed I'm familiar with," Kane said.

"They're very rare," I said.

"Oh, well. Nice dogs," Kane said. "How's the mascot coming?"

"I'll have some stuff for you tonight," I said, feeling a bit uncomfortable, as the work I was doing for the Kountry Pantree had already got me in a bit of hot water, and I wasn't eager to spread the word that I was working for Kane. I needn't have worried. Vic and Sophie had slipped away to the other picnic table, where a veritable banquet had been spread out.

"Grub's up!" someone called. A tiny sneer appeared on David Kane's upper lip, barely perceptible and not very attractive.

"I've got my own stuff in my pack," Kane said quietly, grasping and caressing my elbow. "Caviar, a demi of champagne. Some brie. Would you care to join me somewhere a little more private?"

I wondered if he'd come prepared to hit on a likely female, and I just happened to be handy. I scanned the other members of the camera club and spotted one or two younger women who could also have been likely candidates for Kane's attentions. I was acutely embarrassed. Not that I haven't been propositioned before, but never by someone who was essentially my boss. Kane must have assumed that my "we" referred to the dogs.

"Thanks for the offer, David, but I came with a couple of guys who'd miss me," I said. I could have said I was there with my boyfriend, but I've never been comfortable with the term, and it didn't suit Becker anyway. "Partner" wasn't accurate, and "date" sounded dorky. I've never been very smooth when it comes to rejecting a proposition, which has occasionally resulted in nightmare dates with guys I'm not even remotely interested in. I hate hurting people's feelings. Luckily, Bryan came up and saved me.

"Hey," he said. "They got chicken and cake! Do we have to wait for Dad?"

"I don't see why you can't start without him," I said, feeling warm and strangely maternal. He was a cute kid, and he'd actually treated me like I was somebody important in his life—like it mattered what I thought.

"Cool!" he said, eyeing Kane.

"Hey, big fella," Kane said in a friendly way. "Haven't I seen you before somewhere?" Bryan looked disconcerted for a moment, then decided to ignore the question.

"C'mon guys," he said to the dogs and darted away again. It was Kane's turn to be embarrassed, and he apologized gracefully, replacing one set of assumptions with another. "I'm terribly sorry," he said, standing up at once and stepping out of my personal space, which he had been invading. "I didn't know you were married. Your son's just like you."

I let that go. If I had a son, I thought, he would probably be like me. The fact that Bryan wasn't mine was, under the circumstances, none of Kane's business. I could see Becker approaching along the path which led back to the Jeep. He stopped to have a word with Vic, then headed our way.

"Well, chicken and cake sounds good to me," I said, standing too.

"It's a little early for champagne, anyway," Kane said lightly. "I'll see you at the meeting tonight, Polly." He touched my elbow again as if it were some secret erogenous zone that only he knew about, gave it a little squeeze and let it go. Then he walked quickly over to the picnic banquet, taking the time to tousle Bryan's hair and whisper something to him. What a smoothie. He moved in on Arly, and I could hardly say I blamed him.

"I had an extra pair of jeans in the car," Becker said, handing me a plastic bag and following Kane's retreat with his eyes before turning back to me. "They may be a little big for you, but they're dry."

"Oh, excellent," I said. My jeans were sticking to me in a clammy, unpleasant way, and the sun had gone in again. "I'll just change in the bushes. Thanks."

"I figured you'd be getting into my pants at some point this weekend," Becker said. "It's a little premature, but hey." I swatted at him and he ducked, grinning.

"As you no doubt noticed, David Kane just joined the group," I said. "I don't think there's any love lost between him and Vic Watson. Did you know that Vic almost fell off the Laingford lookout tower during a Camera Club outing last week? His lady friend saved him that time. He suggested he might have been 'helped' over the edge then as well."

"Interesting," Becker said. "You think Kane's trying to do him harm?"

"Who knows? You might tell him to be careful, though. I wouldn't trust David Kane any further than I could throw him." Kane had slipped his arm around Arly Watson's shoulders, and she put her plate down. Moments later they were slipping away from the group and heading for the trail. Champagne and caviar and a rich bachelor to boot. I just hoped she knew what she was getting into.

"Hungry?" Becker said. "I have picnic stuff in my backpack, but there's all that food over there. Vic said to help ourselves."

"Perfect," I said. "You go ahead. Bryan's already in there somewhere. I'll just go do the Superman quick-change thing." Becker had seen the elbow squeeze from Kane, and it had made a tiny worry line appear between his eyebrows. I hoped that he hadn't read anything into it, but just in case, I put my face very close to his and stared into his green-gold eyes.

"My jeans aren't the only thing I'm wearing that's soaked," I whispered in my best phone-sex voice. "I want you to know that when I come out of the bushes in your pants, I won't be wearing any underwear." The green eyes got a shade greener.

"You are an evil woman," he whispered back and kissed me. Kissing is an art that can be taught, but only up to a point. You have to have a natural talent for it, and only instinct will tell you what kind of kisses are appropriate in public. Becker is the greatest kisser I've ever met, and I don't think it was a required course at cop-school. He's a cup-your-face-in-his-hand kind of kisser, as if the lips he's kissing are slightly fragile and require special care. We hadn't displayed much physical affection in public—both too shy, really, and the matter had never come up, so to speak. This was the kind of kiss that you could do in front of your grandmother, but it left me weak-kneed and slightly out of breath. I tottered up the rocks to the trail to find an appropriate bush for changing behind.

As luck would have it, I had just stripped down to my damp gotchies when I heard someone approaching and ducked down out of sight. It was Kane and Arly. I saw the red sneakers and designer hiking boots go by through a gap in the bushes.

"...don't need much experience, because we're going to be computerized," Kane was saying.

"At Dad's we have one of those stupid old-fashioned tills to make the customers think we're, like, pioneers," Arly said. "It's a real pain."

"Why don't you come work for me?" Kane said. "We have a few cashier's jobs left, and the benefits are great. What are you getting now? Minimum wage, I'll bet..." The girl muttered something, and Kane laughed and continued his mesmerizing headhunter pitch as they carried on down the trail. Great, I thought. He's stealing staff right out from under Archie's nose. His own daughter, no less. Vic's brother the grocer was going to go ballistic.

Becker's jeans weren't too big—I'm not exactly a stick-insect myself, and I balled up my own soggy dungarees (along with my undies) and stuffed them into the plastic bag. The jeans were baggy and comfortable, but a bit long, and I had to roll them up at the hem. Something crinkled in the back pocket, and I reached in and found a business card. "K. Johanssen: Custom Jewellery" it said, with an address in Sikwan, the next biggest town south of Laingford.

Now, I am not normally a jealous woman. Far from it. I'm dangerously lax when it comes to keeping an eye out for the signs that most women pick up with internal feminine radar. This has meant that in the past one romantic partner actually drifted away to the point of having offspring with another woman before I noticed. Maybe it's because I've never bothered to invest much in a relationship. In the case of Becker, though, I found myself doing and thinking things that were totally against type. Seeing the word "jeweller" on the business card I found in the back pocket of Becker's jeans set off a peculiar and totally illogical chain-reaction in my brain. 1. Jewellers make personal adornments for women, primarily. 2. Becker had never given me any jewellery, therefore his connection with K. Johanssen had nothing to do with me, therefore 3. it had something to do with another woman who was not me, to whom Becker should not be giving jewellery.

Jeez, Polly, I told myself severely, before my train of thought screamed out of control down the Rockies. Mister K. Johanssen (or Ms.) could have been burglarized and called Becker to investigate. (Nope—Becker didn't wear jeans on duty.) He could have dropped in to the jeweller to order a nice brooch for his mom's birthday. (Nope. His mom died three years ago.) His sister then, the one in Calgary. I applied the brakes, Big Time, and crammed the stupid card back in the pocket from whence it came. Jealously was a new sensation for me, and I didn't like it at all. A great big, cumbersome brain-scrambler, it felt like. A hot and heavy helmet, capable of wiping tender thoughts, like the ones Becker's kiss had left me with, clean off the blackboard of my mind. Unlike jealousy, denial is something I'm used to. By the time I got back to the picnic site, I'd stuffed the jeweller's name into the very back of my mind where I kept my fear of bears, my unhappy childhood and my terror of tax-forms.

The scene which greeted my arrival scattered any remaining thoughts quite effectively. Vic was on the ground again, Sophie was crouched over him, and Becker was on his cell phone.

Eight

Check out our Disney videos! All the latest titles, all the very best in entertainment at prices you won't believe! We also have video games by the truckload that will keep them amused for hours!
—A Kountry Pantree ad in the *Laingford Gazette*

As Becker had predicted, Vic had gone into delayed shock, brought on perhaps by the ecstasy of biting into one of Sophie's lemon squares. He wasn't unconscious or anything—he'd just, as he said, "come over all weak," and Becker was doing his strong-arm act and ordering an ambulance. Vic's protestations were half-hearted, and I don't know about Becker, but I know I felt awfully guilty for not bundling him straight off to hospital in the first place.

Becker put his cell phone away in a pocket and turned to me. "They'll be here in about twenty minutes," he said.

"Couldn't we take him? I could sit in the back with Bryan."

"It might be tricky if he goes into cardiac arrest," Becker said. "Best to wait for the professionals."

"Twenty minutes is an awfully long time," I said. "Do they have to catch the horses first?"

"We're a fair distance into the park," Becker said. "The closest emergency vehicle is the fire truck in Willis Creek, which could get here in five if we needed it, but Vic's in no immediate danger."

"Except he could go into cardiac arrest."

"Which is why we wait for the ambulance," he said. Members of the Camera Club stood around in various attitudes of concern or lack thereof, from Sophie's worried hovering to the relaxed nonchalance displayed by two women piling their plates with potato salad and chattering about film speeds. It was sort of like a car accident in that respect. Those who are directly involved stand or sit by the side of the road, gazing blankly at the scene, or they kneel beside the injured, giving and taking comfort. Passing motorists slow down to gawk, checking for bodies and perhaps for blood, wondering if the victim is somebody they know, then rejoicing that it's not. Still others drive past quickly, eyes averted, cursing the slow-down in traffic.

A fellow human being in distress is interesting, particularly if the situation is already being handled by an authoritative person, Becker in this case. There is no need to step in and do something. Everything that can be done is being done, so the natural adrenaline rush that turns some people into heroes isn't a part of it. Morbid curiosity takes over, guilt dogging its heels. (Is your interest an intrusion? Is your gawking unwholesome? Sick? You'll keep on gawking anyway, though. Betcha.)

Disaster has been packaged as a form of entertainment since the television was invented, and we've learned to be fascinated by it. Action movies, war reports, true crime stories and slasher films have turned us all into cold spectators. When faced with personal horror, we are truly frightened and often traumatized, but when the stakes are lower—the collapse of a colleague, for example, or a roadside fender-bender, it's just another video clip.

The ambulance people arrived in fifteen, not twenty minutes, and quickly bundled Vic onto a wheeled stretcher and hauled him back along the trail. Some of us, including Sophie, followed.

"I'm going in the ambulance to fill them in on Vic's accident and make sure he's okay," Becker said to me. "You drive standard, right? Can you take Bryan back to my place? I'll meet you there."

"Aww, Dad," Bryan said. "I want to come in the ambulance too. I won't touch anything."

"Not this time, kid."

"What about our hike?" Bryan said. If he hadn't said it, I would have. I was as disappointed as he was.

"There are a lot of neat trails around my cabin," I said. "Mark, why don't I take him back there and we can go for a walk in the woods and then have a barbecue?"

"Cool. Can we?" Bryan said.

"I guess so, if it's not any trouble, but don't you have a meeting later?" Becker said.

"It's barely past noon, and that's not until six," I said. "Plenty of time."

Bryan scrambled into the passenger seat of the Jeep, calling to the dogs, who piled in on top of him. Becker drew me aside for a whispered word. "You don't have any pot plants growing around your place, do you?" he said, quite seriously. I shook my head, not daring to open my mouth for fear of what snappish remark might come out. "No rolling papers or hash pipes left out on your desk?"

"Becker, give me a break," I said. He usually completely avoided talking about that stuff. It was a silent agreement we had. Don't ask, don't tell. Now he was asking, and it made me very uncomfortable. I kept my stash hidden away at all times, and I bought my dope from a farmer friend. "Your son shall remain blissfully ignorant of my evil side," I said. "I promise."

"I know he's only eight," Becker said, "but he's no idiot. We teach them about this kind of thing in the schools now, you know."

"I know, Becker. Don't worry. Bryan's safe with me. Now go do your duty, Dudley-Do-Right. Oh, wait. How are you going to get down to Cedar Falls from the hospital? I'll have your Jeep."

Becker grinned. "I'll get Morrison to drive me. He's working today," he said, referring to his beefy partner, Earlie Morrison. Earlie was a close friend of my Aunt Susan's, and of mine, actually. He didn't approve of my relationship with Becker at all (Susan's opinion didn't help), and he'd be just tickled to be asked to drive Becker to my place.

"I'm sure he'll love that. Who's his partner while you're on vacation?"

"Marie Lefevbre," Becker said. "She's new, and they seem to get along okay. I think Morrison has a crush on her."

"Marie? That's not the young constable who was in charge of guarding us after the Steamboat episode, is it? The one who stood over us in the police station, writing down everything we said?" That had been some months ago, but the murder at Steamboat Theatre was still fresh in my mind.

"That's her," Becker said. I was surprised to feel a certain twinge of sisterly concern about Morrison falling for Marie, whom I remembered to have been rather pretty. Morrison was a large man, and more vulnerable than most people gave him credit for. What if she broke his heart? Would Becker be there to pick up the pieces? I didn't think so.

"I've gotta get going," Becker said. "I'll see you back at your place in a while." He gave me a quick peck on the cheek and climbed into the back of the ambulance, which accelerated out of the gravel parking lot with its lights flashing.

Bryan was silent for some time after we hit the highway. I tried very hard not to say the kind of things that grown-ups blither at times like these, when they're forced into close, exclusive association with a small person they don't know very well. I didn't say "So, what grade are you in?" or "What do you want to be when you grow up?" Neither did I ask the kind of questions I was really dying to ask, like "So, what's your mother like?" and "What kind of person do you think your Dad is?" I think children are much more comfortable with silence than adults are.

Finally, Bryan spoke. "Did that man die and then come back to life?" he said.

"Well, sort of," I said. "He wasn't breathing when your Dad pulled him out of the water."

"What do you think about when you die?" he said. I immediately flashed on a moment the year before when someone had tried to shoot me. I had been so scared I'd wet myself. I wondered how much would be appropriate to share with an eight-year-old, precocious as he was.

"I think that sometimes, in an accident, anyway, things happen so fast there isn't time to think," I said. "Your thoughts probably go sort of like 'Uh-oh' and then that's it."

"Would you have time to pray?"

"I guess, if that occurred to you."

"And then when you die, you get to see Jesus, right?" Yikes, I thought. I was not exactly the right kind of person to be getting into a theological discussion with an impressionable child.

"Maybe," I said. I wondered if Bryan's Mom was a church-goer. Did Bryan go to Sunday School? Was he a "Now I Lay Me Down To Sleep" kind of kid? I was out of my element, and strangely, rather frightened. If Bryan had started asking questions about my sex life, I would have been able to handle it. Religion, on the other hand, was a loaded issue for me. Coming from an adult, questions about faith were easy to blow off. Coming from a child, they were important, and I didn't think it right to be flippant.

"So, if you meet Jesus when you die, what happens when you're brought back to life again?" Bryan said.

Why can't he be talking about Jeeps and computers and food? I asked myself. I could deal with those.

"What do you think?" I said.

"On the Internet, there's this website about near-death experiences," Bryan said, sounding efficient, informed and forty.

"What does it say?"

"Some people see a light, and when they come back, they're really sad," Bryan said.

"Why sad?"

"Maybe they were happy meeting Jesus and God, and they didn't want to come back here at all," Bryan said. Or maybe, I thought, they were sad because they got the news that heaven was full of bored people in white robes who all thought they were better than you. I said "Hmmm" in a chicken-shit kind of way.

"My Sunday school teacher says that we all have a job to do on earth, and maybe they're sad because their job isn't finished yet, so they have to come back," Bryan said.

I waited, easing up on the accelerator after I looked down, and discovered that I was speeding. Tension, maybe. I didn't want to usher little Bryan into the next world before his job was done, and I certainly wasn't ready to meet the Big Guy myself, seeing as I was very likely on his "Send to Hell" list.

"You've been thinking about this a lot, haven't you?" I said.

"I was just wondering if the man you and Dad saved got to meet Jesus," Bryan said.

"He didn't mention it," I said and immediately regretted

my tone. Bryan's face fell, and he remained silent until I pulled into the parking lot at the A&P in Cedar Falls.

"We have to pick up a few things for our barbecue," I said. "Hamburgers and hotdogs okay with you?" Bryan became a normal little boy again, much to my relief.

"Can I get a chocolate bar?" he said.

"I don't see why not," I said. I sent him off to locate a bag of charcoal briquettes while I poked around in the meat bin. I don't eat a lot of meat as a rule, not because I'm vegetarian, but because I don't have a refrigerator. Instead, I keep my food cold with an old fashioned icebox, fuelled by big blocks of ice cut out of the beaver pond every winter and stored in a straw-filled ice-house at the back of the cabin. The icebox keeps things reasonably cool, but meat doesn't keep for very long.

Bryan was fascinated by my place, as I'd expected. I showed him how the icebox worked and where the ice was stored. He seemed amazed by the concept of ice being kept solid in straw and sawdust in the middle of summer without electricity, just as I had been when I first tried it. I explained how I used propane to work the small, two-burner stove and how at night I lit oil lamps and candles. Bryan had never seen a wood stove before, which I thought was peculiar, and I explained the theory behind wood heat as well as I could. He wasn't too impressed with the outhouse, but was more than happy to work the hand pump when I needed a bucket of water. After about an hour of explaining and justifying the details of my lifestyle to this twenty-first century child, I was beginning to feel like a pioneer museum exhibit.

Bryan sat at the kitchen table, cracking peanuts and watching me mix ground beef with onion, egg, oatmeal and spices for the hamburgers.

"Wrestling is on right now," he said, nonchalantly.

"Sorry?"

"The World Wrestling Foundation. You know, wrestling. It's on right now. I usually watch it." His tone of voice was kind of hopeful, as if he were asking permission for something.

"Wrestling is on what, Bryan?"

"On TV, silly," he said.

"Uh-huh. And how does television work?" I said.

"I dunno. You know. You use the remote and press the buttons. Like a computer. You turn it on."

"It uses electricity," I said. "Remember, I told you I don't have electricity here."

Bryan was flabbergasted. Gobsmacked. The tour of Polly's cabin had been entertaining in its way, I suppose, but he was getting bored and was hankering for an electronic fix.

"You don't have a TV?" He was thoroughly incredulous.

"Nope. No phone, either."

Now he was looking at me as if I were an alien species, which was probably not far from the truth.

"Everyone has a TV," he said.

"Not everyone. Look, why don't you help me make the hamburgers? It's sort of like clay—you roll it into balls and then mash them down into patties."

"Okay, I guess. But I'd rather watch wrestling," he said.

"Or you could draw a picture. I've got lots of art supplies in the corner," I said. He gave me a look of pure contempt.

"I only use CorelDraw," he said, "or Adobe Illustrator. You need a computer and electricity for that."

Parenting? Count me out.

Nine

Half an hour later, the hamburgers were ready to go, keeping cool in the icebox, and Bryan had finally condescended to try out my best pastels on a sheet of construction paper. He was creating an action scene from his unwatched, sorely lamented wrestling program, and he obviously had a genuine gift for drawing. At the top of the page, he had drawn two burly wrestlers on a tall blue stage, grappling fiercely. Down below, a spectator was showing his disapproval by mooning the contestants. It was pure satire, and I loved it.

"Oh, it's easy," Bryan said when I complimented him. "You're pretty good yourself." I was working on the sketches for my Kountry Pantree meeting.

"I like the cow best," Bryan said. "What are those other ones supposed to be?"

"That's a gopher, and this one's a goose," I said. "A Canada goose."

"The goose looks like E.T.," Bryan said. "Sorry, but it does."

"You're right, and it would be hard for a person to fit into that costume anyway."

"You could make the person inside put their arm up in the air," Bryan suggested, demonstrating. "The arm could be the neck and their hand could be the head part."

"How clever of you," I said. "That's exactly what some puppeteers do in plays."

"I know," Bryan said. "I didn't think it up by myself. It's from the Dudley the Dragon website. There's this picture of the Dudley costume with one side cut out so you can see the guy inside."

"Okay, so the Internet isn't all bad," I said.

"No, it's pretty neat, really. Although there's a lot of garbage on it. You have to be careful."

"What sort of garbage?" I asked, although I had a pretty good idea. I may not have a TV, but I read the papers. I've heard about Internet porn and sick adults picking kids up online.

"Oh, you know. Commercials and yucky romance stuff. My Mom has a census thing on our computer at home, but my Dad doesn't."

"A censor thing, more likely," I said. "So you can't look at stuff for grown-ups."

"Yeah. It's called Kidsafe. It's a real pain. It blacks out words and pictures sometimes so you can't see them, which makes you want to see them more, you know?"

"I know exactly what you mean. So your Dad's computer doesn't have that?"

"Nope. But he trusts me."

"He must."

Bryan made that sort of "tssk" sound that indicates annoyance, and I suppressed a chuckle. There was a pause as we both concentrated on our work.

"You know, grown-ups think that kids are stupid," he said after a while. "They streetproof us and warn us that there are sickos out there, and then they never let us go anywhere to show we can handle it. It's like they give you a skateboard and then say you're not allowed to ride it."

"Do you have a skateboard?"

"Nope. My Mom says I'm not old enough to have an attitude, whatever that is."

"Bryan, I think you have an attitude already. A very adult one."

"So what's an attitude?"

"Look it up. Dictionary's over there on that shelf. Starts with A-T-T."

"I have a dictionary function on my computer," he said. "You just click on the word, and it tells you what it means."

"Uh-huh. I have a dictionary function in hard copy right there," I said. He didn't move.

"I don't read very well," he said. I suppressed the urge to vent aloud about computer literacy having vanquished true literacy, the sort of fuddy-duddy crap that would have alienated my little friend for ever. After all, he was only eight. He was staggeringly sophisticated for eight, but still. I did not tell him that I could read fluently by the time I was four. What good would that have done? Anyway, when I was a kid my family didn't have TV or computers. Books were it.

He looked it up, and we read the entry together. It wasn't an easy one, and I think he was bored by the time I'd explained what "settled behaviour" and "settled mode of thinking" was, but by that time Becker had arrived.

The rest of our Kodak-moment afternoon was lovely. No more near-drownings, no more intrigue. Just the Becker boys and me and a couple of dogs. We went for a long walk along my favourite trail, the one that meanders through towering stands of maple and birch at the north end of George's farm. The trees are lofty, and the leaves rustle in a musical way when the wind passes through them. The sun was out for good now, all the earlier clouds having been blown away by a pleasantly warm wind. We paused for a rest beside a little stream that burbles and sings through the forest and turns into a tiny version of the Oxblood Falls at the brow of the hill. The previous summer, I'd built a toy-sized water wheel on the stream, just before the cascade, where the water picks up speed a little and dances over the rocks.

"How come you built it?" Bryan asked, crouching down to get a better look.

"I wanted to see if it would work," I said. "I have a book at home, a very old one called *Amateur Handicrafts for a Curious Boy*. I found the instructions in there."

Becker's Curious Boy was fascinated. I promised to show him the book when we got back. "There are a lot of neat projects in there," I said. "It was written way long ago when the winters were long, and they didn't have Nintendo." Bryan gave me a look, and I resolved to ease up on the Luddite stuff. He was interested, that was enough.

We followed the path back to the cabin and grilled our hamburgers and hot dogs on the hibachi, electing to eat outside on the deck. The breeze kept the mosquitoes away, and the sun was deliciously warm. After he'd eaten, Bryan disappeared inside, saying he wanted to look at my Amateur Handicraft book. I followed him about twenty minutes later to get a couple of cold beers from the icebox and found him curled up on the futon, fast asleep, with Rosie and Luggy keeping him warm on either side. Boys, like puppies, are irresistible when they're asleep. I patted all three of them gently on the head before going back to Becker.

"Zonked out?" Becker said quietly as I handed him his beer. I nodded. "Thought so. He was wearing that glazed look. I hope the falls episode this morning doesn't give him nightmares."

"He seemed pretty calm about it," I said. "Although he did have some interesting questions about the afterlife, which I found rather difficult to answer. He has an interesting mind. Like his Dad."

"He's way smarter than I am," Becker said. "I think he'll turn out to be another Bill Gates type, which would be good. He can keep his old Dad in the lifestyle to which he would like to become accustomed."

"A yacht, maybe? A country estate and lots of fast cars?"

"I was thinking more of a retirement villa on the B.C. coast, but yeah, a yacht would be nice." We sipped our beer in companionable silence, but I could feel him beside me, working up to something.

"He likes you, you know," Becker said.

"I like him, too. Thank God."

"What do you mean?"

"Oh, just that I was worried he'd hate me or he'd turn out to be a brat that I couldn't stand. That would have been tricky."

"You thought my kid could've been a brat?" He was bristling.

"Oh, Becker, relax. You know I'm not crazy about kids. I've dropped lots of hints in that department. At least, I thought I had, which was why I figured it took so long for you to introduce me to Bryan—which is fine, by the way. Totally understandable."

"Well, yeah, I did kind of wonder just how much you disliked kids, eh? But this kid is different. He's mine. So I didn't want to rush things."

"Anyway, that hurdle's over with. We like each other."

"So I don't have to keep you two in separate cages," Becker said, taking a swig of his Kuskawa Cream Ale. "That's a relief." It was my turn to bristle.

"I'm not big on cages," I said.

Becker laughed. "Aren't we just tiptoeing around the issues?" he said. "Look, I know I don't talk about my feelings very much—I'm not the new-age sensitive guy you should be going out with, I'm a big divorced cop with a kid who can't figure out what you see in me."

I leered at him suggestively until he blushed. "That's not fair," he said. "There's got to be more to it than that, Polly."

"Sorry," I said. "I'm not used to serious talk coming from you, of all people. Scares the hell out of me."

"Me too."

"But Mark, this thing we have—of course it's based on more than sex. It has to be, doesn't it? I mean, neither of us is a teenager any more, but we're both capable of cruising the bars for an occasional pillow buddy if that was all we wanted. It would be easier than stumbling around in boyfriend/girlfriend-land like we've been doing."

"True."

"But as to what I see in you, I've been asking myself that for months. Actually, so have several other people."

He laughed, a little nervously, but persisted. "I can just imagine who. What did you tell them?"

"That you're honest and decent and a bit of a hunk," I said. He rolled his eyes but didn't try to stop me talking. I guess he really wanted to know. I don't think he was fishing for compliments or anything. Becker's not like that. "What I didn't tell them, because I've never tried to, you know, make a list until now, is this—" I thought for a moment. "You give me a lot of space, you're not demanding and you have your own life. You're not needy. Your sense of humour is just like mine. You can be bossy sometimes, but you make up for it by being—I have to say it—really great in bed." Becker was so red now, he almost matched his hair. Well, he asked for it. "So," I said, "I made you blush. Your turn, O big divorced cop-with-a-kid who's being sensitive all of a sudden. Quick, before the spell wears off. What do you see in me, then? A flaky Luddite, I think you said once?"

Becker moved in for the kill. Here it comes, I thought. This is where he tells me that he's seeing someone else, but he'd really like to stay friends.

"I think you're the most amazing woman I've ever met," he said, speaking rather quickly. "Your independence drives me crazy, and I've always been attracted to women who need me, so go figure. You're gorgeous and smart and funny and I don't want to be your pillow buddy any more, I want to marry you." He reached into the breast pocket of his shirt. "I wanted to give you this at our picnic, but a body got in the way, as usual," he said. Keep talking, I thought fiercely at him. I can't say a word.

"Don't say anything yet—not yes, not no, okay? I've been practising this, and I'll lose my place. Just keep this—wear it if you want, or keep it for a while and think about it. I just want you to know where I stand. It won't kill me if you just want to keep things going as they are, and I know I've kind of sprung this on you. So it's your move, Polly."

The little box was damp. I guess he'd had it on him when he fished Vic Watson out of the Oxblood River. The ring was pretty, a thin gold band set with a modest diamond, simple and really very tasteful, if you like diamond rings. I gazed at it.

"You look sad," Becker said. "This is not good."

Polly Deacon, queen of the gentle rejection, struggled to

say something honest that wouldn't sound like a kick in the balls. It wasn't easy.

"Oh, golly," was all I could manage. "Oh, the irony" would have been more accurate. I had just finished telling Becker that one of the things I really liked about him was that he gave me my space and wasn't demanding or needy. Not that he hadn't just given me a really easy out at the end of his proposal, if that's what it was, but my problem was that I wasn't sure I wanted to take it. My inner Spinster was running screaming for the hills, but a large part of me was saying "why the hell not, you idiot?" As well, my inner Cinderella was whining that he hadn't said "I love you" and, ridiculously, that he hadn't got down on one knee like they do in the movies.

My silence was freaking Becker out. "Can we see if it fits, anyway?" he said softly. I nodded. The box had a label inside—"K. Johanssen", the Sikwan jeweller whose card I had found in the back pocket of the jeans I was still wearing. That flash of jealously I'd felt earlier was replaced with a complicated mixture of doom and delight. With infinite care, he took the ring from its wet velvet nest and slipped it on The Finger. Perfect fit.

I think that one of the reasons for the tradition of the ring is that it gives the proposer and the proposee something to concentrate on while they struggle with imminent heart failure. Our hands were shaking. Wedding images scrolled across my private movie screen; white dresses, organ music, the sweet proud face of Becker waiting at the altar, a bouquet of something expensive trembling in my hands. Quickly, though, the movie turned surreal. Lug-nut and Rosie bounded down the aisle and jumped up on the priest, Bryan as ring-bearer wore a face of thunder, and suddenly the church was full of goats and policemen.

"I'm sorry, Mark," I said. "I can't possibly give you an answer right now. I'm floored. Confused. Flattered. Bewildered."

"Enough with the thesaurus," Becker said. "I didn't expect you to throw yourself into my arms yelling yes, yes."

"Really?" I said.

"If you had, I would have called 911 to have them take you away."

"That's a relief."

"But you didn't throw the ring in my face either, and that's something."

"Did you really think I might do that?"

"I had considered the possibility. But I didn't want to just casually ask how you felt about marrying me, because I was afraid you wouldn't take me seriously." He poked my finger. "This is to show you that I'm serious, that's all." Then he gently removed the ring, put it back in its box and handed it to me. "Hold on to it, Polly. Think about it. I'll know what your answer is when and if I see you wearing it."

"Way too symbolic," I said. "Can't I just tell you?"

"Yup. That would be good. Can I kiss you now?"

During the next few moments, I think Becker might have whispered that he loved me, but I'm not absolutely sure, and anyway, I've never believed in *amor vincit omnia*. More like amor screws everything up so it's impossible to think straight.

We heard little footsteps on the deck and disengaged ourselves. Bryan was standing there, his hair tousled and a look of distress on his face.

"Ms. Deacon," he said, "your puppy just pooped on your bed."

Ten

Do you like eating at your meeting? Call our deli section for a tray of goodies to make your business get-togethers go with a bang!
   —An ad in the *Laingford Gazette*

Duke Pitblado's real estate office was housed in a Victorian mansion in the west end of Laingford, overlooking Lake Kimowan and the town girly bar, Kelso's. The mascot focus-group was scheduled to meet in Duke's boardroom at 6 p.m., but I was early, as the hired help is expected to be. I had my drawings with me, rolled up in a mailing tube, and I'd requested one of those flip-chart things so I could pretend that I was making a presentation to a multi-national executive assembly.

The door of Pitblado Kuskawa Enterprises was locked, so I pressed the buzzer and waited, sweating in the July heat. I wore a mildly businesslike get-up, a biscuit coloured linen jacket and matching walking shorts that a friend had given me "in case you ever get a real job." Beneath the jacket and red silk tank-top, Becker's ring hung on a thin gold chain. I had tried it on again after he left, but my mind was still too scrambled to do more than stare at it and marvel at how a little bit of gold and rock could represent such a huge fork in my personal road. The chain was long enough that the ring dangled well below the cleavage line. I didn't want anybody asking about it.

Actually, I didn't want anybody knowing about it at all. At least not for a while. I knew, though, that I would blurt it out to George or Susan fairly soon. I am, as Susan has said many a time, an open book.

My buzz was answered by a precise female voice.

"Yes?" she said.

"Polly Deacon here for the Kountry Pantree meeting," I said, sounding as official as I could. Obviously, if you wanted to buy Kuskawa real estate from Duke, you had to have an appointment. No "just browsing" here, kiddies.

"Oh, yes," the disembodied voice said. "Please come up." Another buzz followed, and I pulled the door open and stepped inside. Immediately, goosebumps appeared on my arms, and I tugged down the sleeves of the jacket, which I'd rolled up. It was freezing in there. I'm not a big fan of air conditioning to begin with, but this was ridiculous. Talk about conspicuous consumption. Shivering, I climbed the thickly carpeted stairs to the second floor, following the discreet brass signs. Antique prints of old Kuskawa homes studded the walls, sepia tinted and beautifully framed. Someone had done an exquisite job with the restoration of the interior. The staircase was one long, beautiful sweeping curve, with finials and spindles—polished oak, maybe—heavy and luxurious. The wallpaper was period and the woodwork around the windows glowed in the early evening light. It occurred to me that if I had been entering this building in the 1800s, I would probably be using the back stairs, the servants' entrance. Know thy place, an inner voice said to me. There is big, old money here.

At the top of the stairs, a receptionist behind a vast, polished desk greeted me with a cool smile. She was dressed for mid-autumn, in a boiled wool cardigan (Chanel, probably) and discreet pearls at neck and ears. She wasn't much older than I was, but she exuded sophistication and poise. Her ash-blonde hair was swept artfully back into a thing I think they call a chignon.

"Ms. Deacon? You're early," she said.

"Sorry, it's a habit I have. I should have brought a sweater, though. You could catch cold in here."

"I know," she said, thawing suddenly and dimpling at the cheeks. "It's Arctic, isn't it?" She pronounced it "Ardic" and slipped a notch or two on the social scale. I liked her better for it. Her face was somehow familiar, and we exchanged that "do I know you from somewhere" look.

"Wait—you're Polly, aren't you?" she said. "Polly from drama?"

"Linda? Linda Stewart! Well, long time no see!" I said. Linda and I had been in the same Grade Nine drama class at Laingford High. We hadn't known each other very well, but we'd played opposite one another in some obscure play that went to the Sears Drama Festival and won an award. We'd shared a room in Peterborough, where the festival was held, and gotten drunk on apple wine together. At least, I thought it was apple wine. It might have been lemon gin. We'd puked our guts out, anyway, both of us. It was a long time ago. I had lost touch with all but a very few of my high-school contemporaries.

"Still drinking lemon gin?" she said, confirming the evil beverage and bonding us instantly in that peculiar high school reunion kind of way.

"Well, not as such. I seem to recall lemon gin being decidedly dangerous."

"I'll say," Linda said. She came out from behind her elegant desk and hugged me.

"So, what've you been up to in the past twenty years or so?" I said.

"Oh, you know. The usual," Linda said, looking rather wistful. "I'm married. Three beautiful kids. I'm not Linda Stewart any more. I'm Linda Kirschnick."

"Not Doug? You married Doug? You lucky thing." I swear that for a moment, Linda and I were fifteen again, staring into the past as if a veil had been lifted. Our voices had risen into the stratosphere, shrieking and giggling. We practically bounced up and down. Doug Kirschnick had been the hunk actor guy, the Grade Twelve Bogart with the bedroom eyes. We'd all had a massive crush on him, and Linda had married him. Gosh.

"Yup. I snagged him," Linda said, smiling proudly. "And we have three boys, Polly." She snatched a framed photo from her desk and showed me—three young hunklets, all looking exactly like Doug had at various stages all through public and high school. All looking smug and self-satisfied.

"So what's Doug doing now?" I said, after admiring her brood. "Did he ever pursue his talent? He was an amazing actor."

"In more ways than one," Linda said but did not elaborate. "He works here, actually. Real estate. A sales representative. He tried to be an actor, Polly, but never got anywhere. Real estate's been good to us, though. We're doing pretty well."

"I'm glad to hear it," I said, but there was a feeling of cold melancholy in the room, suddenly, as if the air-conditioning had been turned up a notch or two, if that were possible. Linda herself had been a brilliant math and physics student, destined we had thought for a PhD and a life of scientific research. I didn't ask her about that. Her Chanel sweater and shiny receptionist's desk were all the answer I needed.

"What about you?" she said. "Married? Any kids?" I briefly sketched my life to date. I didn't have any offspring to show her, but I did pull out a snapshot of me and the dogs on the front porch of the cabin.

"You're so lucky to be independent," Linda said. "You can do anything you want. I find that hard, sometimes. The responsibility of a family." I suddenly saw myself living in Mark Becker's apartment, wearing a June Cleaver dress and fixing an after school snack for Bryan, Cheez Whiz and Ritz crackers, with the soap operas droning away on the TV in the background.

"Independence can be lonely," I said, surprising myself. There was no time for more, as the buzzer downstairs sounded and Linda became the Pitblado Kuskawa Enterprises receptionist again. After she had buzzed in whoever it was, she gave me a bright smile.

"We'll have to get together sometime," she said.

"Sure, that would be fun," I said, but we both knew that was unlikely. In high school, all we'd had in common was drama class. It wouldn't be any different now, and there's nothing more depressing than playing "Whatever happened to so-and-so?" after you've realized there's nothing else to talk about. Different circles, different lives.

I followed her directions to the boardroom and began to set up my Kountry Pantree mascot sketches, feeling rather nostalgic and very slightly antique, as if I and my peers had all squandered our early potential and had nothing much to show for it.

The Elliots, Winston and Serena, arrived with Duke Pitblado right behind them. Linda came in with fresh coffee and a tray of cheese, fruit and pastries from the French Loaf in Sikwan. I knew this because all their little petits fours have French Loaf logos on them in gold icing. Not exactly within the budget for the cheezie set. I hadn't had dinner because my walking shorts, though fashionable, were a bit snug around the middle, so I'd planned to eat later. (A note to those of you on fixed incomes who sometimes have to show up at cadillac-class meetings. Eat lots of Kraft Dinner first so you don't have to do battle with hunger when they bring out the high-end nibblies.) I waited until the men had loaded up their napkins with brie, stilton and strawberry tarts, then took a couple of grapes and a slice of perfect camembert on a whole wheat cracker. Ladies don't pork out on the genteel finger food, I told myself, willing my tummy to stop gurgling.

Serena Elliot, rail thin and possessed of a face that had been lifted more times than I've lifted a beer mug, contented herself with a black coffee and two carrot sticks. Duke Pitblado, who is a very big man, worked steadily through the food that was closest to him, eating with a mindless determination that I found a little embarrassing. Winston Elliot ignored the food but filled his coffee cup almost half full of cream and added about seven sugars. We were waiting for David Kane, who, being the head honcho, could be as late as he damn well pleased. We made small talk, about the weather, the traffic congestion downtown, and how wonderful it must be for the local retailers but how dreadful for the locals, etc. Pitblado boasted about skyrocketing real estate prices, and Elliot offered the information that the resort had been booked solid since May. I could have talked about the bumper crop of zucchini in George's garden, but I didn't think they'd be interested. Serena just looked at her nails and said nothing.

When Kane arrived at almost a quarter after six, all the nibblies on the tray in Duke's corner were gone, and he was starting in on my sector. Oddly, I had lost my appetite.

"Sorry I'm late," Kane said. "Got held up at the construction site."

"Everything going smoothly?" Duke asked, spraying

shortcrust pastry across the table. Serena flinched, and an expression of distaste passed briefly across her smooth, shiny face.

"Absolutely!" Kane said. I've never really trusted people who use that word instead of "yes". "We should be ready to open on September the first, if everything stays on schedule. We've got almost a full complement of staff now, and our marketing campaign is ready to move into full gear." Kane looked at me expectantly. "Which is why we're here, of course. Polly? I believe you have some sketches to show us."

"Absolutely," I said. I didn't mean to, it just popped out. I saw a flicker of amusement in Serena's eyes, but her face remained immobile. I presented my three sketches. First there was Grocer Goose, a cheerful fowl (the one Bryan thought looked like E.T.) with a nice white apron and huge yellow feet. I pointed out, however, that if they went with that one, they'd probably have to schedule several staff members per shift to wear the costume, as the head piece was as Bryan described— held aloft, which would be hard on the arms.

"We can't have that," Duke said. "We'd have people coming down with repetitive stress or arm injuries, and we could be sued." Kane agreed. The word "sued" made him go pale.

The second option was Willie Gopher. I had to explain the pun. "Willie Gopher…you know, as in the question 'will he go for groceries?' You could have fun with it in your ad stuff."

"I don't get it," Winston Elliot said.

"You never get jokes," Serena said. It was the first time I'd heard her speak. She had a lovely voice, all bell-tones and treacle.

"Aren't puns the lowest form of humour?" Duke said. This, in retrospect, when you looked at the ad campaign that eventually emerged, was ironic.

"What about the cow? I always liked the cow idea the best," Kane said. I showed them Kountry Cow. Or Kow, as they would have it. They loved it, as I knew they would. The vote was unanimous. Kountry Kow it was.

"Dairy nice choice," Serena said, looking pointedly at Duke.

"How soon can you have the costume made?" Kane said. "The Bath Tub Bash is next Saturday and we want to put a Kountry Pantree tub in the race, to show our community support. I want the mascot to be driving it." The Laingford Bath Tub Bash is an annual publicity stunt that's been a highlight of the summer tourist season for about twenty years. The racing vessels—a bunch of fibreglass tub-shaped boats with small outboards, sponsored by practically every business in the area—run an obstacle course on the Kuskawa River, with much kibitzing and merriment. It's a major deal—a big attraction, loved by many, loathed by some. It pulls about eight thousand people into the downtown core for an afternoon, always makes the regional TV news and creates the mother of all gridlocks on Main Street. Wahoo.

"It could be dangerous for the person inside the costume if the tub capsizes," I said. "The foam rubber padding would take on water and sink like a stone."

"They've got all those safety people on Sea-Doos standing by," Kane said. "It'll be fine. So, can you finish the costume in a week?"

"Oh, jeez," I said. "A week? I can try, I guess. There would have to be an extra charge for overtime, if I have to make it waterproof as well." I had given Kane an estimate for the job when I got the go-ahead to make the sketches, but we hadn't signed anything. "I'd thought I had until the end of August."

"Oh, we can throw in an extra couple hundred for time and

trouble, can't we, Dave?" Duke said. "Don't worry about it, dear." Now, I don't much like being called "dear", but the fact that these folks could talk about throwing in a couple of hundred like it was a sneeze made me regret my modest estimate at the beginning of the business. Live and learn, I guess.

"Just invoice us," Kane said. "We're good for it." He snickered then, and I realized that they were making fun of me. Well, a couple of hundred may be a joke to the Kountry Pantree magnates, but it wasn't to me. I resolved at the next meeting to gorf out on all the pricey stuff on the goodie tray before anyone else got there.

Ten minutes later, I was out in the parking lot with an advance on my fee burning a hole in my pocket, while the muggy July air burned a hole in my brain. I had one week to build a full-body cow costume, complete with detachable head, out of fun fur and foam rubber, and teach some poor teenager how to stumble around in it without falling on his butt. In addition, it appeared that I was also required to make the costume waterproof (which ruled out using hot-glue, my old standby) and provide enough visibility in the head-piece so that the person inside could see well enough to pilot a Bath Tub around a watery obstacle course without drowning. A puppet maker's work is never done.

Eleven

I am not, as you may have gathered, a deeply religious person, but I do have some regard for the Sabbath. I like the notion that on one day out of the seven, a person is more or less forbidden to do any work. Not that I work particularly hard during the rest of the week, compared to the wage slaves who nine-to-five it in offices or factories, but a day of sanctioned idleness is welcome nonetheless. On Sunday morning, I closed the cover of my sketchbook and ignored the insistent whispering in my brain telling me I had less than seven days to create a cow. Instead, I lounged on the deck with L.R. Wright's last book, *Kidnap*, and a cup of coffee with Bailey's in it.

Eddie Schreier and his girlfriend, Robin, found me snoozing there in the late morning.

"Hey, Polly!" Eddie called from the path. Lug-nut and Rosencrantz, who had been dozing on my feet, scrambled up and went to meet them. I offered them coffee, and they joined me in the sun, sitting close together on the foldout patio lounger I'd scrounged from the dump. They were both a bit grubby, having spent most of the morning working in George's vegetable garden.

"We came up to deliver a message," Eddie said. "Constable Becker called this morning. You and him are supposed to go to the police station."

"The station? I thought he was on vacation."

"Yeah. He said you had to go in to give a statement about the man that you guys rescued yesterday. He said to tell you that the guy died in hospital last night."

"Vic? Oh no. That's terrible. He must have had a heart attack after all. Oh, poor Vic."

"Yeah, that sucks," Eddie said. Both he and Robin had that sorrowful but slightly avid look you get when you hear about the death of someone you don't know. It's not that you're glad they're dead by any means, but the details are interesting. I told them about the river rescue and what kind of man Vic had seemed to be.

"It'll be a big loss to the town," I said. "Vic was a councillor, and according to Becker, one of the only guys on council who really questioned things that everybody else blindly accepted."

"Susan says somebody probably bumped him off because he was against the Kountry Pantree project," Eddie said. "That big store is sure making a lot of people mad, isn't it?"

I nodded. "Having a heart attack in hospital can hardly be construed as foul play, though," I said. Vic had suggested the day before that someone was perhaps trying to nudge him off into the afterlife, but I didn't mention it. I would definitely remind Becker, though. I sighed and tipped up my coffee cup to get the last drops of Bailey's. My sabbath was over, I guess.

"We also came to ask for your advice," Eddie said, as I

began to haul myself up out of my chair. His face had gone dead serious, and Robin's had turned pink. I sat back down.

"Ask away," I said.

"Ummm, well, it's kind of hard," Eddie said.

"Anything I can do for you, I'll do," I said. "You know that, Eddie."

"Well, promise you won't get mad? We can't talk to Susan about this because she'll go postal, and Robin's dad's going to kill her."

Uh-oh, I thought, guessing what was coming.

"I can't promise I won't get mad, but if I do, I promise I won't lecture you," I said.

"See, I told you she was cool," Eddie said to Robin, who looked ready to hyperventilate. "Go ahead, Robin." I waited. There was a long pause. Eddie was holding Robin's hand very tightly, as if to give her strength for the next part, as they had obviously agreed that she would do the telling.

"I think I'm pregnant," Robin whispered. Yup. Figured.

"We were always real careful, eh?" Eddie said. "It's not like we're a stupid couple of kids, you know?"

"You just think you're pregnant?" I said, gently. "You're not sure yet?"

"Well, my period's late and everything," Robin said. "I can't go to the doctor because he'll tell my Mom, and there's no clinic around here."

"Your doctor isn't allowed to tell her," I said. "They're supposed to keep that stuff confidential."

"Oh, right," Robin said, her voice weighted with sarcasm.

"Well, they're not," I said, but I didn't sound all that confident myself. Small town and all that.

"So what do we do now?" Eddie said.

"Well, I guess the first thing to do, before you both flip out completely, is to find out for sure," I said. "Then when you know, you can start to look at your options."

"I'm so scared," Robin said.

"You know I won't let you go through this alone," Eddie said. Well, that was a blessing anyway, I thought. There were plenty of teenaged boys who would disappear like smoke at the first whiff of fatherhood. I spent a moment swallowing the speech that popped into my mind—the "if you're not prepared to take responsibility, why the hell did you have sex in the first place" speech, which is what they'd have got from Susan. I was flattered that they'd decided to confide in me, but I also wondered if they did so because they thought I approved of teen sex.

"How old are you, Robin?" I asked.

"Seventeen," she said. Same age as Eddie.

"Well, if you are pregnant, you won't be the first seventeen-year-old mom on the planet," I said. "In some cultures, you'd be an old married lady with three kids by now. Juliet was about twelve, you know. So was the Virgin Mary." Robin smiled wanly.

"Robin and I love each other," Eddie said. "And we're going to get married some day."

"That's great," I said. "But you'd probably like to have some control over the timing, eh?" They both nodded.

"So, how are you going to find out for certain whether or not you're pregnant?" I said. I wasn't going to lead them by the hand.

"Ummm, there are tests you can get, right? I've seen them in magazines," Robin said.

"Yup. That's right. You can pick them up at the drugstore for about ten bucks," I said. "And the Downtown Drugstore's open on Sundays. You can go right now."

"But what if somebody sees?" Robin said. "Then they'll tell my Mom. She knows a lady who works there."

"Ah," I said. "Eddie, you two have been using condoms, right?" He nodded, blushing. "And how do you acquire those?"

"Ummm, a friend gets them for me."

"Uh, huh. And I expect that the drugstore checkout person blabs it all over town that he's buying condoms, right?"

"I don't know. But he's never made a big secret of it," Eddie said.

"I see. So it's cool to be seen buying condoms, because that means you're 'getting it', right? But it's uncool to be seen buying a pregnancy test, because that means you're getting it, but you messed up."

"Sort of. I guess."

That was as far as I was willing to go in lecture mode, for now. Although I had plenty more where that came from. We all make mistakes, but they were so young, dammit.

"So, you need a pregnancy test, but you're too scared to go buy one." They nodded and looked at me beseechingly.

"I'd do it, but I just know Mrs. Hillman would tell my Mom," Robin said. "And everybody knows that Eddie's my boyfriend, so he can't either."

"Well, I suppose it's not illegal to procure a pregnancy test for a minor," I said. "That's what you're hoping, isn't it?" They both nodded, doing the kicked-puppy-eyes thing. I felt like a sucker, but then I am one.

"Okay, but I want you to pay me back the ten bucks, Eddie."

"Oh, I will, Polly. Right away. I'd pay you now if I had any money on me."

"Would you help us, you know, do the test?" Robin said. "I'm not very good in science."

"Me either," Eddie said.

"I don't think they're very complicated, Robin, but yes, okay. It doesn't take more than a few minutes, and then we can talk about what to do next. Meet me here tomorrow morning, and bring a urine sample with you."

"What?" Robin looked totally grossed out.

"A urine sample. You know what that is, for pity's sake. These tests measure the hormone levels in your pee. Best to save some of your first pee of the morning. You can do that, can't you?"

"I guess."

"Good. Pee into an apple-juice bottle and then nobody'll know except you." Sad, really, that these kids can deal with the messy, sticky business of copulation, but they can't deal with talking about urine. Go figure.

"Now, I suppose I've got to go and call Becker and find out about Vic. Just what I wanted to do with my Sunday." An hour earlier, I'd been feeling fresh and relaxed. Now I felt like a grumpy old bat.

"I got a call this morning from one of the nurses in the cardiac unit at Laingford Memorial," Becker said, when he picked me up an hour later at the farm. "I know her. She was there when we brought him in yesterday. She said that Vic died last night around six p.m., but she thought there was something funny about it, so she called me. That's all she would say, and she asked that we didn't use her name. So I called Morrison, and he said he would look into it. About two hours later, he called me back and said we'd better go in, you, me and Bryan, too, and tell them about what happened at the falls yesterday."

"Sounds awfully fishy," I said.

"They're not going to arrest you, are they, Dad?" Bryan said from the back seat. "Can they arrest a police officer?"

"No, son—I mean, yes, of course they can arrest a policeman if he's broken the law, but no, they're not going to arrest any of us. They just want a statement about what happened, like I told you."

"And they probably want you to tell them exactly what you saw when Vic went over the falls," I added. "You're an important witness, Bryan."

"Cool," Bryan said, but he didn't sound like he meant it.

"You're sure you didn't see anybody else up there, eh?" Becker said.

"Well, I wasn't looking there, I was finding a stick to throw for the dogs," Bryan said. "I don't know what made me look up—maybe he yelled or something. I can't remember."

"You'd better try and remember, Bryan," Becker said, rather sharply, I thought. "It could be important." Bryan didn't respond, and I stole a sideways glance at Becker. His face was hard, and his lips were set in a thin line. It was probably difficult, I reflected, having a cop for a father.

The Laingford OPP station wasn't exactly a hive of activity when we arrived. All the police cruisers were lined up in their spots outside like sleepy cows, and there was nobody at the front desk.

"Nobody commits any crimes in Kuskawa on Sundays, I take it," I muttered to Becker, who had let us in with his key. He frowned at me.

"If you call 911, it's patched through to the Barrie office, and there are local officers on duty at all times," he said with some severity. When Becker's in cop-mode, his sense of humour disappears completely. It's one of the things I don't much like about him. What would it be like living with him, I wondered? Would he slip in and out of cop-mode in a domestic setting? Would he go all official and disapproving over his breakfast egg? I'd seen him do this eerie switch from sensitive lover to arresting officer a couple of times already, and it wasn't pretty.

We found Earlie Morrison and Marie Lefevbre, his temporary partner while Becker was on vacation, in the desk area in back. Morrison was typing one-fingered on an old IBM electric, and Marie was sitting on the edge of the desk, leaning over him in what I thought was a slightly flirtatious way. Morrison had a besotted look on his face and barely noticed when we came in.

"Oh, hi, sir," Lefevbre said to Becker, slipping off the desk and coming to a kind of attention. She said "sir" in a way that meant, while she may have been obliged to address him as her superior, she didn't really consider him one. Aunt Susan, if she'd been there, would have called her tone insolent.

"Thanks for coming in, Becker," Morrison said. "And thanks for calling us about Vic Watson. We got a statement from a couple of the nurses on duty at the hospital, and for sure there was something weird about his death. They're still trying to figure out what killed him, but I'd bet it wasn't a simple heart attack." Morrison eased his considerable bulk out of the small police-issue chair into which he had been squeezed and stood up. "Hey, Goat-girl," he said to me. "How's it goin'?"

"Not too bad, Earlie," I said. "Eddie and Susan send their love." Morrison was Eddie Schreier's unofficial Big Brother, having taken the kid under his wing after Eddie's real father had abandoned him for a life of sin with a holy roller in the States. Eddie's mom was out of the picture for some rather complicated reasons I won't go into here, and my Aunt Susan had invited him to go live with her. Earlie, a former professional wrestler, coached Eddie in the sport at Laingford

High, as well as privately. Earlie maintained that Eddie was Olympic material—a kind of prodigy, although the kind of wrestling Eddie had been doing with his girlfriend would, I thought, burst that bubble pretty handily. I could just imagine Earlie's reaction if Eddie told him he was giving up wrestling to become a teenage dad. Ouch.

"Sorry to drag you in here on a Sunday," Morrison said. "Thing is, that if Watson's dive into the Oxblood Falls yesterday was no accident, and Becker here gives me the impression that it wasn't—well, we may have a murder investigation on our hands, so we gotta get all the details we can."

"Have you interviewed the Camera Club yet?" Becker said.

"Now Becker, you're on vacation, eh? And you're a witness, not the investigating officer, so don't you worry how we're handling things." This was not a remark calculated to put Becker's mind at rest. I could see that Morrison was enjoying himself. "Marie, why don't you take young Bryan here into the coffee room and get his story, and I'll interview the adults?"

"I don't want Bryan interviewed alone," Becker said.

"Why not?" Morrison said. "We won't use the tactics his dad uses. We'll do everything nice and easy."

"What the hell's that supposed to mean?" Becker said.

"Nothing, nothing. Just a little joke. But Becker, no kid tells the whole story when his dad's in the room. Ain't that so, Bryan?" Bryan, mesmerized perhaps by Morrison's deep, chocolate-covered voice, nodded.

"There. What'd I tell you?"

"What are you pulling here, Morrison?"

"Just going by the book, Becker."

"Let Polly go too, then," Becker said. "She won't coach him. C'mon, Morrison. Ease up." Morrison gazed at Becker for a long moment, maybe weighing how far he could push his colleague. I wasn't sure why he was playing this game, except that Becker had pulled rank on him more than once, and I supposed that the temptation to do the same was too much to pass up.

"Okay, I guess that'd be all right. Marie?"

"Fine by me, Earlie. You want me to get a statement from her, too?" "Her" was me. I knew this because officer Lefevbre poked a thumb in my direction as if I wasn't there. Morrison nodded.

"So, kid, you go with the ladies, and I'll have a chat with your dad, okay? I think you may find a box of Timbits on the table in there, too. Help yourself."

Bryan looked to Becker for guidance. Becker nodded, although he didn't look terribly pleased.

As Bryan and I followed Constable Lefevbre down the corridor to the coffee-room, I heard Morrison begin the interview. "Now, for the record, you are Detective Constable Mark Becker, living at 67 Lakeview Crescent in Laingford?" I just hoped they wouldn't come to blows.

Twelve

Got your groceries? Need a stop?
Rest your feet at our in-store coffee shop!
—A sign in the Kountry Pantree bakery section

The coffee room at the Laingford cop shop was a miniature version of the Tim Hortons donut shop across the highway. There were orange plastic chairs and several small round formica tables, a Tim Hortons coffee maker and, on a shelf over the sink, a number of cans of Tim Hortons coffee and Tim Mugs hanging on cup hooks. It was like a shrine. Constable Lefevbre must have noticed my astonishment and said "when they renovated the Tim's last month, they gave us a lot of their old stuff."

If you're not from around here, you probably don't know about the Canadian love affair with coffee and donuts. We have more donut shops per capita than anywhere in the world. The town or village you're in may only have a population of 500, but you can bet your bippy that it has a Tim Hortons, or a reasonable facsimile thereof. Tim Horton was a popular hockey player who died suddenly in a car crash in the 70s, not long after establishing the franchise with a partner. His death shocked the nation. Presently a curiously church-like atmosphere crept into each Tim Hortons outlet and reverent fans met there to comfort each other. The coffee and cruller became a sacrament, the terminology (large double-double and a maple dip to go, please) morphed into a kind of liturgy, and a Canadian institution was born. Now, when you invoke the Horton name, every Canadian from coast to coast knows what you mean, although they won't think of hockey. Homesick Canadian peacekeepers on a mission to the Middle east were comforted not long ago by a much publicized shipment of Tim's coffee to their warship, and many weary world travellers have made the Tim's at the Toronto airport their first stop after customs. The relationship between Tim Hortons and Canadian police officers is likewise the stuff of legend. Wherever there's a police station, a Tim's beacon shines nearby, and if, in the dead of night, you want some constabulary help, all you have to do is follow your nose to the source of hot fat and caffeine.

Constable Lefevbre put a pot of coffee on and handed Bryan a box of Timbits, the bite-sized donuts purported to be the "holes" left over from making the big ones.

"Now," Lefevbre said when we were settled at one of the round tables, "can you tell me in your own words what happened yesterday, Bryan?" Bryan's mouth was full, and he waited a long time before he answered her.

"Do you have a napkin?" he said. "My hands are sticky." With a "tsk" of impatience, Lefevbre found one and handed it to him. He wiped each finger carefully.

"We were on a hike, right?" I said. The police officer frowned at me and made a little "shush" motion with her mouth. Oh, yeah. No coaching. Bryan reached for another Timbit, but Lefevbre moved the box out of his reach. "In a sec, Bryan. Tell me the story first, okay?"

"Not much happened," Bryan said. "We were on the path to the falls and I went ahead with Polly's dogs and saw the guy fall, that's all."

"You saw him fall over the falls?" Lefevbre said.

"Uh-huh."

"Was he by himself, Bryan?"

"I forget. I didn't see."

"Either you forget, or you didn't see...you can't have it both ways."

Bryan looked away. There was something he wasn't telling us. I shifted uncomfortably on my plastic seat.

"Did the man yell before he fell?" Lefevbre said. Bryan nodded. "Is that why you looked up?" He nodded again.

"He did a kind of somersault into the water," Bryan said. "I saw him go over the falls and then he disappeared and then he came up again and he wasn't moving and I ran back to get my dad."

"Okay, good," Lefevbre said, turning to me. "And you, Ms. Deacon, you were back along the trail with Detective Becker, right?"

"That's right," I said. (I didn't say we were playing photographer and model, and maybe we weren't thinking about Bryan much. I felt guilty about that. It could have been Bryan in the water, and the story could have been a lot worse.)

"How far back on the trail were you?"

"Oh, a hundred feet or so, I guess. It didn't take us more than a moment to run to the bottom of the falls. Becker had him halfway hauled out by the time Bryan and I got there."

"Did you hear anything while you were on the trail?"

"Just the roar of the falls, sort of muffled by the trees," I said, then I turned to Bryan. "Hey, Bryan. How could you hear Vic yell over the sound of the falls? He must have yelled pretty loud, eh?"

Bryan then nodded enthusiastically. "Real loud," he said.

"So you're sure there was nobody with the man at the top of the falls, Bryan?" Lefevbre said.

"I was looking for a stick to throw for the dogs," Bryan said. "I wasn't doing anything wrong, and I didn't see anything."

"Why would anyone think you were doing something wrong?" I said, but Bryan had reached out to the donut box and was choosing another Timbit, ignoring me.

"I guess that's all we're going to get," Lefevbre said. "The guy slips, Bryan sees him go over the falls, and he gets rescued by our hero, Mark Becker. Good thing you folks were there." I felt a twinge of annoyance that she had left me out of the rescue equation, but it wasn't worth mentioning. Remembering the triumphant moment when Vic had yacked up river water all over Becker and started breathing again—that was enough. Although Vic had died anyway, later, which I supposed meant that Becker and I would have another ghost to add to our growing collection. Hooray.

"You two stay here for a minute, okay? I'll be right back." Lefevbre said and left the room. Bryan continued to work his way stolidly through the remaining Timbits, chewing mechanically and obviously not tasting them.

"Bryan," I said, very quietly, "I think there's something you saw that you're not telling us for some reason. Nobody can make you tell, but just think for a second. If the police don't know about it, they might make a mistake. It would be like trying to do a jigsaw puzzle without having all the pieces."

"What's a jigsaw puzzle?" Bryan said. I sighed.

"It would be like trying to log on to the Internet without knowing what the password is," I said.

"Oh," he said and lapsed into silence again. I gave up, for the moment. Maybe he hadn't seen anything at all and was just revelling in the extra attention. I didn't want to tell Becker my suspicions for fear that he would start grilling the boy. I had a pretty good idea that Bryan could be as stubborn as Becker, and I wasn't keen to start a war. Bryan might just come up with the missing piece (if there was one) on his own when he had ceased to be the star attraction.

Becker was in a less than charming mood when we all met up again in the reception area of the station.

"Everything go okay?" he said to Bryan, who gave him a sullen nod. "Did you remember anything more?" Bryan shook his head.

"Morrison's not telling me a goddamned thing," Becker said to me. "I was the one who called him after that nurse called me, and now he's acting like I'm a civilian. I feel like ploughing him one."

"That's probably what he wants," I said. "To get you mad, I mean."

"What he wants is to impress that little blonde copette," Becker said. "The sooner this week's over and I can get back to work, the better. I should talk to the staff sergeant and see if I can come back earlier. Morrison could botch this whole thing."

Bryan was looking apprehensively at his father. "What would happen to me, Dad?" he said. "Mom's in Calgary, remember?"

Becker looked at him, then at me. Hoo boy, I thought. Instant Mom I ain't.

"I have this Kountry Pantree project to do," I said, apologetically. "Deadlines, eh?"

"He'd be no trouble," Becker said.

"I don't want to be with her at that stupid old cabin," Bryan said. "I want to do stuff with you."

"Watch your mouth," Becker said. "Polly's home is not stupid."

"It is so. She doesn't even have a toilet, for Chrissake." Hearing "for Chrissake" coming out of the mouth of an eight-year-old is not nice. I flinched. Becker lost his temper.

"That's enough!" he shouted. "One more word and you're spending the rest of the week in bed." We drove into town in heavy silence. I could feel Becker's ring, like a cold question, lying next to my skin. The unanswered marriage thing reminded me of Eddie and Robin and the favour I had promised to do for them.

"Can you stop off at the drug store for a moment?" I said. "I have to pick up a couple of things." Becker waited with the engine running while I crossed the street and went into Downtown Drugs. I guessed that he might want to have a word or two with his son while I was gone, so I didn't hurry.

The store was quite crowded, and I exchanged polite greetings with several people I knew. I got a basket and put into it some toilet paper and toothpaste I didn't need and a large package of sanitary napkins. I was perfectly well aware that I was stalling, waiting until the coast was clear. I had been the one to tell Eddie and Robin that it was childish to skulk about in a drugstore, but of course now that I was there, I understood their reluctance perfectly. The lineup at the till was thinning, and I wanted to time it so that I was alone, one-on-one with the cashier, whom I didn't know. I scuttled down the aisle to the pregnancy tests, chose one quickly, buried it deeply in the basket between the Kotex and the Cottonelle, and then lurked at the end of the line, feigning interest in the chocolate display. O, cowardice.

Moments later, Theresa Morton, Aunt Susan's assistant at the feed store, emerged from the cosmetics aisle and joined the queue. We chatted about this and that, and I decided to brazen it out. After all, the pregnancy test wasn't for me, but to point that out would have drawn attention to it. One doesn't automatically observe what one's friends are buying at the drugstore, does one?

Making sure my shaming purchase was well camouflaged by its companions, I bade a cheery farewell to Theresa and headed back outside to Becker's Jeep. Becker was tapping his fingers impatiently on the steering wheel, and Bryan had been crying. More silence. What fun family life must be. I yearned for the calming, unconditional companionship of Lug-nut, Rosencrantz and the squirrels in my roof.

"Do you want to get together tonight?" Becker said, as we pulled into the driveway at the farm. "Bryan's going to bed early, and we could watch a movie or something. I make a mean batch of popcorn."

"I don't think tonight, thanks," I said. "I have to get a head start on the mascot, and I have a meeting at nine tomorrow." I hadn't forgotten that Robin was supposed to come over to my place with her apple juice bottle. What Becker and I had not said, but both understood, was that if I went over to his apartment to watch a movie, I would very likely spend the night. Of course the prospect of curling up in bed with a good policeman had its attractions, but Bryan's presence would have made me feel inhibited, and I wasn't sure I wanted to be around when the Becker boys were bickering.

Becker told Bryan to stay in the Jeep and came around to the passenger side as I was clambering out. "See you later, Bryan," I said, and Bryan gave me a quiet "Bye" just before I closed the door. He looked small and lonely sitting there, and I felt a faint tug in the heartstring region. Poor little guy. All he wanted was to spend some quality time with his Dad. What was so wrong with that?

"Have you given any more thought to what we talked

about yesterday?" Becker said, his face close to mine.

"I've hardly thought of anything else," I said. "But I can't answer you yet. Give me some time, okay?"

"All the time you need," he said and did that thing he does with the hair on the back of my neck that makes my knees go funny.

"Becker, ease up on Bryan, eh? He may have the brains of a university student, but he's only eight."

"I know. Don't worry. This will blow over in about half an hour. We fight a lot, Bryan and I, but we work it out. The temper's in the genes, eh?"

"And in this corner, wearing the green trunks, we have Bryan Becker, weighing in at almost sixty pounds..."

"Polly, I'm not asking you to be the referee, you know."

"I know," I said, and he kissed me.

The passenger window rolled down, and there was Bryan sitting where I had been. He was holding my drugstore bag. He waved the pregnancy test at me before cramming it in with the rest of the stuff.

"This tipped over, but I put it all back," Bryan said. "You forgot it. Here." I took the bag, hoping that Bryan wasn't savvy enough to have been interested in reading the labels. Giving Becker a final peck on the cheek, I headed up to the cabin to commune with my dogs in solitude.

Thirteen

The shots of a lifetime: Who is doing your wedding photos? Why not make sure they're perfect? Our photo team at Kountry Pantree will coordinate your wedding shots and present you with a dream album at the end, at a fraction of the cost you might expect! Call us now!

—A Kountry Pantree ad

I am on a storm tossed cruise ship on the high seas, and I am struggling to keep upright as I lurch down the aisle of what seems to be a grand dining room. I am dressed in a 1920s sailor suit which is a little too big for me, and I'm about to get married to the captain. The wedding guests are holding on to each other for support, but there are only a few of them, and I know instinctively that a lot of passengers have abandoned ship already. I wonder why I haven't.

The captain, in a white dress uniform, has his back to me and appears to be steering, looking out of a large porthole at the end of the room. Through the porthole I can see waves that are miles high—it looks like we're going through a mountain range. Oddly, I'm not seasick. I stumble and drop my bouquet, a cunningly arranged bunch of carrots, and I hear the band leader call out to his musicians to "keep on playing, chaps."

When I get to the end of the room, the captain turns around with a big smile on his face. He is very short. It is Bryan. He reaches out his hand towards me and at the same moment, I see the iceberg looming up in the porthole behind his head. The band strikes up the theme song to the movie Titanic. I wake up just before impact with Celine Dion's wretched, saccharine bellow reverberating in my brain.

As I swigged my first coffee of the day, I congratulated my subconscious for its lack of subtlety. In my sleeping state, at least, marriage to Becker spelled certain disaster. I lit a cigarette and looked at the list of pros and cons I'd written out (albeit in a somewhat chemically-altered state) the night before. The Pro list went like this:

REASONS TO MARRY MARK BECKER
1. If I love him, marriage is logical. (I wasn't sure if I did, though.)
2. I'd have financial security for the first time in my life. Becker could take care of the bills, and I'd never get another knee-capper letter from Petrocan again.
3. It would be a chance to be intimately connected with a partner and share everything with him. (This also appeared on the Con list.)
4. Marriage to Becker is a guarantee that I would never again be the "extra single person" at dinner parties. (And I went to so many, eh?)
5. If I ever decide I want children, I will have a stable family relationship in which to bring them up.
6. I would get to practice parenting on Bryan before I had one of my own. (This was where I started to go into surreal-mode. Having children was right up there with sticking needles in my eye and being set on fire.)
7. In sharing my life with Becker, I would have support and

comfort during the bad times and get to share the joy of the good times. (At this point in making the list, I wondered if there might be a job for me at the Hallmark card company.)

8. In case there really is a God, marrying Becker would save us both from hellfire, seeing as what we were doing on a regular basis could be classified as textbook fornication.

9. I would get unlimited sex whenever I wanted it, without the complication of arranging places and times.

10. I would get to keep Becker's pretty ring and wear it on my finger. I would also get to star in "Wedding Day, the Movie".

The Con list was longer:

REASONS NOT TO MARRY MARK BECKER
1. The institution of marriage holds little, if any, importance for me. However, perhaps it does for him. If I said yes, I would have to rethink my values.

2. Although there would be financial security, I'd have to start being responsible about money.

3. It would be a chance to be intimately connected with a partner and share everything with him. It would mean giving up some things, like dope and cigarettes and take-it-when-you-want-it solitude.

4. Marriage to Becker would mean I could never lust after anyone else again, or at least I couldn't act on it. (Not that I'm easy or indiscriminate, you understand, but I like my options to be open.)

5. I get bored easily. What will happen if I get bored with Becker?

6. I bet I would have to wash his socks.

7. I might feel pressured to have a baby with him.

8. I'd become the wicked stepmother of Bryan.

9. As far as bad times and good times go, I kind of like to enjoy them on my own. Face it, Polly. You're a hermit and you like it. Hermits shouldn't marry.

10. I am reasonably certain that if there is a God, he doesn't much care about the rutting practices of his human creatures. I think he's more concerned with whether or not they love each other and treat each other with respect.

9. What if my husband wanted sex and I didn't?

10. I'd have to use the expression "my husband". And I'd be "wife". Yikes.

11. I would wear Becker's pretty ring on my finger, and I wouldn't be able to take it off. "Wedding Day, the Movie" could turn out to be a turkey.

12. I would have to leave my cabin and join the twenty-first century. I would have to have a TV in my home and a telephone. I know damn well that Becker wouldn't seriously consider moving into the cabin with me. Or would he?

13. Lug-nut would be very pissed off.

All in all, the Con list was more compelling than the Pro list. Aunt Susan had taught me to make lists like that when I was faced with a major decision. I considered telling her about Becker's proposal and showing her the list, but I wasn't sure what her reaction would be. A year previously I would have put money on her saying "Marry that policeman? You've got to be kidding!", but now I wasn't so sure. She seemed to be more concerned with my security and my future than she used to be. I guessed she was feeling her age.

The thing is that for me, an attachment has always been something to be choked down, a cocktail of conflicting desires with the sweetest taste to be found in the dregs.

The weaving together, the knitting of affections, has always been a challenge, a complicated obstacle course of cause and effect, clash and compromise. It isn't that I set myself up for failure; I've always built my domestic constructions to last. They're robust, towering things cemented together with plans for the future and constant reassurances of fidelity. My partners have trusted me, always. I don't trust myself, ever. Discontent gathers like saliva, making whatever is good taste bitter. The biggest rush of all is cutting loose.

I loved the idea of loving Becker, but that's as far as I was willing to go. I knew that marrying him wouldn't work, and if I was going to hurt him by saying no, at least that was better than going along with it and then screwing up after the deed was done.

I burned both lists and resolved to give Becker's ring back, with a grateful, loving and gentle "thanks but no thanks."

Robin arrived on the dot of nine, apple juice bottle (still warm) in hand. She was pale and alone.

"Eddie's working this morning," she said. Eddie worked in the bakery at Watson's General Store in Laingford. I wondered suddenly whether David Kane would try to headhunt him for the Kountry Pantree.

"So, let's do the test," I said, trying to be cheerful. After having come to my decision about Becker, I felt a little melancholy, as if I'd just buried something or someone I cared about.

The pregnancy test included a couple of plastic swizzle sticks with little pill-sized orbs embedded in a mesh cage at the bottom. Sort of like a Q-tip with a candy at the end. There were two of them, and the accompanying literature explained that this was a two-for-one deal, in case you wanted a second opinion.

The instructions were extremely simple but written in such

a way that made it obvious the manufacturers assumed that the question of yes or no was a joyful one.

"If the ball turns blue," the pamphlet said, "congratulations! See your physician right away to confirm the results!" It didn't say "Better luck next time" with reference to the ball not turning blue.

"Oh, God, I hope it doesn't turn blue," Robin said.

"Me too," I said. "Now, what it says we have to do is put the swizzle stick here into this little test tube, with a slug of your apple juice. You do that part, okay?" I watched her perform the experiment with shaking hands.

"We've got to wait for five minutes then put the stick into the other test tube with the stuff in this other bottle. Then we wait another ten minutes and then we'll know. If it turns blue, we'll figure out what to do next."

I put my watch on the table so that we could both observe the minutes ticking by.

"We were careful, you know," Robin said.

"So Eddie said," I said.

"It was just that the condom came off once, eh? We were so scared. It got stuck inside me, and he had to pull it out. I guess it leaked. It was so gross."

"Are you using anything else? Spermicidal foam or anything?" I felt like Doctor Ruth and suppressed the urge to speak in a German accent.

"What's that?"

"It's like hair mousse. You spray it in and then if the condom breaks or comes off, the foam kills those little sperms dead like bug spray."

"Eeew."

"Look, Robin, the whole sex thing is 'eeew' if you look at it that way. You have to protect yourself, though. Eddie—and yes, I know he cares about you a lot—but Eddie isn't the one who would have to deal with pregnancy directly if it happened. You would."

"He loves me."

"I know he does, honey, but being a parent is hard work. It's for life. Have you thought about what you'll do if this swizzle stick turns blue?"

"Yeah, I guess. There are some girls at school who had babies."

"Are they still at school?"

"One is. She's a friend of mine. Tanya. Her Mom takes care of Tyler when she's at school. And I've met her for coffee downtown a couple of times. Tyler's really cute, and Tanya really loves him."

"I bet she grew up really fast, though."

"Oh, yeah. She can't go out with us any more, and she wears sweats all the time now. She used to be this really hot dresser, you know? Now she doesn't even wear her nose ring any more."

"Would your Mom help take care of your baby, if you had one?"

"I don't know. I doubt it. She works full-time."

"I see. So you would probably have to find a daycare space and the money to pay for it," I said.

"Yeah, I guess, if I stayed in school."

"Do you have plans to go to university or anything?"

"Well, I'm in Grade Twelve now. I wanted to take international business. I don't know now, though." I thought of Linda Kirschnick at the Real Estate office and her promise of a career in physics. The five minutes were up, and we transferred the swizzle stick from the pee solution into the test tube with the clear solution that came with the kit. Now we had to wait for another ten minutes.

"Let's get a breath of air," I said. Robin and I did a circuit of the cabin while Lug-nut and Rosie gambolled about, bringing us sticks to throw. It was one of those golden mornings when the sky was a heartbreaking blue and the birds were twittering like demented opera singers.

"Did you ever think of having kids?" Robin asked me.

"Well, I've thought about it, Robin, but I'm not the maternal type. The noise drives me crazy, and I honestly don't like being around babies. I'm always afraid I'm going to drop them."

"Really? I just love them. I do a lot of babysitting, eh?"

"Good for you. But I think that having one of your own is a bit different. You can't, you know, go home at the end of the evening."

"Yeah, there's this one little guy, Adam, who's a real handful. I charge extra when I go there."

"Think of how his mother must feel."

We went back inside. I'd put the test tube out of the way on top of the ice box.

"You look," Robin said. "I can't. I'm too scared. Is it blue?"

I looked. I held the test tube and swizzle stick up to the light and shook it a couple of times.

"Robin," I said, "the little ball-thing is as white as it was when we put it in. According to the whatever-it-is company, you're not pregnant." I held her while she cried.

Robin had not wanted to use the back-up second-opinion stick. "No way I want to go through that again," she said. She said she thought that her period might have been late because she'd been dieting lately.

"I actually feel that I could get my period tonight, you

know? I sort of feel heavy down there." She left, beaming, after having promised to visit her doctor to get a prescription for the pill. Maybe after this scare, she and Eddie would be more careful. If I had my way, kids would be kept segregated until they were thirty.

I poured the contents of the apple juice bottle out on the ground and threw the test stuff in my bathroom cabinet, then fed the dogs and prepared to head out. I was supposed to meet the members of the Weird Kuskawa Art group at noon in town, because the show was now being advertised in the *Laingford Gazette,* which meant it had to happen. We had planned it to coincide with the Bath Tub Bash on Saturday, to take advantage of the crowds. With the new Kountry Pantree cow deadline, I was in crunch time, but that was for later. For the time being, it was still a figment of my imagination, like Robin's baby had been. I also had to get in touch with Becker, so I could tell him about my decision while causing him the minimum of pain. I was feeling full, pressured to complete too many tasks in too short a period of time. Never mind that I thought Vic Watson had been murdered in his bed at the Laingford Hospital and agreed with Becker that constable Morrison, distracted by the charms of Constable Marie Lefevbre, might make a botch of it. Whatever happened to the back-to-the-land puppet-maker thing I'd dedicated my life to? How did it all get so complicated?

Fourteen

The Kuskawa region, several hours north of Toronto, is a rugged, exquisite landscape full of deep, cold lakes, pink granite bedrock and dense forests. It's a tourist-magnet, a resort developer's wet dream and a haven for artists. The creative urge seems to lurk in the soil and in the air, and the local "find-it-here" maps are dotted with galleries and art supply stores. In the autumn, the hardwood forests of Kuskawa vibrate with fluorescent oranges, yellows and reds, impossible colours, really, the kind that you have to see to believe. The trees seem to give off a light of their own.

For a few weeks every September, Laingford hosts thousands of Japanese and German tourists who wander blissfully through the streets, expensive cameras festooned around their necks like garlands. Vistas and lookouts become crowded with portable easels, the painters jostling for position and eyeing each other's work with varying degrees of admiration or contempt.

It's not only the fall colour that inspires art here. The winters are magical; thick snow blankets everything and glitters in the cold sun, softening the sharp outlines of tree and cliff. Icy mists lift from the rivers and lakes, clothing the naked shoreline with silver. In spring, there are always a few days of tender beauty, when leaf-buds hover like smoke in the tops of the birch trees. The melting snow finds its way down to the lakes, forming merry brooks and rills that meander their way through the forest, catching the light in unexpected places. When summer hits, as it always does with a quick backhand we never expect, the forest floor bursts into a carpet of trilliums, red and white, and the ferns grow so fast you can almost hear them.

In mid-summer, the artists turn to cottage life for their subject matter; "Still Life With Canoe" is a popular theme, as are "Kuskawa Chair on Dock" and "Child Fishing". Not all of the art produced in this Mecca is what you'd call quality. Some of it is frankly awful, but almost all of it finds a market, which means that there are plenty of people in Kuskawa calling themselves artists. Every community holds an annual art show, usually outdoors in the local park. On any given weekend in August, you can usually find one, although finding a piece of art you actually might consider buying and hanging on your wall is another matter.

Okay, so I'm an art snob. You try carving out a living as a puppet maker in any Ontario town north of Toronto and see if it doesn't make you bitter.

The Weird Kuskawa Art Show was Yolanda's idea. Yolanda is an old friend from high school, one of the out-crowd with whom I spent my traumatic teenage years. The out-crowd were those of us who couldn't afford designer clothes, did reasonably well in school, were interested in the arts rather than sports and who all, to varying degrees, suffered from acne, braces or corrected vision. We were so uncool we had to band together to keep from being crushed like bugs under the feet of the jock elite. Yolanda Kristopoulos is a painter, a real one, whose work actually gets shown in Toronto galleries, which, as we all know, is the only true measure of success. She does commercial artwork to pay her rent, and she's a wacky person who doesn't really care what people think of her. Lately, she's been working on a series of surreal Kuskawa landscapes with incongruous things like businessmen, computer keyboards and bananas inserted into the picture, hovering in the air or half-buried under some leaf mould. I really like her work.

The third member of our Weird Kuskawa Art project was Dimmy Cox, who is a photographer. Dimmy doesn't belong to any photo clubs. She works alone and creates elaborate, set-up shots with lots of props, using local people as her subjects and putting them into emotion laden situations. One of my favourites was taken on George's farm. She placed two adults in Edwardian dress inside a pen in the goat barn (the resident goat didn't seen to mind much) and on the outside, peering in, was a child in a silvery Star Trek outfit, talking on a cell phone.

We met in the storefront space where we had planned to set up the exhibition. In Laingford's early days it had been a family run men's clothing store, specializing in tailor made suits and beautiful shirts. It had thrived for several generations until the advent of Tommy Hilfiger, the rise of the baseball cap empire and the availability of cheap off-the-rack dress jackets at the Bargain Hut.

Many of the fixtures were still in place, including a bedraggled mannequin which Dimmy immediately decided would be part of the show.

"We can dress him up and park him in front of one of your

pictures, Yolanda, as if he's studying it. An art critic. See if anyone notices."

I found a broken clothing rack from which I could hang some of my marionettes, and after some discussion we chose the centre of the room to display Audrey. Audrey is an enormous foam rubber body-puppet I built some years ago for a production of *Little Shop of Horrors*. When the company went bellyup, I had bought the puppet back from the prop shop, because anyone doing the show needs an Audrey, and the market isn't exactly flooded with them. I'd rented her out a couple of times, and when she wasn't on the road, she lived in a plastic-lined fridge box in George's barn. Audrey is a man-eating pitcher plant, about seven feet tall—a big mouth, basically, with tentacles. The puppeteer climbs inside, hangs onto the interior aluminum frame with both hands and levers the mouth open and shut in coordination with Audrey's dialogue. Playing Audrey is kind of like working out on a Nautilus machine for two hours while stuffed inside a pitch black, foam rubber bag. Not for the faint-hearted.

"Maybe we could get somebody to work Audrey during the art show," Yolanda said. "You know, just sit there inside until someone comes close enough to get eaten. Performance art."

"You'd probably have to pay them union scale," I said. "It's hot, and it stinks in there. Good idea, though." I wondered if David Kane had chosen which poor teenaged employee was going to be forced into wearing the Kountry Kow costume. Maybe we could give the kid a foretaste of the job by hiring them to do Audrey for our art show.

"By the way," Dimmy said, "I wanted to ask you two if we would consider letting any other artists into the show. I know it's kind of late in the game, but a couple of people have approached me."

"Is it weird art? Our kind?" Yolanda said. "I don't want this to degenerate into a craft fair."

"Well, there are two," she said. "A sculptor, a young girl from Laingford High who does neat compilation pieces, and another photographer, Sophia Durette."

"They give you slides or examples?" Yolanda said.

"Yeah. The girl, Arly Watson her name is, gave me these, and Sophia asked me yesterday if she could drop by with a couple of pictures." Dimmy passed over a couple of crumpled colour photocopies.

"I've met Arly," I said. "She's Archie Watson's daughter. She belongs to the Camera Club, but I didn't know she was a sculptor as well." Her sculpture was interesting, certainly. It looked like she was working with "found objects" (the term we art-types use for garbage) which she glued and bolted together into human figures and then shellacked. The figures were proportional and kinetic, some of them obviously designed to make a political statement. The masculine genitalia on one, for example, were fashioned from a tiny toy pistol flanked by Christmas tree baubles.

"I like it," I said. "How big are the sculptures? Have you seen them?"

"They average about two feet high," Dimmy said. "She works in a corner of her Dad's garage, and I went to visit. I think she's got something—she's a peculiar kid, but she's disciplined. This is not just a hobby for her."

"Well, I don't see why we can't bring her on board," Yolanda said. "She's weird enough, wouldn't you say, Polly?"

"Yup. Maybe we should make a deal with her. She can show her stuff if she's willing to do Audrey for us." The others nodded. Arly might not go for the idea of baking inside a foam rubber puppet for the duration of the show—not exactly the ideal celebrity status a budding artist might imagine, but it was worth a try. We decided that even if Arly nixed the Audrey idea, we'd still offer her some space. Her sculptures would help smooth the transition from my three dimensional stuff to the flat planes of Yolanda's canvases and Dimmy's photos.

There was a knocking on the papered-over window at the front of the shop, and I could see the shadow of a person standing outside.

"That'll be Sophia," Dimmy said, moving to the door.

"What if her stuff isn't what we're looking for?" I muttered to Yolanda.

"We'll tell her so, I guess," Yolanda said, but she looked uncomfortable. Dimmy returned with an older woman in tow, whom I recognized at once as the late Vic Watson's friend, Sophie. In the dim light of the empty shop, her face appeared unnaturally pale, her grey hair was unbrushed and her expression was one of pure misery.

"Oh, hello, dear," Sophie said to me. "I suppose you've heard about Vic."

"I have, Sophie, and I'm awfully sorry," I said.

"You two know each other?" Yolanda said.

"We met on the weekend," I said. "A friend of hers was in some trouble, and we helped out a bit."

"You saved his life," Sophie said. "Not that it made any difference in the end. Kane got him anyway." When she spoke David Kane's name, her eyes flashed and her face contorted in a grimace of pure hatred. Yolanda shot me a questioning glance, and I frowned quickly in response. "Tell you later," I thought at her. She got it.

Dimmy had missed the exchange, having become distracted by her mannequin, which I could see she was just dying to photograph.

117

"Did you bring some work for us to look at, Sophia?" Dimmy said, tearing herself away from her *Art Critic*.

Sophie nodded and produced a slim portfolio of photographs, as well as a package of prints from Shutterbug.

"I just picked these up," she said. We leafed through the portfolio together. Sophie's pictures were very good, but conventional, as I'd feared. Her landscapes and close-ups of plants and flowers were hasty-note or postcard material, very slick and professional but hardly what you'd call weird. Yolanda and I exchanged worried glances. How do you tell a freshly bereaved senior citizen that her art wasn't weird enough? Sophie shoved the package of snapshots at me.

"You might find these more interesting," she said, as if reading my mind. I looked through them. More of the same, I thought sadly, gazing at a nice composition of rushing water over rocks and another looking down over a cataract. She must have taken these on Saturday, at the Oxblood Falls. Then one picture made me gasp aloud. It was a long shot across the top of the falls. A figure crouched in the distance at the very edge of the precipice, slightly out of focus, leaning over the water—a large man, with grey hair. Behind him, obscured by a tree, was another figure. The blurry photo gave no clue as to who the other figure was, but the big man could only be Vic Watson.

I looked up to find Sophie staring at me. "Interesting, isn't it? Look at the next one," she said. I did so. The next photo didn't look like anything at all. It was completely unfocused and at an odd angle. There was water and rock, a dark blur which could have been the crouched figure, and a small blurry patch of red behind it.

"I wasn't looking," Sophie said. "I was advancing a new film, and I didn't bother to take the zoom lens off. There was nobody there when I looked up again."

"This was at the top of the falls, I take it?" I said. Sophie nodded.

"David Kane was wearing a red sweatshirt that day," she said, with meaning.

"That's weird," I said without thinking.

"Weird enough for the show?" Dimmy said. She had been looking through Sophie's portfolio and was obviously hoping that the pictures I held in my hand might save us all from having to reject Sophie's work.

"Not really, just weird," I said.

"I'll just leave those prints with you, shall I, dear?" Sophie said. "I know your friend the policeman would be interested in looking at them. And never mind about the others. I can tell by your expressions that my photographs aren't appropriate for your show, which is more or less what I expected, but I thought I'd chance it." Her voice was brisk and unaccountably perky, as if her job was done and she was ready to move on. She took the portfolio gently from Yolanda's hands and advanced toward the door.

"Call me if something develops, won't you?" she said, adding "Pardon the pun" at the end as a kind of afterthought before sailing through the door and out into the street. Dimmy, Yolanda and I were left staring at each other.

"What the hell was that all about?" Yolanda said.

"I think I have to talk to Becker," I said.

Fifteen

I heard it through the grapevine! Have you heard that Kountry Pantree offers premium Canadian vintages right on site in our own Wine Shoppe?
—A Kountry Pantree ad in the *Laingford Gazette*

Of course, as soon as I said it, I realized that it wasn't Becker to whom I should be taking Sophie's snapshots, it was Morrison. After all, Morrison was the one leading the investigation, if there was one, into Vic Watson's death. Morrison and that cute, blonde rookie cop called Marie. I wasn't quite sure why I felt so much antagonism towards her. She hadn't done anything to me, she'd been perfectly polite and sensitive, even, in her dealings with me and with Bryan. Deep down I suspected that my mistrust was based on Morrison having the hots for her, but I didn't want to examine that one too closely. Still, I would have to come to some sort of conclusion about the photos, and soon.

I invited Yolanda and Dimmy to join me at the Slug and Lettuce Pub for a pint to talk it over and perhaps to solicit some friendly feedback about Becker's proposal. Dimmy begged off, explaining that she was shooting a wedding the next weekend, and had to go meet the bride and groom and talk about locations, shot lists and all that complicated stuff that professional photographers have to nail down before the big day. In my "what if I actually said yes to marrying Mark Becker" moments, I had fantasized about Dimmy being the official wedding photographer. Me on soft focus in a frothy white gown, gazing wistfully into a mirror, the veil held in trembling hands. Dimmy called that the "sucky mirror shot" and said every sentimental bride insisted on it. Sucky? Sentimental? You bet. Who was I to stand in the way of tradition?

The Slug and Lettuce overlooks the Kuskawa River in downtown Laingford. It has all the qualities that I insist on in a watering hole: plenty of English beer and Kuskawa Cream on tap, old jazz playing not too loudly in the background, comfortable booths where friends can get intimate without making a spectacle of themselves, deep ashtrays on every table and a bartender who knows what you drink without having to ask.

Yolanda and I grabbed a booth by the window. The screen doors let in a cool breeze and Nick, the barman, drew us a couple of pints of Kuskawa Cream as soon as we walked in the door.

"Afternoon, Polly. Caught any murderers lately?" Nick said, wiping the table and depositing the beer in front of us with a flourish.

"Hot on the trail of a new one, Nick," I said. It wasn't as if I bragged about it. It's true that I had been connected with a couple of suspicious deaths (well, four) in the past year or so, but I didn't hand out little cards with "Polly Deacon, Private Eye" on them. It's just that word gets around in a small town and I did (ahem) occasionally take a drink at the Slug and Lettuce, eh? Nick went back to the bar, and Yolanda and I clinked glasses.

"Here's to weird Kuskawa art," she said.

"Cheers," I said.

"I'm glad that Arly Watson is on board," Yolanda said, "but that was very strange about Sophie Durette. It was like she didn't really even want to be included at all—she just wanted you to have those snapshots. So what's up with that?"

I filled her in on the Vic Watson thing, including the suspicion that David Kane had something to do with it. She had heard about his death, but none of the details. Yolanda's a safe confidante. I know this because in Grade Ten I told her that I had a crush on Fish Gundy, which, because he was four foot nothing and had really bad acne, would have been dangerous information in the wrong hands. She never told a soul, and I've always appreciated her discretion.

"I don't even know how Vic died," I said. "All I know is that the nurse at the hospital said there was something funny about it and that Morrison and Lefevbre are looking into it."

"So why did you say you had to talk to Becker?" she said.

"Well, Mark's on vacation right now, but normally he would be investigating something like this."

"Uh-huh. You're still seeing him, I take it."

"Yup. More than that, Yolanda." I whispered the next bit. "He wants to get married."

"To you?" she said and hooted like a fog horn.

"Thanks a bunch," I said.

"Oh, jeez, I'm sorry, Polly," Yolanda said, straightening up as soon as she saw my expression. "I thought you'd find that as funny as I did. I just can't see you as the marrying type. Your dogs and your, you know, lifestyle."

"It's not that far-fetched," I said. "I could adapt. He's a nice guy, you know."

"Of course he is," she said. "Or at least, he's not a criminal and he has a steady job, which is more than I can say for the last two men I went out with, but honestly, Polly, the thought of you going through with a marriage just tickles my funny bone. You told him no, didn't you?"

"He put you up to this, didn't he?" I said. "He's working on all my friends, getting them to tell me how crazy the idea is so that I'll consider it just to be perverse." Yolanda narrowed her eyes.

"You're not serious?" she said. "You're really considering it? Who have you told?"

"You're the first," I said. I showed her the ring I wore around my neck.

"Oh, God, you're wearing his ring?" she said.

"Around my neck, Yolanda. I haven't given him an answer yet."

"Around your anything is bad," she said. "Listen, Polly, I'll be frank, okay? None of us, your friends I mean, think it's a great idea that you've been dating a cop, although we haven't said anything, mainly because you automatically do the opposite of whatever advice you get. If you marry this guy, you won't be Polly Deacon any more. You'll be a police wife. God."

"Of course, I would still be Polly Deacon." This was not, I discovered, what I wanted to hear from Yolanda, or from anybody. She knew me too well—I am a sucker for reverse psychology. What I wanted to hear was the conventional "Oh, Polly, congratulations…when's the wedding?" so I could tell them that I was flying in the face of convention and would rather perform self-surgery than marry him. What I wanted was to hear people trying to convince me that marrying Becker was a good idea, so that I could argue against it. What I didn't want to hear was a validation of my own gut feelings, because—why? Because that would make me predictable? Because that would mean that I was actually taking the advice I was being given? Heaven forbid.

I wondered suddenly if my self-image as a goer-against-the-norm was entirely healthy. Splashing around in a sea of confusion, I downed my beer and waved at Nick to bring us another round.

"Polly, Mark Becker may be a nice guy, but he sleeps around, or at least he used to," Yolanda said. "After he got divorced, he went through about half a dozen women in less than a year."

"I'm not exactly a saint myself, you know," I said. Actually, I was rather more of a saint than were most of my single contemporaries, and Yolanda knew it. She quirked an eyebrow at me.

"He's just looking for someone to look after that kid of his," she said. "Everybody knows that his ex is involved with Duke Pitblado. Duke's got enough kids as it is. He won't want another one."

"What?"

"You don't gossip nearly enough, Polly. Duke's wife moved to Toronto a couple of months ago, but their five kids are staying in Laingford with him. He's got a housekeeper and a nanny, but Catherine Becker is on the bench, just panting to play," Yolanda said. "She may be next in line for the Pitblado millions. Little Bryan Becker is the wild card. The grapevine says that Detective Mark Becker would get custody whether he wanted it or not."

"How the hell do you know this?"

"The grapevine, Polly. You're completely out of the loop. We need to see each other more often." I wasn't so sure about that.

On the way home, I thought about Yolanda's unkind suggestion that Becker was just looking for a live-in babysitter. I was hardly the ideal candidate, if it came to that. Becker had already made it clear that my "lifestyle" as Yolanda called it, (which was code for being a dope-smoking, alcohol-sodden bohemian back-to-the-lander) was not something he was eager to let Bryan share. Hadn't he double-checked that I didn't have any dope lying around before he'd let the kid come home with me? He was hardly expecting me to transform myself into Martha Stewart in the twinkling of an eye. Or was he? I pictured my pro and con list and added another con. *"Item #14"*, I wrote on my mental notepad, *"Concessions. Is Becker willing to make concessions about his own lifestyle, or does he want me to play Eliza Dolittle to his Henry Higgins?"* As I parked George's battered Ford pickup in the farm driveway, I found that I still wanted to give the photos to Becker, not Morrison. I'd use them as a bargaining chip in the "discussing our future" game. Not very laudable, but then I was stressed. I also found that Yolanda's advice was at work within me, percolating in reverse, like one of those cheap metal espresso pots. I wasn't ready to tell Becker I wouldn't marry him. In fact, I was searching for ways to make it a possibility. I am such an idiot.

There were several cars in George's driveway, Stan Herman's yellow Camry with the plastic camera on the roof, Emma Tempest's purple, posy-splashed mini van and a big old vintage van I didn't recognize. I came in the back door of the farm house with some supplies Susan had asked me to pick up while I was in town. Archie Watson, Emma and Stan were in the kitchen with Susan, sitting around the big pine harvest table with coffee and donuts in front of them, obviously having a League of Social Justice meeting. There was no sign of George, and they clammed up as soon as I walked in.

"Don't let me interrupt anything," I said. "Just go on as if I'm not here." I headed for the fridge to deposit the eggs and the beer. Archie took me at my word.

"That bastard'll be at the funeral," he said. "I know he'll be there—he already sent us a big bunch of flowers and a card and he'll be there, all right, pretending Vic was his best friend, although we all know otherwise." Oh, right. I'd forgotten that Vic was Archie's brother. Although Vic's remarks on Saturday had suggested that the brothers weren't exactly close, losing a sibling was a horrible thing. I went over to clasp his hand.

"I'm really sorry to hear about Vic, Archie," I said. "My condolences to your family." Archie's eyes misted up as he nodded his thanks and I wondered why, the day after a death in the family, he was sitting in George's kitchen having a political meeting.

"It was a shock, all right," Archie said. "He was a healthy fellow. Nothing wrong with his heart, far as I knew." He gave me a challenging look as if daring me to tell him otherwise. I did, kind of.

"Well, he did fall in the river on Saturday," I said with as much sensitivity as I could. "He nearly drowned. I expect that weakened him a good deal."

"He was pushed," Archie said. "I know it and you know it. Everybody knows it, and everybody knows who did it. What I can't figure out is why David Kane is still walking around a free man."

"Why do you think David Kane pushed him in?" I said.

"I heard it from one of the camera club members," Archie said. "Kane was mad that Vic voted against the Kountry Pantree project and wanted to get him back."

"What good would it do to kill a council member after the project has been approved?" I said.

Archie laid one finger beside his nose, nodded and winked at me. I've never actually seen anybody do that in real life before, and I've always wondered what it meant. "There's a

126

detail or two you don't know about, Miss Deacon," Archie said. Oh. The international symbol for "I've got a secret", I guess. Susan put a restraining hand on Archie's arm.

"Archie, that's enough. It's best if Polly doesn't know about our plans," she said.

"I wasn't going to tell," Archie said, sounding like a wounded child.

"Susan, I frankly couldn't give a damn what the League of Social Justice is planning," I said with some heat. I've always hated being left out. "But if you're looking to stop the project, you're leaving it kind of late. The grand opening is slated for the first of September, and they're already hiring staff."

"We know that," Susan said.

"If you want to find out more, come to the town council meeting tomorrow night," Archie said, as if he were giving me a stock tip. "Should be quite interesting." He pronounced it "innerestin" and did the nose/finger thing again.

"Maybe I will," I said. "If only to be there when you guys get arrested for disturbing the peace, and I have to bail you out."

"Oh, what we have planned is quite legal," Susan said. "Anyway, Polly, you're hardly in a financial position to bail us out of jail, are you?"

"Speaking of which, you owe me twenty-three bucks for the beer and eggs," I said. She paid up.

I left the Social Justicers to their coup planning and slipped into George's living room to make a phone call.

Becker picked up the phone before it rang at his end. It was one of those weird Ma Bell moments you can't explain.

"Becker?"

"Polly? How bizarre. I was just calling you."

"We have a psychic link, eh?" We blithered about how strange that was for a while, then got to the point.

127

"I've signed Bryan up to spend a couple of days at Camp Goomis," Becker said. "He's driving me crazy."

"I thought you guys were supposed to be having some quality time together," I said without thinking. "Isn't eight a little young to be doing overnights at camp?" Rule Number One in relationships where there's a kid who is not yours: Don't criticize the parenting. Ever.

"You don't know Bryan," Becker said through suddenly clenched teeth. "He wants to go. He's not a baby."

I backtracked. "Of course not. When's he going?"

"I just dropped him off. You want to get together?"

"Sure. Actually, I have something I want to run by you. Have you talked to Morrison today?"

"Nope. He's not returning my calls. He's treating me like a civilian, dammit."

"Well, I guess it's because you're off duty, eh?"

"That's no excuse. Anyway, I'm back on as of Thursday."

"What about Bryan?"

"If he likes the camp, he'll be staying there until Sunday night, when my ex gets back."

Poor little guy, I thought, but I didn't say it out loud. If his Mom was truly planning to hand him over to Becker so that she could join Duke Pitblado's family unencumbered, Bryan and his Dad were in for some rough times. Especially if they couldn't last four days together without fighting.

"I see. So if you go back to work on Thursday, does that mean you'll be taking over the investigation of Vic's death?"

"I hope so. Before Morrison messes it up too bad."

"You don't have a lot of faith in your partner, do you?"

"Look, Polly, I know he's your friend and all, and he's a good guy in his way, but he's not the most brilliant police officer in the world. Why do you think he's still a constable?"

Earlie Morrison had once told me that he had been passed over for promotion so many times he hardly thought about it any more. Detective Constable Becker had been parachuted in from Toronto about four years previously, and had, according to Morrison, been stealing the limelight ever since. Morrison said he didn't care, but I suspected that he did.

"Maybe it's because Morrison isn't very glamorous," I said.

"Maybe it's because he's fat and kinda slow," Becker said. "He's muscle, Polly. That's why we make a good team—he's the brawn, I'm the brains. By himself, or with that fluff-ball Lefevbre, it's just meat without the heat."

How unkind, I thought. Catchy, but mean. Becker said he would pick me up at the farm at around seven and take me out for a night on the town.

"There's one of those chick flicks playing at the Laingford Odeon," he said, "and I've already made reservations at the Mooseview Inn, if that's okay with you." The Mooseview meant candlelight and wine, big time. And a "Chick Flick" to boot. Gosh. My suitor was pulling out all the romantic stops, no question.

The scene that played across my mind wasn't Cinderella and Prince Charming, though. What I saw was a live trap, baited with honey, with me in the role of skunk, scent glands fully-armed, waddling in with my eyes wide open.

Sixteen

Our closed circuit camera is watching you!
—A sign at the entrance to the Kountry Pantree superstore

I spent the rest of the afternoon with Kountry Kow, wrestling with bits of foam rubber and wire as I constructed the cow's head. The framework was basically an inverted wire basket (try putting a large lampshade on your head and you'll get the idea), over which I laid canvas pieces, then contact-cemented foam rubber to create the proper cow-like contours. Because the costume was supposed to be more or less waterproof (damn David Kane and his wretched Bath Tub Bash) I had to abandon my usual liberal application of hot glue and use a needle and thread instead. This put me in a rotten mood. I'm not a bad seamstress—I made my share of Annie Hall outfits (with matching bow ties, God help me) in the seventies, but working with light cotton and a nice little Butterick pattern was easier than sewing bits of heavy canvas and fun-fur to a wire frame. The inside of the cow's head was dotted with charming little splodges of Polly-blood by the time the frame was complete.

At around four, the dogs alerted me to an approaching visitor. Luggy gave his "There's someone coming and I don't know who it is" growl, a sort of deep rumble that sounds like thunder a long way off. Rosie, who was too young to have

130

learned how to growl yet, let her hackles rise (which on a Lab puppy isn't threatening, it just made her look like a sheepskin ottoman), and yipped once or twice. I was trying on the cow head at that moment, and I went to the door still wearing it.

"Gracious," said Emma Tempest's voice, as I opened the door, holding onto Luggy's collar in case he decided the visitor wasn't friendly. "How ceremonial," she said.

Through the eye-holes of the cow head, I could see Emma's soft, pink cheeks, her pearl earrings and part of her neck, which had a loose, wrinkled look like crushed velvet. I realized that if the mascot costume were to be worn by someone who was expected to steer a motorized bath tub around a watery obstacle course, I would have to enlarge its field of vision.

"Come on in, Emma," I said, my voice echoing in its foam-rubber chamber. "Let me get this thing off." Luggy and Rosie bombed her with love as I struggled to doff Kountry Kow.

"I take it that's the project you're working on for the Superstore," Emma said. I nodded. "I do understand why you're reluctant to have anything to do with our protest, even if the rest of the group doesn't," she said.

"Thanks," I said, and offered her some tea.

"No thank you, dear. I just came up to give you something that belongs to you, something that I should have given back to you years and years ago, but then you moved away and I forgot all about it until I saw you again at Susan's the other night."

"Oh, yes. Susan mentioned you had something you wanted to give me." I couldn't think what it could be. Something of my mother's, probably, some memento that Emma thought I would appreciate. How could she know that I had deliberately discarded all such reminders of my parents, all knick-knacks, mementoes and gee-gaws that might whip me back to a quarter century ago when my parents were alive and I was desperately trying to get them to notice me?

Emma reached into the enormous purse she carried and extracted a dusty manila envelope, which she handed over.

"You left these, I think, tucked away in a gap in the back wall of my shop," she said. "I came across them sometime in the eighties, when I was doing renovations. One of them has your name on the inside, dear, and I'm afraid I read a bit of it, because I just couldn't help myself. I guess you were looking for a good hiding place, hmm? It was, you know. I could easily have missed them."

I knew at once what "they" were, although I hadn't given them a thought since hiding them, and my stomach did a little back flip.

"You read them?" I said.

"Well, you wouldn't believe me if I said I hadn't, now, would you?" Emma said, which was perfectly true. I was crimson with shame, and I think she was as embarrassed as I was.

"Did you show them to Susan?" I said. I was nine years old again, hot all over, and my knees were trembling.

"Of course not, Polly. They are obviously very private. I kept a diary myself when I was a girl. I would have been aghast if my mother had seen it."

"These are hardly diaries," I said.

"Well, perhaps not, but they are your business, nonetheless. And they were important enough to you to want to hide them somewhere, weren't they? Why did you hide them? In my shop, I mean?"

"I haven't the faintest idea," I said, which was true. "It was a long time ago." I hadn't opened the envelope, which was wrapped in a rubber band. What was the reason for having hidden the envelope in Emma's shop? I could see myself doing it, but the why of it was buried somewhere in my brain.

"Well, anyway, dear, that's all I came about. I'm sure it's just a silly, trivial thing to you now, and I could easily have burned them, I suppose, but I thought that you might like to dispose of them yourself." She was looking very sharply at me, and I returned her gaze with as much honesty as I could muster.

"I assure you it's not silly or trivial, Emma. At least, it wasn't then, and it doesn't feel like it now. Thank you for returning them to me."

"My pleasure. And Polly, your secret is safe with me," she said and slipped quietly out the door. She wasn't talking to the adult Polly, I realized, as I walked a little unsteadily to the kitchen table. She was talking to nine-year-old Polly Deacon, the little "flower girl" who had accompanied her mother the "Glad Lady" on her flower delivery rounds twenty-five years ago.

Lug-nut nudged my hand as I sat down, and I patted him absently on the head as I touched the envelope with the tip of one finger. It wasn't as if it could bite me. For heaven's sakes, it wasn't evidence that would send me to jail or to hell or anything. In fact, it was laughable. Why wasn't I laughing?

I made a cup of tea, first. I could, I suppose, have lit a fire in the woodstove and burned the envelope, contents and all, but now I was curiously eager, as if I were about to open a Christmas present. I removed the elastic and reached inside, pulling out two small, spiral-ringed notebooks, about three by four inches square. They were very dusty, and wrapped round with a thin cord of white crocheted Phentex, a kind of cheap, polyester yarn that was all the rage in the early seventies. One book had a picture of flowers on it, the other a dog.

On the inside cover of the first, in careful printing that was not mine, were the words "Gabrielle and Polly, 5C, partners since Nov. 6, 1975." I flipped open the second, and the same words were printed in my book, in my childish hand, on the inside front cover. On the facing pages we had inscribed "Polly's and Gabrielle's S.S.C. for two." S.S.C. stood for "Secret Stealing Club", and Gaby and I were its only members.

In my mind's eye, I could see Gaby as if she were sitting next to me. She was pale and small, a nervous child who was bullied at school for her home-made clothes and her infuriating meekness. She was the principal's daughter, but her golden-haired, adored younger brother was a star whose ascendency she couldn't hope to compete with. Gaby was brought up to know her place, to behave like a lady, to serve her brother at the dinner table and to obey authority. In Gaby's world, authority came to mean every single person she met, including me. I knew, sitting there with our Secret Stealing Club notebooks open on the table in front of me, that the idea had been mine, not hers. I had probably coerced her into it, offered her a rare friendship in exchange for conspiracy, although my memory of the details was cloudy.

"Our first assignment," my wretched little notebook said, "was on the date of November 6, 1975, when we went on a spree at Knight's. We 'got' these notebooks, at 39 cents each." The pages that followed listed our plunder. It began with little items pilfered from the drugstore and the stationery store, the price-stickers peeled off and re-stuck onto the lined pages like trophies. Further in, the items became more costly, the risks greater. A $1.49 china squirrel from the high-end gift shop on Main Street, a $4 box of bath beads from the Five and Dime. We never used the word "steal" in our club. The "S.S.C." was the only tacit admission of our guilt. Gaby's book said "On our next mission, I missionaried a beatiful pair of earings (peirsed)." I preferred the euphemism "I got."

On the inside back cover, Gaby's book included this statement: "I promise on my honer, to be Polly's Loyal and trusted friend for ever and ever until death do us depart. I promise to do my best in every way. Together we fit like Two Pea's in a fresh pod. If I don't keep my promise I will first apologise then I will make myself write this out 100 times!" On the back cover of my own notebook, I'd written "I pledge to have a bonded partener and friendship with Gabrielle Kelly Murchison. I am sinning, I know, but it's fun!" I had totted up the value of every stolen object in my book, like a bank manager.

Gaby's book was blank after the first few pages. Perhaps she had seen the error of her ways and told me that my friendship wasn't worth it. I hope that's what happened. I can't remember. For some reason, I kept her book. Perhaps in the hope of future blackmail. My notebook, the one with the picture of the dog on the cover, was full.

I remember the thrill of shoplifting. The heart-crushing, excruciating wait for the right moment. The quick slip-it-in-your-pocket. The sick, sweet pleasure of getting away with it. And I did, for what seems like ages, but was probably only a few months. I showered my parents with pocket-sized gifts at Christmas. I had a never ending supply of notebooks, pencils and erasers. All hot.

I was never caught. If shoplifting is supposed to be a cry for help, as most psychologists would have us believe, how devastating it must be, and must have been, to have the cry ignored. I stopped stealing one day, when, after lifting a chocolate bar on my way home from school, the owner of the store followed me all the way to the door, his eyes boring into mine, his face full of suspicion and sorrow. I was not willing after all, it seems, to step over the line from petty theft to public disgrace. That's the way I remember it, anyway.

As I flipped through the pages of Gaby's and my pathetic little testaments, my shame was strong, but I found I had little compassion for the child I had been. There was something else about the whole thing, too, something that transcended the disgrace of the theft, but my mind refused to cough it up.

I closed my eyes for a moment and could see my small hands pushing the wrapped up notebooks into the secret hiding place I'd found in Emma's shop, but I couldn't recall when I'd done it, or why. Obviously, I wanted to avoid being found out, but that was not the whole story.

I thought suddenly of confession—the churchy kind. I'd made my first confession when I was eight. What followed, since my parents were singularly devout Catholics, was a weekly routine of confession, penance and absolution before going to mass on Sunday. My confessor was Father Douglas, a gentle old priest who was an associate at St. Margaret's Church in Laingford. The main priest was Father Christopher, a young, dynamic fellow with thick black hair and piercing blue eyes. Father Christopher scared me silly, but Father Douglas was very sweet, and when I thought about God at all (which was a struggle, as I wasn't convinced that he was any more real than Santa Claus), I pictured him as a very large Father Douglas.

Of course, seeing as I was too young to have any good, juicy sins under my belt, I made most of them up, as I imagine most Catholic kids do. I didn't have brothers and sisters, so I couldn't confess the "I was mean to my brother" kind of sin that Gaby padded her list with. I told Father Douglas that I had been mean to some person at school instead. I'd pick a schoolmate at random and weave a tale—usually one in which I had been wronged by this person and had lashed out in righteous indignation. I was a natural storyteller, sometimes even convincing myself that it had happened. When Father Douglas gave me a couple of Hail Marys to say in penance, I did them fervently, with only the very tip of my mind telling me that, if anything, I was doing the penance for having lied, not for having snapped at a friend.

I had absolutely no intention of telling the priest about the Secret Stealing Club. For one thing, I knew that stealing was a mortal sin, and that it would turn my soul as black as licorice. In my mind, it wasn't a sin unless you admitted it, and if nobody found out, your soul was safe. I knew that because the club was secret, I was technically receiving communion in a state of mortal sin, which compounded the offence, but there was no turning back. I had this theory that the holy wafer the priest put on my tongue somehow would fix things, like a kind of internal detergent.

When my parents died, I was certain at once that my mortal sin had set them up. Maybe that's why I hid the books. It certainly was why, after the funeral, I never darkened the door of the Catholic Church again. I had burned my bridges, and was, essentially, a murderer. To my relief, my Aunt Susan, who became my guardian, was an atheist.

All this diving into the past and splashing around in long-buried guilt left me exhausted. It was late afternoon by then, and I was supposed to be getting ready to whoop it up with my beau. Somehow, I didn't feel like partying, but I could hardly call up Becker and say I wanted to cancel because I had just remembered I was a thief and a murderer and I was kind of depressed. I put the Kountry Kow head away, cleaned up my work table and went to the well to pump up some water for a bath. As I poured hot water from the big kettle into my portable zinc tub, a line from Shakespeare's Macbeth popped into my head. Lady M., sleepwalking after the murder of Duncan. "All the perfumes of Arabia could not sweeten this little hand…"

I poured a bit of Body Shop musk bubble bath in instead.

Seventeen

Dine at home in style and win an evening out! Fill in a ballot every time you purchase a Kountry Pantree Pre-cooked Shrimp Ring, and you have a chance to win a free dinner for four at Kuskawa's finest resort: the Mooseview!

—A sign on the freezer-bin in the frozen fish
 section of the Kountry Pantree superstore

"You're quiet this evening," Becker said. We were sitting in the main dining room at the Mooseview Inn, Serena and Winston Elliot's masterpiece. Our table was right next to a huge window overlooking the Kuskawa River. Below us, the Mooseview's private dock glowed like a highly polished dance-floor, reflecting an artful tangle of white fairy lights festooned in the trees beside it. The lights glinted in the mirror-still water, and a lone canoe, backlit by the tail end of a glorious sunset, slipped past the end of the dock. I suddenly wanted to be there, in that boat, not where I was, making awkward conversation with a man whose personality seemed to have changed overnight. A tea-light candle floated in a brandy glass full of blue liquid between us, casting oh-so-romantic shadows over Becker's face.

"Are you growing a moustache?" I said.

He fingered the faint red stubble that adorned his upper lip and cleared his throat. "I was thinking about it. Do you like it?"

"It's a little early to tell. Ask me again in a week."

"I can shave it off if you don't," he said. Lordy. Mark Becker was seeking my approval about his facial hair. He had been treating me like fine china since picking me up, deferring to my opinion over how long it would take to get to the Inn ("d'you think we should take the back road? The reservation's for seven…"), complimenting me on my outfit, which was nothing special, and even asking if I minded the walk after parking a hundred metres away from the front door. We had made small talk—really small, the kind people make when they hardly know each other. The unanswered proposal hung between us like the proverbial Elephant in the Room. I didn't want to ask about Bryan, because that had already revealed itself as a touchy subject, and Becker had already asked me about the Kountry Pantree project. (I'd said it was going "fine", which is really all one can say about a creative thing in the early stages.) In the intervening days since Becker had asked me to marry him, a weird reversal of status had occurred. I realized that, for as long as I had known him, he had been the bossy, opinionated half of the equation. I had responded in my usual feisty, "don't you dare tell me what to do" way, and the resulting electricity had fuelled our fire. Or mine, anyway. To my horror, I was discovering that when Mark Becker was being solicitous and sensitive, he wasn't sexy any more. Yeesh.

I toyed with my wine and lit a cigarette. "You going to the town council meeting tomorrow?" I asked.

"I wasn't planning on it. Why?"

"I think you should. The League of Social Justice is planning some sort of coup, I think." Oh, great, Polly. Champion secret keeper, that's me.

"Coup? You mean they're going to take over the council chambers?" Becker said.

"It might not be that funny," I said, cutting off his laugh. "They've apparently got hold of some information about the Kountry Pantree. Something that they seem to think will kill the project. It may get ugly." Becker's eyes lost their kicked-puppy look, and my heart sang.

"Ugly, how?"

"Well, Archie Watson was over at George's this afternoon with a couple of the other members, and it looked like they were having a meeting. Odd, don't you think, when his brother has just died? He told me they were planning something, but he wouldn't tell me what. Susan wouldn't let him. It was all very hush-hush."

"How did Watson seem? Was he as torn up about Vic as you'd expect him to be?"

"Well, he was emotional, but then that seems to be a permanent state for him. I don't think he and his brother were very close."

I looked up to see Serena Elliot herself bearing down on us, carrying two sizzling plates.

"Now these are very hot," she said, placing my escargot order in front of me with a flourish.

She was wearing a screamingly expensive black sheath, which probably cost more than Becker's Jeep, and the diamonds adorning her long, thin fingers were too big to be fake, if you know what I mean. As she leaned over me, a waft of her perfume caught me squarely in the sinuses, and I sneezed.

"Gesundheit," she said. "It's Poison. My scent, I mean. It makes Winston sneeze, too. Heeeere you go, Detective Becker." She deposited Becker's plate in front of him and squeezed his shoulder. "Now you two be careful with these plates. We always have our staff say that because some jerk from the States tried to sue us once after he burned his little pinkies." She immediately went off into peals of delightful laughter, and it occurred to me that she might be a mite tipsy.

I muttered a thank-you, and Becker just stared at her.

"Oh, you're probably wondering what I'm doing playing waitress," she said. She really had a lovely voice. "I just told Rachel I'd bring them over, because I wanted to make sure everything was all right. We do like to check in with our important clients, you know." Important clients? A puppet maker and a policeman?

"Thank you kindly," Becker murmured, sounding exactly like Constable Fraser on *Due South*.

"Everything's great, Serena," I said. "You guys have done a beautiful job with the place."

She ignored me and squeezed Becker's shoulder again. "And I just wanted to tell you how sorry I am, we all are, about poor Vic Watson's death," she said. "Such a tragic thing. Such a good man." It wasn't as if Becker was related, I thought. She hovered for a moment, looking as if she might just pull up a chair and sit down.

"It sure was sad, ma'am," Becker said. His face was totally blank.

"And I expect you've heard the rumours by now," Serena went on. "About how someone, um, hastened his death in hospital. Why, everybody's talking about it. But I can't see it myself. I went to visit him, you know, Saturday evening, and he looked just awful. I told Winston I thought he would probably have another heart attack pretty soon. He was just white as a sheet. I suppose there's going to be an inquest, is there?"

"I don't know about that, ma'am," Becker said.

"Well, if there is, I just wanted you to know that I was one of his many, many visitors that day," she said, smiling so widely her plastic face took on a sudden sheen in the candlelight, like a polished apple. "There was quite a line-up after me, you know. Victor Watson was a popular man. If you want a list of who was there, you only have to ask. Now, enjoy your snails, darlings, before they get cold." She sailed away, a galleon in full glory, tottering slightly on her three-inch heels.

"Gosh," I said.

"Interesting," Becker said, and began to splutter, the kind of sound one makes to hold back inappropriate laughter. The escargots smelled divine.

"It's Poison, you know," I said in a Serena-voice.

"Only for our most important clients," Becker said in a strangled falsetto and beckoned Rachel, our real waitress, over to order another bottle of wine.

We didn't go to the movie. In fact, we decided to abandon the Jeep, as well, because there were two bottles of wine sloshing around inside us, plus a couple of Armagnacs we had with dessert.

"We're fried, you know," I said, as Becker plunked down his Visa card.

"Like eggs," he said. "Taxi, I think."

"Gene's playing tonight," I said as we passed the piano lounge on the way to the front desk. It was a Monday, and the lounge was almost deserted. We exchanged a look, which translated into the agreement that "one for the road" was okay if the Laingford Cab Company was part of the deal. Gene greeted us like old buddies (which we were) and played to us like he was our own private troubador. He's tall and thin, with a repertoire that would shame the biggest jukebox in the world. He dredged up several Beatles tunes, old Creedence Clearwater Revival stuff and even some Elton John, although I'm not saying which one of us requested "Candle in the

Wind". I will say, however, that Becker holds a secret, vaguely maudlin regard for Lady Diana, Princess of Wales (may she rest in peace). I made a mental note to probe further at a more opportune time.

We were kicked out of the place long after last call, when our waitress Rachel from the dining room started putting the chairs upside down on the table next to us. Gene gave us a lift back to Becker's place, saying it was the least he could do, seeing as we'd saved him from the Monday night Bingo Ladies, who usually swarmed him, demanding Elvis and Buddy Holly to go with their margaritas.

Becker's apartment was as bleak as ever. It was a good-sized, reasonably appointed two bedroom on the ritzy side of Lake Kimowan, but he had never bothered to make it more than a place to put his stuff. He'd moved in three years previously, on a trial separation from Catherine, his ex-wife. I think that a lot of people end up living in places like those—the "I've moved out for a while" kind of dwelling that begins as a temporary refuge and ends up being permanent. There were cardboard boxes in his laundry room that he'd never unpacked. Most of the furniture was Ikea stuff, an indication that Catherine had kept the honeymoon suite, and the only things on the walls were a framed Bateman poster (the lurking wolf one) and an abstract thing by Bryan (aged three) that would have been stunning if it had been framed properly. He had books, lots of them, which always help to furnish a room, but it was still bleak.

"You interested in a nightcap?" Becker asked, fumbling for the light switch. What he actually said was more like "Yinneres dinna nicap?" (we were really rather sloshed), but I knew what he meant. I complied, but we had hardly had more than a sip of whatever it was he splashed into two glasses before we were tangled together on the Ikea sofa, making the kind of noises that

143

would have made Bryan, had he been there, say "eeew, gross."

I will pull a discreet veil over the rest of the evening, or morning, I guess. There is nothing remotely interesting about booze-sodden coupling, although the participants may think so at the time. Usually, though, they don't remember much about it. I didn't, anyway.

The next morning found us both standing in front of the open door of the fridge, guzzling liquids directly from the cartons: me, orange juice, him, milk.

"Have we actually ever made love completely sober?" I said. He suppressed a belch and grinned like a jack-o'lantern. "C'mere," he said.

Later, he called a cab and went to pick up his Jeep from the Mooseview Resort, while I snooped around his apartment. There was ample evidence of Bryan—comic books, small clothes strewn here and there and the remains of a bowl of breakfast cereal on the coffee-table, one lone Froot Loop palely loitering in a sea of pink milk. As I took the bowl to the kitchen and dumped it into the sink, I heard Bryan's voice in my mind, complaining, "I was saving that."

The second bedroom was his: a small rumpled bed with a bunched-up Pokemon coverlet, a bookshelf full of children's classics (most of which had "Mark Becker" written neatly on the flyleaf in a childish hand) and the usual assortment of stuffed bears and mangled action figures. In fact, though Bryan didn't live permanently with his father, he had made his room far more homey than his Dad had managed with the rest of the place. I wandered back into the kitchen, made myself a piece of toast and ate it standing up against the counter, surveying the scene and drifting off into a daydream. What would it be like to live here? Where would my stuff go?

I envisioned my worktable set against the wall by the

window that looked out over the lake. I placed my books next to Becker's on the shelves and hung my pictures on his walls (mentally sending Bryan's abstract to the Framery to get the gold-label treatment and banishing the Bateman print to the bathroom.) I imagined my toothbrush in the Ducky cup with Bryan's and Becker's and filled the closet in the bedroom with my shirts and trousers. I let Rosencrantz and Lug-nut curl up on the sofa and stepped back. Not bad. Just weird. Alien.

I turned around and looked at the sink, the dishwasher, the monster fridge. No more getting water from the handpump. Hot showers. A clothes washer, for heaven's sake. A dryer. A freezer. A big TV and a stereo system. A computer and e-mail. A vacuum cleaner and a housedress. The possibilities were endless. Outside, a Sea-Doo screamed past on the lake and in the apartment below, someone started up the tunes—heavy metal, it sounded like, the bass coming up through my feet and making my teeth ache. No squirrels. No woodpile. No solitude. I couldn't make it work, not in my head, anyway.

Becker returned, and I asked him to drive me home.

"You don't want to stay for a while?" he said. "I picked up a video for later."

"I'm hung over, and I have to get back to the Kountry Pantree thing," I said. "Besides, the dogs need me."

"The dogs? Aren't they with your aunt?"

"George and Susan are looking after them, yeah, but it's not fair to ask them to dog-sit all the time."

"We could go get them and bring them back here," he said.

"They'd tear your place apart, Mark. Anyway, I have to work."

"Are you okay? Is everything okay?"

"I'm fine. Just hung over is all—nothing to do with you. Nothing personal." Everything personal, actually, but I wasn't going to say so.

In the Jeep on the way to Cedar Falls, the silence was thick.

"I had a good time last night, Becker."

"So did I," he said. "I—ah—I'm going to go into the station today and talk to Morrison. Find out what's happening with the Vic Watson thing." I remembered the blurry photograph that Sophie had given me, that I had been meaning to pass on to Becker. It didn't seem to be the time, although it was right there in my jacket pocket. Later, maybe, when I had more energy to explain what I thought it might or might not mean.

"Does that mean you're back in harness again?" I said. He nodded. Sad, really. This was supposed to be a week off for Becker, and he had lasted less than a day. Perhaps he had some workaholic issues that he needed to clear up before he thought seriously about committing himself to a domestic partner. I considered saying so, but it would just have turned into a fight.

"Don't keep me in the dark, Becker, okay? I want to know why they think Vic's death in hospital was suspicious."

"We'll see," he said.

"Are you going to tell Morrison what Serena said about visiting him? That there was a line-up to see him? You think that was true?"

"I'll tell him if he's prepared to give me the background," Becker said.

"This sounds more like a macho one-upmanship thing than an investigation," I said.

"I won't grace that remark with a reply," he said, after a tiny little pause. I guess I was going to get my fight after all. Lucky me.

"Well, aren't you guys supposed to be sharing information? Isn't that the way it works?"

"You seem to think police work is all nice TV cop-buddy stuff, with the clues coming in on cue like the goddamn daily newspaper," he said. "It isn't like that. We don't sit around a King Arthur table and hold hands. We collect information and draw our own conclusions, and if one of us gets a lucky break, he also gets the credit. That's the way it works, Polly."

"Every man for himself, you mean."

"That's not far wrong."

"Charming. How just."

We were almost at the farm, and the cab of the Jeep was filling up with resentment, as if one of us had broken wind. We'd had this kind of conversation before, and we never got anywhere with it. It was old ground, like an ongoing battle between neighbours over a long disputed fence line. The thing that bothered me most about it was that, in the middle of a fight with Becker, I found that he was attractive again. Suddenly, I was very tired. I could feel Becker's ring rubbing against me on the inside of my shirt, directly over my heart like a cold metal finger, and I decided I'd take it off as soon as I got home. There was no point swinging this way and that over the issue any more. It was a doomed notion. Marriage was a dance I would not be doing any time soon—not with Becker, at any rate.

"Will I see you at the council meeting tonight?" I said.

"Probably. Don't save me a seat, though. I'll be at the back."

"Consider your seat unsaved, then," I said. I did kiss him before I got out of the Jeep. After all, we had spent an intimate night together, and though we were snarling at each other, we were still technically sweethearts. Heh.

I collected my dogs from George's farm house and trudged up the hill to my cabin. First I would smoke a joint to get rid of my headache, then I thought I might just take a wee nap. Sometimes life just isn't worth staying awake for.

Eighteen

And the winner is…! Why not visit our engraving shop at Kountry Pantree, located right next to the bakery. Get your daily bread, and then pick up that trophy for your little league tournament! Why waste time downtown when you can get everything you need at Kountry Pantree?

—Another ad in the *Laingford Gazette*

A couple of hours before the council meeting, Aunt Susan's League of Social Justice met for a final briefing at George's place. I was not invited, and George had requested diplomatic immunity, so we decided to go together in the same vehicle. I offered to drive the farm truck, as George's eyesight was deteriorating and his driving technique, while lawful, combined a firm determination not to go more than 40 km per hour, with a disturbing propensity for exploring the road conditions in the oncoming lane.

"So, do you actually know what they're up to?" I asked as he climbed into the cab of the pickup.

"I have some idea," George said, "but I have deliberately stayed out of it. Your Aunt believes that the fewer people who know, the better."

"They're not planning anything illegal, are they? No dynamite or anything?"

George chuckled. "They have a lot of papers, documents

they have obtained from what Susan says is an inside source. That could be dynamite, maybe. But I don't know."

"Well, whatever happens, I just hope she doesn't embarrass herself."

"I think your Aunt is old enough not to worry about embarrassment," George said, craning his neck as I inched the truck past the bumper of Emma Tempest's purple van. The driveway looked like the parking lot of Downtown Business Folks' Association (DBFA) meeting hall: every single vehicle was an advertisement on wheels. "Emma's Posies are Bloomin' Lovely" on the purple van, "Downtown Drugs: Your Family Drugstore" on Joseph Olszewski's sedan, "Smile for the Shutterbug" on Stan Herman's yellow Camry with the camera on the roof, "Go Crazy: It's Pizza Madness" on Pete Holicky's battered compact (with a license plate that said PIZA PIE), "Make Every night Movie Night at Homerun Video Den" squeezed onto the driver's door of Florence Levine's Tempo, and "Watson's Old Fashioned Service" on the side of Archie Watson's vintage panel van.

"If you are concerned about embarrassment," George said, "perhaps it is your own that you are thinking of, no?" The wheel slipped in my hand, and I just slightly grazed the side of the pizza car. A faint noise accompanied the action, as if someone had just torn a small strip of velcro off a tin can.

"Holicky won't notice," I said. "It looks like he's a regular at the Sikwan demolition derby already."

"And my truck? I will not notice either?" George said. Normally, this kind of incident would have had me apologizing in fourteen different positions and offering to go to jail. I don't know what was wrong with me. I sighed rather obviously and hopped out to examine the damage. George stayed where he was, gazing at me with a bemused expression on his face. There wasn't a scratch on the pickup truck, but its front fender had scraped a four-inch hairline of paint off Holicky's car, just above the wheel. The scratch blended in quite happily with the dozen or so other ones in the immediate area, stopping just short of a large, rusty dent that looked to be a couple of years old.

"Hand me my notebook, would you, George?" I had brought it along so that I could doodle if I got bored. George passed the book out to me and I scribbled a note and left it under the windshield wiper of the pizza car. "Pete—There is a new scratch on this car. If you can tell me which one it is, I'll give you $50. Polly Deacon."

We drove for a while in silence.

"There is something bothering you," George said. I shrugged. "There was a time once when you would have told me about it."

"We used to be together more," I said. "Now you've got a full house most evenings, and Susan and Eddie have taken over the goat stuff, so we don't hang out in the barn like we used to." I could hear a little whine begin in my voice, like a miniature sewing machine.

"That is true," George said and waited.

"And it isn't as if I can just come down there and say I want to talk to you privately and not have Susan wonder what I'm telling you that I'm not telling her, because it would just hurt her feelings, wouldn't it?"

"Perhaps."

"And anyway, there's a lot of stuff that she's not telling me because she thinks I can't keep a secret, and who's to say she can keep one either?" I went on in this vein for quite a long time, George prompting me with the occasional "I see" and "Ah" in just the right places. By the time we got to the

Laingford Town Hall parking lot I had brought him up to date on Vic's near-drowning and subsequent death, David Kane's flirtatious behaviour with me and with Arly Watson, Becker's problems with Bryan and finally, Becker's proposal. I left out the part about the Secret Stealing Club and Eddie and Robin's pregnancy scare, because they were both, in different ways, too private. As I turned off the ignition and killed the lights, it suddenly occurred to me that I hadn't felt such a curious lightness in my chest since my going-to-confession days with Father Douglas. I glanced over at George and pictured him suddenly in a clerical collar, seen through a screen in profile.

"But enough about you, let's talk about me," I said. He laughed.

"I miss our talks," he said.

"Me, too. No advice, then? No magic solutions?"

"I could tell you about my dear first wife, Kaarina, or about how wonderful it is having your Aunt Susan live with me," he said, "or I could tell you about how difficult it was, and is, sometimes, but I do not think you need a testimonial about marriage. I think you need to make a decision on your own, Polly."

"I've already made up my mind," I said.

"Uh-huh," was all George said as he got out of the truck. I've never heard an "uh-huh" that had so many words in it.

The Town Hall in Laingford was built in 1872, back in the days before television and radio, when the townsfolk relied upon each other for entertainment. Because of this, the building featured a lovely auditorium with a brave little stage and proper audience seating, perfect for community concerts, amateur theatricals and edifying lectures. Of course, by the dawn of the twenty-first century, the good citizens of Laingford had long abandoned the concept of gathering in one place for culture's sake. They had hundreds of television channels beamed into their homes by satellite, millions of films available to them at the drop of a Homerun Video Den card, billions of musical recordings stashed away inside personal CD collections and an infinite array of temptations on the Internet. The theatre had slowly succumbed to neglect, its original dimensions eaten away by the municipal need for more office space, and was now used primarily to accommodate the overflow of Disgruntled Taxpayers at controversial public meetings. The stage was used as a storage space for broken chairs, cardboard boxes full of tax files from the 1980s, obsolete flip-charts (the Town had invested in a power-point computer program for special presentations) and several retired overhead projectors, whose tall necks reached up out of the clutter, the lens-contraptions at the top looking like the heads of browsing brontosaurs in a museum installation.

Regular Laingford council meetings were held in the council chambers on the ground floor of the Town Hall, but when the agenda included an issue that was likely to attract attention, the meeting was scheduled to take place in the second floor auditorium.

At the top of the stairs leading up to the theatre, a woman sat at a table beside a stack of council agendas and a sign-in book.

"Good evening," she said, smiling in a hostessy kind of way. "You are with the Kountry Pantree deputation or that other one?"

"Er, neither," I said. "Just a couple of taxpayers. This meeting's public, isn't it?"

"Of course it is," she said, "but we would appreciate you signing in. For the record, you know."

We both signed the register and took an agenda. I half

expected to find an usher on the other side of the door, who would ask us in a hushed voice whether we were with the groom's party or the bride's. I just couldn't get my mind off the marriage thing, I guess.

The place was pretty full, but there were quite a few empty seats on the right in Row A, within spitting distance of the action. I would have been happier at the back, but unless we wanted to stand, there wasn't much choice. George headed for them, and I followed.

The stage, of course, was not being used, as it was full of second hand furniture, but someone had set up a long table in front of the stage with chairs for all the councillors and the mayor. A big screen had been pulled down where the curtain used to be, and there was a computer off to the side, which, presumably, would impress us all with hi-tech displays at some point.

On the way down the aisle, I saw several people I knew. Theresa Morton, Susan's assistant at the feed store, waved to me from a couple of rows over. Beside her was Peter Kastner, a guy from Wiarton who had a cottage in Cedar Falls, and was one of those summer people who actually took an interest in local politics. My old friend Rico Amato, a Cedar Falls antique dealer, was there with a young man I think worked for the Town as a clerk of some sort, and Sophie Durette, Vic's friend and camera club buddy, was with them. I could see Linda Kirschnick seated in the front row off to the left, with the Elliots and Duke Pitblado. There was an empty seat beside Duke that was probably being saved for David Kane, if the entire Kountry Pantree contingent was to be in attendance. We settled in at the end of the right front row, checking first to make sure there weren't any "reserved" signs anywhere that we'd missed. I felt eyes on the back of my head and scrunched

153

down small. Calvin Grigsby from the *Gazette* sat at a rickety card-table set up way off at our side with a little hand-lettered sign on it that said "Press". Nice of the Town to accommodate the media, I thought. I gave him a little wave, and he grinned at me. His camera was ready to go, sitting on top of the table with a powerful-looking lens in place. He'd be able to get extreme close-ups, I thought.

I glanced down at my agenda. At the top, it said: *"Corporation of the Town of Laingford—Regular Council Meeting"* and gave the date and time.

1. Adoption of Agenda

2. Disclosure of Pecuniary Interest

3. Closed Session-Personnel matter (By resolution)

4. Deputations

   a) Mr. David Kane, representing Numbered Corporation 000997-467-43. Re: Update on the Kountry Pantree Development Project

   b) Ms. Susan Kennedy representing the League of Socialist Justice. Re: The Kountry Pantree Development Project

5. Bylaws and Approvals.

It looked like a big bundle of fun from start to finish.

"How come there are so many people here?" I said to George.

"I think Susan and her group put the word out," George said. "And I suppose if there is going to be a presentation by the people who are building this superstore, many locals will be interested."

"What, you mean because they want jobs?" I said.

"Or they are worried about their own," he said.

Behind us, the League of Social Justice filed in, walked down the aisle and (I should have guessed it) filled the rest of the front row where we were sitting. Susan lifted an eyebrow and gave me a huge "I knew you'd come around" smile. I was marked now. I had inadvertently put on the uniform of the anti-Kountry Pantree faction by sitting where I was sitting. I knew this, because I glanced over at Linda Kirschnick and the Elliots on the other side, and they were frowning at me. I lifted my hands at Linda, trying to tell her it was a mistake, but she turned immediately to Duke Pitblado and made a remark that made him look up. In my mind's eye, I saw the Kountry Pantree cash cow slipping away. Would they cancel my contract? Delay payment? Ask for the advance back? Sue me? I felt frightened, somehow, although it was only a stupid mascot job and losing it would not be the end of the world.

A side door opened and David Kane entered, smiling with the confidence of a man who has never in his life paid attention to signs that say "Authorized Personnel Only". He gave a vague, friendly wave and a wink to someone at the back, and I was not the only person to turn my head to see who he was waving at. I suspect that it was one of those deliberate, politician's gestures, the kind that spin doctors and handlers coach their protégés to use. It was a kind of "working the room" thing. One or two of the standing-room-only people near the door smiled in a bewildered way, but I would bet that when Kane waved, he was looking directly at nobody at all. Kane took his seat with the rest of the Kountry Pantree party, and was immediately absorbed in a confab. He glanced my way, so I winked and waved.

Seconds later, the Laingford town council trotted out from the same door Kane had used and took their places at the head table. Each councillor had his or her own nameplate, facing audience-wards, to remind us of who they were. These nameplates could be had for $7.95 from the Framery, which also did engraving and trophies on the side. (I knew this because I once had a nameplate made for Susan, for the feed store. Hers said "Susan Kennedy: She Who Must Be Obeyed".)

The mayor, the Honourable Phyllis Lunenburg, carried a box of Kleenex in one hand and a briefcase in the other. The tip of her nose was red and shiny, and I could hear her breathing through her mouth. Either she had a wicked cold or the death of one of her council members had hit her very hard indeed. Lunenburg was into her second term as mayor, which in Laingford is officially a part-time job. Her other sphere of work was law. She was an extremely successful real estate lawyer, and there were several people in the community who had recognized that if they dealt with Lunenburg and Associates, things like minor variances and municipal planning issues seemed to go very smoothly. The mayor was in her mid-fifties and had clearly made a recent stop at Katie's Cut 'n Curl. Her hair was a most unlikely shade of bronze.

There were five councillors for Laingford, but of course, only four of them were present. The fifth, Vic Watson, was represented by an empty chair and a nameplate. Councillor Stephanie Barnes, who looked about twelve (I think she was in her early twenties, the youngest person ever to be elected to council in the history of Laingford), placed an ostentatious bunch of roses on the table behind Vic's nameplate before she sat down. This caused a mild sensation in the audience, and I risked a look over my shoulder at Sophie Durette. Sophie was not amused.

The others were Andrew Jackson, who represented Cedar Falls and area and was effectively "my councillor", Tom Southwell and Bernie LeBlanc. Bernie and Tom had been councillors since the dawn of time and were both well into their eighties. I have no idea what kind of careers they had enjoyed before retirement allowed them to dive headfirst into the delights of municipal politics. Andrew, who ran a marina on Stanfield Lake (in lovely downtown Cedar Falls) was middle aged, and liked to speak for the "working family man" on controversial issues. Stephanie was a young dot-commer who had sold her search engine company, "WooHoo", to some multinational corporation for untold millions and now lived by herself in a mansion next to the Elliot's Mooseview Resort. Rumour had it that she drank, a little.

In addition to the councillors, the Town treasurer was present, one Richard Wayman, according to his nameplate, and next to him was the Town clerk, a sour-faced woman called Frances Berry, who was dressed from head to toe in red, with long, nasty-looking fingernails painted to match.

Phyllis Lunenburg banged her gavel on the little wooden gavel-thing, and the meeting began.

Nineteen

Let our valet parking service make your grocery shopping experience something special. Not only will we park you car for you, we'll also load your purchases and wash your windshield! At Kountry Pantree, the customer is King!

—A sidebar in the *Laingford Gazette* classified
    section, right next to the auto ads

"Before we get dowd to buisdess," Lunenburg said, "I want to express, od behalf of council, our condolences to the fabily of councillor Vic Wadsod. Let's all stad and have a bobent of silence." We did so, although the solemnity of the occasion was marred slightly by a monstrous sneeze that shook the mayor from head to toe. Nobody could fake a cold like that.

"She should be at home in bed," George muttered.

"She's gonna wish she was," Susan muttered back.

The first order of the meeting was the adoption of the agenda, which would only take a moment (or bobent, as the mayor would have it). Susan raised her hand.

"We don't take comments from the floor this early in the meeting," Lunenburg said. (I won't keep substituting the letter "b" for all her "m" sounds, but you get the picture.) Susan stood and spoke anyway.

"I would just like to respectfully point out," she said, "that the name of our organization is the League for Social Justice, not Socialist Justice, as it is spelled here on the agenda."

"I thought it was the same thing," Bernie leBlanc said. "Communists, the lot of youse."

"Bernie, that will do," Lunenburg said. "Strike that from the record, please, Emma," she said in an aside to a young lady who was busily typing on a laptop in the background. I heard a little snicker from Calvin Grigsby and saw him scribble something in his notebook. Bernie's remark may have been struck from the public record, but I would bet it would appear in the *Gazette*, nonetheless.

"Point taken, Ms. Kennedy," Lunenburg said. "It will be amended in the minutes." Susan sat down again.

"That was a deliberate mistake," she whispered to George. "I just know it."

Item Two was the disclosure of pecuniary interest, which didn't mean a thing to me. "I have an interest to declare," the mayor said. "In the matter of the Kountry Pantree project, I will be handing this meeting over to Andrew Jackson, the deputy mayor, and I will be leaving the room." Another mild sensation in the audience, although none of the council members, nor the KP party, I might add, looked particularly surprised.

I leaned over George to talk to Susan. "What does pecuniary interest mean?" I said.

"It means that she stands to gain from the business under discussion," Susan said, her eyes glued to the mayor in a narrow, deadly stare. "It means she's working for them, probably as their lawyer, though I hardly think that can be legal." She put up her hand and stood without waiting to be acknowledged.

"Madam Mayor," she said, "does this mean that you have been working for the Kountry Pantree corporation all along? Without declaring an interest?"

"Of course not," the mayor snapped back. "If I had, I

would have declared a conflict back in May, now wouldn't I? The group has retained the services of my firm very recently on an unrelated matter which is of no business of yours, Ms. Kennedy, and I am declaring an interest now because I like to abide by the rules. And I wish you would do the same and not keep interrupting these proceedings." Susan sat down again.

"If she was involved with the legal set-up of the Kountry Pantree at the beginning, when they were starting to get planning permission and zoning bylaws and so on, and didn't declare an interest, that would make all those things doubly illegal," she said, almost to herself, though we all leaned in to hear her. Her eyes were shining. "This just adds to what we already know. We can take it to the Ontario Municipal Board, and they'll have to start all over again."

"We will now go into closed session on a personnel matter," the mayor said. "This shouldn't take long."

"A closed session? You mean, like a secret meeting?" I said to Susan.

"It's in the municipal rule-book somewhere," she said. "If they have to discuss something about staffing, hiring and firing and disciplinary actions and so on, it's not allowed to be public."

"Why do it now, when everybody's here?"

"Because it makes them feel important, I suppose," Susan said. "If this was a session in the council chamber, we'd all have to leave, but they're not going to try and clear the auditorium, are they?"

Obviously they weren't, because the council got up from the table and filed out through the side door they had entered by. Emma, the stenographer, followed, carrying her laptop. The audience began talking and moving around.

I leaned over Calvin Grigsby's little desk. "You don't get to sit in on this one, I take it?" I asked him.

"I wish," he said. "But if they're going into closed session to fire somebody, I usually hear about it anyway. It's just hard to get the facts."

"Is that what they're doing? Firing someone?"

"So rumour has it," he said.

"Who?"

Calvin looked pointedly over at a small knot of people a few rows back. It was the little group with Theresa Morton, Rico Amato and the young man from the Town office.

"Brent Miller," Calvin said, "that thin guy in the blue shirt. He works with the Town clerk, Mrs. Berry. I don't know what he's done, but someone I know in the municipal office told me that he was suspended a couple of days ago, with pay, pending some sort of investigation."

"Investigation? You mean the police were involved?"

"God, no. Nothing so official as that. An internal investigation. The worst kind." He smiled a bit sadly. "I doubt we'll ever hear the details."

"Poor guy," I said, wondering if it would be tacky to go over there and commiserate. Probably it would, as I didn't know the man, although Rico was a good friend of mine and appeared to be a good buddy of Brent's as well. Besides, it was all rumour at this point, so what could I say? "Hi, you don't know me but I hear you're being fired. So what did you do?" Not, as they say, done. Anyway, the most important thing right then was to find a washroom. I had to pee in the worst way.

The line-up for the ladies' public loo at the back of the auditorium was miles long, as it usually is at these things. The queue for the men's was shorter, but it was still a line-up, and my need was very great. I discreetly asked the hostessy lady at the door if there was another facility I might use. I told her it was one of those "woman's things". She responded at once, with a sympathy that I found rather touching.

161

"There are more washrooms on the other side of the building," she said. "Just go out the door the councillors used and turn right." I went back into the auditorium and headed for the "Authorized Personnel" door, hoping I wouldn't be seen. Unlike David Kane, I am not one of those people who is comfortable stepping into restricted territory. I needn't have worried. There was a crush of people around the front row where the Kountry Pantree people were sitting, lots of milling around and schmoozing, and the side door was effectively masked by bodies. I slipped through quickly and found myself in a dimly lit, carpeted hallway.

I turned right and headed in what I assumed to be the direction of the facilities. Halfway down the hall was one of those soft, accordion vinyl doors, the kind that folds back like a curtain. It was closed, but light streamed out from the gap at the bottom, and I could hear the subdued murmur of voices. This must be where they're having the closed session, I thought to myself, tiptoeing past.

"He wouldn't dare!" a woman's voice said suddenly, quite loudly. I froze. "That's classified information, not for public eyes or ears. Goddamnit, I'll sue the pants off him!"

"Calm down, Frances," came the mayor's voice. "There would be no point suing him, because it would be admitting that there was something funny going on. Better to let him go with a severance package that'll make him keep his mouth shut."

"Isn't it too late for that?" a man's voice said. Sounded like Andrew Jackson.

"If those commies have got hold of it, it'll be all over the *Gazette* by Wednesday morning." That was Bernie LeBlanc.

"If you call them commies again in public, I'll tell your wife about that Toronto convention incident," the mayor hissed.

"You wouldn't."

"I would, so button your lip. Now, listen, people. The next part of the meeting is going to be tricky, but it will be fine if you all just remain calm and businesslike and stick to the rulebook. No discussion of votes. No discussion of personnel matters. A bland, slightly surprised attitude, as if the whole thing is a bunch of fuss over nothing. Got it?"

"Where will you be?" someone asked.

"I'll be in here, of course, listening on the intercom," the mayor said. "So don't try any clever stuff. No grandstanding. Especially you, Franny."

"What I don't get is why we have to let them commies say anything at council at all," Bernie said.

"It's a democracy, so we have to, Bernie."

"Huh. Bleeding heart liberals, the bunch of them. Trudeau-lovers."

"Trudeau's dead, Bernie."

"Can we get on with it?" That sounded like Stephanie Barnes. "I mean, like, what are we doing about this Brent guy?"

"We could demote him to bylaws. Make him work with Sam giving out parking tickets," Andrew said. There was a general chuckle, and their voices lowered.

"Excuse me, young lady? Can I help you?" A hand touched my shoulder, and I jumped about a foot in the air and turned around. It was Tom Southwell, the councillor who, like Bernie LeBlanc, could remember Laingford when the horse and carriage reigned.

"Ummm, hi. Sorry. Looking for the washroom," I said.

Southwell jerked a thumb down the hall. I heard running water, the sound of a recent flush, and headed quickly towards it, muttering my thanks. How long had he been standing there? Did he know how much I'd heard? I couldn't wait to tell Susan. But first, I had to pee.

Twenty

This way to the Kountry Pantree Beachside Patio and play area. Light lunches served daily. Licenced by the LLBO.
  —A sign at the side entrance
    to the Kountry Pantree complex

On my way back down the hallway a few minutes later, I noticed that the light from under the accordion door was gone, and everything was quiet. That must mean the councillors had gone back into public session, I thought, and hurried the rest of the way. I didn't want to miss anything, especially after hearing what had sounded like a cover-up of some sort. Whatever had happened, the mayor had talked about "something funny going on", and they all seemed to be concerned about what "the commies" were about to disclose. I couldn't wait to hear it.

When I got to the little side door which led into the auditorium, though, I found it was locked. I could hear some muffled applause and then the patrician tones of David Kane. Oh, right. The KP presentation was first, anyway. If I banged on the door for someone to let me in at that point, it would be like blundering onstage in the middle of a concert performance. Worse, really, as Kane would assume I was doing it on purpose. I didn't want him madder at me than he probably was already. I would have to find another exit, I supposed, and then go all the way around the building to the front entrance and back up the stairs, then sneak quietly into the auditorium from the back.

The corridor led to a staircase and I took them two at a time. At the bottom, there was not, as you'd expect, a door leading outside, just another hallway leading off into the interior of the municipal offices. I was beginning to feel like a rat in a maze, and a panicky one at that, seeing as I had absolutely no business being there. Most of the office doors were closed, but there was one on the left that was wide open, with a light on. I could hear a noise that was vaguely like a vacuum cleaner, and figured that there must be a night custodian on the job. I poked my head in to ask where the nearest exit was.

The Honourable Phyllis Lunenburg looked up, startled. She was standing behind a large square bin with a machine on top, which hummed. She held a thick bundle of papers in her hand and was in the process of feeding one into the maw of the machine. With a mangled, munching sound, the machine gobbled it down.

"Oh!" she said.

"Oh, sorry," I said, noting that she continued feeding the papers into the shredder, one-by-one. "Can you tell me how to get out of here? I seem to be lost." I had to raise my voice, as the shredder in action was a noisy sucker.

"End of the hall. Turn left," she said.

"Catching up on some paperwork?" I said. I couldn't help it, it just popped out.

"That's right," she said, putting the papers down and striding over to the door with a determination that made me back up into the hall. "A personnel matter. Strictly confidential." She closed the door firmly in my face. I stood there dazed for a second and heard the shredder start up again. Whatever she was doing, being interrupted didn't seem to phase her one bit. Her confidence spooked me. Hadn't I, a taxpayer, just caught her in the act of destroying documents that could have been connected to the Kountry Pantree project—perhaps something incriminating? Or was it just personnel files of some sort, something to do with Brent Miller? If so, why was she bothering to shred them?

Not that I could do anything about it, I thought, as I ran down the hall, found the exit door and crashed outside. Even if I could convince Susan, or even Becker, (if he'd bothered to show up), that she was destroying evidence of some sort, by the time someone went to investigate, all the papers would be confetti.

I raced round the side of the building, in the front door and up the stairs. At the top I paused to catch my breath, and my hostessy friend, who was still sitting at her station, looked at me with concern.

"Are you okay?" she said. "Did you find the ladies' room?"

"Yeah, thanks. Just got locked out. Had to come around. Did I miss much?"

"Well, the Superstore people are just finishing up their presentation, I think," she began, but I didn't wait to hear the end of it.

It was crowded at the back of the hall, people standing three deep near the doors.

"You're late," said a voice in my ear. It was Becker, leaning against a pillar with his arms crossed.

"Actually, I was here from the beginning," I said. "I got stuck in back by mistake."

"Shhhh," the man beside me said.

Up at the front, David Kane was narrating what looked like

a slick, Ontario Tory-style television commercial playing on the screen, complete with upbeat music. This was the power of modern media, I supposed. The people around me were gazing at the screen with their mouths half-open, mesmerized.

"The Kountry Pantree Complex will offer Laingford an increased consumer base that will create a spinoff economy for neighbouring businesses," Kane said. On the screen, a picture of a full parking lot dissolved into a photo of Downtown Laingford in the busy season. The happy music contained, for one tiny moment, the "cha-chinggg" of a cash register. I wonder how many people consciously heard it. Maybe lots of us did, but were too stunned by its overt greed to comment.

"In addition, we'll be creating a special Kountry Pantree beachside fun area," Kane continued, "with a sand beach, pedal boat rides and a full-time lifeguard." The screen showed an artist's rendering of something that looked like a theme park, with a number of buxom, bikini clad babes in the foreground. "When the whole project is complete, we'll be providing over two hundred full time jobs and probably about a hundred part-time positions as well." Picture of happy, healthy, clean cut teenagers.

"A similar project in the town of Beswick, in Southern Ontario, has resulted in quite a boom, economically speaking," Kane went on. A graph appeared. "One year after the Beswick Magic Mart was built, the unemployment rate went down four per cent, new home building stats increased significantly and the town got a new arena." Picture of a minor hockey team holding up a trophy.

"All in all, the Kountry Pantree project will benefit the community in dozens of ways," Kane said. "Jobs, the economy, the tourist industry, the whole bit, as well as increasing your tax base. Anyone who tells you otherwise is still thinking inside the box—the box that keeps Laingford from becoming the hub of the Kuskawa wheel. Whoever tells you that Kountry Pantree will harm the community is the kind of person who thought computers were just a fad." Here, the audience laughed warmly and looked at each other to make sure that everybody knew that they, at least, thought computers were just wonderful.

"What an asshole," I said. Becker poked me. "Well, he is. See ya." I started working my way back to my seat at the front.

The music swelled to a heart warming climax and the final picture on the screen showed a family gathered around a loaded grocery cart, Daddy, Mommy, boy, girl and baby, all holding up items that they'd found at Kountry Pantree, all grinning as if they'd just seen God. Then the screen went blank and the lights came back on. "Any questions?" Kane asked.

"Yeah, when do you open?" somebody called from the back.

"In exactly one month," Kane said. "Saturday, September the first. We're gonna have a parade, a community barbecue and fun fair, the whole bit. Completely free, of course."

"Where can I pick up a job application?" somebody else asked.

"Hey, Bob, you wanna be a lifeguard, dontcha? Hang out with the babes on the beach?" another voice called out. Laughter.

"Well, I have some with me," Kane said, over the general hilarity. "Come see me after the meeting, or you can pick them up at the *Gazette* office in town here, if you'd rather." I glanced at Calvin and saw a tiny frown appear on his face. Surely the *Gazette* was supposed to be an objective organ, so to speak? Just how involved was the publisher of the newspaper, anyway?

Andrew Jackson stood up to shake David Kane's hand.

"Thanks for your report, Mr. Kane," he said. "I'm sure we're all eagerly awaiting the opening of your superstore, and all the commercial benefit it will bring to Laingford." Kane resumed his seat to a round of applause.

"Now, for the next item..." Jackson said, picking up his agenda and reading from it as if, in all the excitement, he'd forgotten what came next. "The League for Socialist—er, Social, I mean, Justice. Miss Kennedy? You have the floor."

Susan stood up and turned to face the audience.

"Thank you, Deputy Mayor," she said. "Ladies and gentlemen, I'm sorry I don't have any audio-visual accompaniment to our presentation. If I did, I'd be trying to show you another side to the glowing picture that Mr. Kane has entertained us with. I wish I could show you a photo of the main street of Beswick, two years after the Beswick Magic Mart opened its doors. You would see closed and 'For Sale' signs on a disturbing number of the old, established community businesses. You would also see, if I could show you a graph, that the unemployment rate in that community went down because a lot of people had to move away, having lost their livelihood. I might also tell you that the new arena in Beswick was made possible by a government grant that was announced three years before the Magic Mart appeared on the scene. However, the League for Social Justice is not here to argue about the so-called benefits of the Kountry Pantree Superstore, but rather to raise one or two questions about procedure."

Susan held up a piece of paper. "I have here a photocopy of the last will and testament of Silas Gootch, whom many of you will know was one of the founding fathers of Laingford. He died in 1942. In his will, he bequeathed a parcel of waterfront property, Lot 4, concession 6, to the Town to be held in perpetuity as community parkland. The will also states that if the Town, for any reason, decides it does not want to retain title to the property, it automatically reverts back to the Gootch family, or its descendants. This town holding was sold to the proponents of the Kountry Pantree in February, 2000. What I would like to know, for the public record, is who sold the Gootch property, where the Kountry Pantree is now being built, to Mr. Kane and his friends? And for how much?"

This caused more than a mild sensation in the audience. Calvin Grigsby was writing so hard his pen was a blur. Andrew Jackson conferred with Richard Wayman, the treasurer, for a moment and then spoke without standing up.

"A fair question, Ms. Kennedy, although hardly relevant to a Town Council meeting. If you paid attention to the newspaper, you would have seen back in January of last year in the classified section that the Town gave up the deed to that property, er,..." he bent his head to Wayman, who whispered to him "...for tax purposes and it reverted back to the Gootch descendent in question, an individual whose identity we are not at liberty to say."

"Who brokered the Real Estate deal?" Susan said.

"I did," Duke Pitblado said, standing up. "Got a problem with that?" More mutterings and excited murmurings from the audience. It was like a trial in a John Grisham book, without the expensive suits. I was loving it.

Still, Susan seemed nonplussed. If that was the extent of their "secret weapon", the LSJ was dead in the water. "No, Mr. Pitblado, I don't have a problem with it as such, though I would be very interested to find out who the vendor was, and how much he or she got," she said.

"I'll just bet you would, lady," Pitblado said and sat back down to laughter and a smattering of applause.

"Go to the land registry office in Sikwan," someone called

from the back of the room. "They'll tell you if you give them enough money."

Susan turned and nodded, grim-faced, at the crowd. "I'll do that," she said.

"You have anything further to add, Ms. Kennedy?" Jackson said. He looked like he'd just swallowed a spoonful of something really sweet.

"Oh, yes, Councillor Jackson," Susan said. The room hushed again. "This is about the planning permits that the Town approved in March of last year. The permits for the Kountry Pantree development."

"Were you present at those planning meetings, Ms. Kennedy?" said Richard Wayman, unexpectedly.

"No, Mr. Wayman, I wasn't. I have the minutes here, though," she said.

"Those were very complex meetings," Wayman said, as if he was telling a small child not to bother trying to understand quantum physics. Susan went just a little pink, and her left eyebrow shot up into her hairline. Uh-oh, I thought. I felt George shift uncomfortably beside me.

"I have here," Susan said, waving another piece of paper, "a copy of a memo from the MNR—that's the Ministry of Natural Resources, for those of you who don't know. In it, the official in question, a Mr. Henry Blakeny, sends a very strongly worded message. He says the development can't possibly be permitted at that site, as it's too close to the shoreline, and involves an important stream, thereby endangering a certified sensitive area of fish habitat. Out of the question, he says."

"I wouldn't know anything about that, Ms. Kennedy," Wayman said, a little warily.

"No, of course, you wouldn't. But your mayor would, as it's

addressed to her, but she isn't here, is she, because she's declared a pecuniary interest in this project. Funny, that."

"I don't see that this has got anything to do with an open session of council," Bernie LeBlanc said.

"Oh, but it does," Susan said. "You see, this other piece of paper is a letter addressed to the clerk, Mrs. Berry, from the same MNR office. In it, Mr. Blakeny thanks her for the Town's donation to the Save the Kuskawa Pike Fund and refers to a phone call received from our local MPP, Kenneth Rivers, in support of the development proposal. In this letter, Mr. Blakeny waives all MNR rules and restrictions previously cited. Now, Ken Rivers is the Mayor's brother, isn't he?"

"Where did you get those?" Frances Berry roared, erupting up out of her seat.

"Mrs. Berry, do you mean to deny that you sent a cheque from the Town, using our taxpayers' money, to the Kuskawa Save the Pike Fund, in order to influence the decision of the Provincial environment authority regarding the Kountry Pantree development?"

"It wasn't taxpayer's money, it was a collection taken up in council!" Mrs. Berry shrieked.

"For twenty-five thousand dollars? That's a hefty sum on a councillor's salary, isn't it?"

"You bitch! You don't know what you're talking about!" Mrs. Berry said and launched herself at Susan, all ten crimson nails extended. I jumped up to help, not wanting to see my dear aunt get shredded like the mayor's papers downstairs, and several other people joined in. I felt a "poof" as the flash on Calvin Grigsby's camera went off, saw Becker pushing his way down the aisle, and then the Town Hall fire alarm started with a howl that would break your eardrums. The meeting, you might say, was effectively adjourned.

Twenty-One

Extra! Extra! Visit our extra-ordinary newsstand in the Kountry Pantree Food Court, for national and international magazines, newspapers and books—the KP newsstand, where you can pick up all the news that's fit to print!
—An advertisement in the *Laingford Gazette*

Nice picture of you in the paper, Polly," Nick said, plunking a pint of Kuskawa Cream down in front of me. It was Wednesday afternoon, the day after the fiasco at Town Hall. I had just bought the *Gazette*. I had endured a number of similar comments from everybody who even slightly knew me since the moment I'd left my truck.

"Hey, Polly. Nice picture!" "Hey, remind me never to piss you off, Polly!" "Look, it's the Polly-nator!" I had marched straight into the *Gazette* office to pick up a copy and marshal my defences.

So far, I'd only looked at the picture and the headline, "Brawl at Town Hall"—a big, 52-point screamer at the top of the page. You could hardly blame Calvin. Usually, this time of year, the only hard news the paper saw was the occasional ugly Sea-Doo accident ("Tragedy on Lake Kimowan") or a traffic story ("Highway Clogged at Weekend"). The Kountry Pantree kerfuffle was a gift, and I wasn't surprised that the *Gazette* had made a meal of it. There was a big front page story and a timeline thing in a boxed side-bar, with a flag saying "for background, see page 17." I was interested, though, to see how much of the policy stuff the League for Social Justice had disclosed would make the paper, given that the publisher, Hans Whiteside, might be one of the KP silent partners. The picture was a doozy.

Calvin had captured Frances Berry's attack on Susan at the very moment before impact. I guess I had seen it coming, because there I was, on the other side of Susan, in what I can only describe as a battle ready pose, crouching, fists raised, with a snarl on my face worthy of Skinny Minnie Miller, my childhood Roller Derby hero. Yikes.

Susan looked somehow dignified, standing erect with her famous left eyebrow well above resting position, not a hair out of place, holding aloft a piece of paper. To her right, flying out of the frame like a banshee, was Frances Berry. She was actually airborne, her fingernails curled in readiness, her arms in Catfight Position #1. Her face was truly terrible—quite nutso, really, and I'm glad that I hadn't been looking into her eyes at the time, because I would probably have wet my pants. It was a great picture. I resolved to ask Calvin for a blow-up of it for the Weird Kuskawa Art Show.

I was supposed to be meeting Yolanda and Dimmy at the Slug and Lettuce for lunch, after which we were planning to scrub the storefront area from top to bottom, in preparation for Saturday's show. I was early, for once, which gave me some time for a little quiet reading.

I reached for my Kuskawa Cream and took a swig, but found I could hardly swallow it. My stomach did a triple back flip, and I set the glass down again. Obviously, the tension in my life was taking its toll. Normally, I didn't have an anti-beer bone in my body. I have had beer for breakfast, often. I picked the glass up and took it to the bar.

"Nick, honey," I said, "I'm sorry, I can't drink this."

"What's the matter? Is it flat? I just started a new keg."

"No, it's not that."

"The glass dirty or something?" He seemed really upset.

"No, no. I just don't seem to feel like beer today. You know what I'd really like?"

"What?"

"A—milk. A Kahlua and milk."

"A brown cow? At noon?" He stared hard at me. I lifted an eyebrow. "One brown cow, coming up," he said.

I took my drink back to the booth by the window and gave my attention to Calvin's coverage of the council meeting. He had obviously done his homework before going to press. There were quotes from the 1942 will of Silas Gootch and from the tiny newspaper announcement of the Town's giving up the deed to the property. (I guess that was some legal requirement, but nobody at the paper had picked up on it. Nobody actually reads the classifieds, do they?) Cal had got copies of the leaked MNR memos from Susan, as well as some pretty juicy quotes, and as far as I could see, he hadn't been muzzled by his publisher. Susan was quoted as saying that, based on the evidence, the LSJ had submitted an official request to the Ontario Municipal Board, asking for a stop work order to be placed on the development project, and a request for a full OMB inquiry. However, Calvin's article did give equal billing to David Kane's presentation, and to all the happy prognostications the Kountry Pantree Project people had made in terms of economic growth. Basically, he just reported the news, which was, I suppose, his job.

The editorial, however, written by Hans Whiteside himself, came down firmly on the side of the developers.

On A Learning Curve

Recent developments in the saga of the Kountry Pantree project may make readers of this newspaper wonder about the honesty of our municipal government. Allegations have been made that any responsible newspaper should follow up, and we will do so. However, we must not lose sight of the fact that this town is on a learning curve, economically speaking. If we are to remain competitive in a modern market, that is to say, in the District of Kuskawa, we must be open to progress. It is the opinion of this newspaper that a development of the magnitude of the Kountry Pantree project can mean nothing but good for this community, both in terms of jobs and tourism.

While it is regrettable that the Town decided, many months ago, to give up its rights to a piece of land that an honoured citizen had bequeathed to it, it is understandable. Tax revenues are down, and maintaining our vibrant community is costly. However, the decisions of a private citizen (the descendant of the original benefactor) are not public business. Supporting a forward-visioning development is.

In terms of fish habitat, that matter is a provincial one, and we all know that Lake Kimowan remains a healthy, clean body of water, teeming with fresh water fish of all kinds. (Note the success of last year's Pike Tournament, where a 25 lb. pike was caught right off the Town docks!) The allegations raised by one interest group should not distract us from the benefits offered by the generosity of the Kountry Pantree proponents. It is to be hoped that the accusations made in this matter do not hinder the upcoming opening of the Kountry Pantree, and the gala parade and community barbecue prepared for the enjoyment of every citizen.

—Hans Whiteside

I took a big gulp of my brown cow and felt the cold milk and coffee liqueur slide soothingly down my throat. Aaaaah! Why had I never recognized the qualities of this particular tipple? I resolved to buy a bottle of Kahlua and a litre of homogenized on my way home.

"Polly, what the hell are you drinking?"

"Hi, Yolanda. It's Moo juice. Kahlua and milk, in honour of my pact with the devil—that is to say, David Kane, proponent of the development that will either destroy this town, one small business at a time, or turn us all into millionaires."

"Yeah, I read it," Yolanda said, dropping her massive purse on the floor and sliding into the booth. "Nice picture, by the way."

"Thanks."

"So, is David Kane still talking to you? Seeing as you're like, associated with the Socialists now?"

"Social Justice, Yolanda, not Socialists. And yes, he is. We chatted on the phone this morning, and everything's fine. I told him about my aunt and everything, and he just thinks it's hilarious, which it isn't, but I still have the job. They don't have any choice, really. They want the mascot in three day's time, for the Bath Tub Bash."

"Good. Is it done yet?"

"Almost. I have Eddie coming up to my place tomorrow to try it on. He's about the size of the average teenage grocery clerk, which will be the poor kid who has to wear the thing in the store."

"Who's going to wear it for the Bath Tub Bash?"

"I don't know," I said, "but I don't envy them."

"Hey, kids have a higher tolerance for pain than we do, you know. So, really, what's with the milk drink? You got an ulcer or something?"

"No. Just off beer, I guess. Oh, good, here's Dimmy."

Dimmy had brought a floor plan she'd made of the show space, and we spent a pleasant hour gorfing down a super-size plate of the Slug and Lettuce's excellent nachos and arguing about where our pieces would go. After lunch, we moved over to the storefront and started cleaning. It was Dimmy who found the old newspaper, stuck in the back of the display cabinet we'd decided to use as a ticket counter.

"Hey, look, you guys, the *Laingford Gazette*, 1942. In perfect condition." She pulled it out gently, but it wasn't brittle at all—just a little yellowed. Well, it was only sixty years old, but still. We flipped a coin to see who would get to take it home and read it first. I won and slipped it carefully inside my bag. I love old stuff, especially old newspapers. Reading them makes me feel sort of sneaky, as if I'm looking into lives I'm not supposed to see.

Later, back at the cabin, I mixed up another brown cow, lit a joint, and settled down to look into the past. The first thing I came across, on the second page, was the obituary of Silas Gootch.

FORMER MAYOR WAS PILLAR OF THE COMMUNITY
The Union Jack at Town Hall flew at half mast this week in honour of Silas Gootch, a former mayor of this town, whose legacy will remain forevermore.

Mr. Gootch passed away at Dr. Bennett's Hospital last Saturday evening, after a lengthy illness. He was ninety years old. The funeral took place on Wednesday at St. Margaret's Catholic Church in Laingford.

What followed were the usual details of Mr. Gootch's life and family, his career as a politician and pillar of the community (do you have to take a course for that?) and the clubs and associations he belonged to. There was no mention, of course, of his bequest to the town, as that would not have come out until the will was read, probably some time after his funeral. What interested me was the next bit.

Mr. Gootch is pre-deceased by his first wife, Edna, and his daughter, Kate. He is survived by his widow, Rachel, and his daughter Selma (Gregory) Watson.

Watson. One of Gootch's daughters had married a Watson. Did that mean that a Watson was the unnamed descendant of the Town's benefactor? That would make him or her the owner, and possibly the vendor of Lot 4, Concession 6, on the shore of Lake Kimowan in Laingford.

Twenty-Two

Back in the horse-and-buggy days, Laingford's grocers knew a thing or two about service. Picture a butcher in a clean apron, offering you the choicest cuts, the freshest, the best. You can find the same Old Tyme courtesy at Kountry Pantree. Our fully trained staff are in touch with the past, and at the same time offer you the future. Service, the modern way!

—A particularly fulsome Kountry Pantree
    ad, playing on MEGA FM Radio

Many people believed that the Laingford Public Library had been ruined by its renovation in 1986. Originally a stately, red-brick Carnegie institution, it was now all open-concept, with soaring ceilings and nubby, burnt-orange sofas. The decorum was gone, they said, replaced by a notion Evan Price, the chief librarian, called accessibility. A few stiff and elegant leather chairs had been salvaged from the main research area and placed in the Kuskawa reading room, which was set apart from the rest by a wall of plexiglass, like the terminal ward in a rest home. That is where I found Herbert T. Reilly, Laingford's resident historian. He practically lived there.

The reading room shelves were full of soft-bound, low budget books on local history, several of which were written by Herbert himself and presented to the library in small ceremonies to which, he once told me, nobody came. There were personal memoirs: *Rick's War*, penned by Herbert's old friend Richard Clarke, who had died last year at the age of ninety-two, and *Maid of Honour*, painstakingly researched by Edwina McHattie, who had worked as a servant in the grand Kuskawa hotels during the early 1900s. Family histories, typed on old Underwoods and photocopied, had been placed in three-ring binders and left to gather dust next to genealogical studies written in spidery copperplate. Against one wall, heavy steel cabinets (locked) held the Kuskawa files—clippings, grainy photographs, brittle playbills and advertisements for long-forgotten church socials. A yellowing notice instructed commoners to ask the head librarian for the key, but Herbert had his own.

In the main part of the library, the local history section included half a dozen slick coffee table books, beautifully produced with glossy photos and the kind of chirpy, poetic text designed to lure rich tourists to the area, but the documents in the Kuskawa room could not be taken away. They were there for good, safe under Herbert's single, watchful eye.

When I walked into the Kuskawa reading room, Herbert was at the microfiche machine. He was nose-up to the screen, humming and clicking along with it, like they were playing music together.

"Umm...Herbert?" I said. His head turned slowly to see who it was. He wore an eyepatch, which covered the gap in his face where his left eye had been, once, before the war.

"Polly Deacon, I do declare! Long time no see, my dear. How have you been?"

"Good, thanks, Herbert. You're looking well." Herbert gave a brief bark, like a seal.

"That's as may be," he said. "I'm still alive—just. Working

on a family history for the Campbells. Keep coming across police reports. All the old Campbells were crooks, but I hardly like to tell them that. Can't find a respectable one anywhere." He barked again.

"Never mind. There's a certain cachet inherent in having criminals in your past these days," I said.

"Really, now? I'll have to tell Helga Campbell that. It's hip, is it? The in thing?"

"So I've heard."

"Congratulations on getting your picture in the paper, by the way. You look like a youngster I used to box with in the war."

"Thanks. Actually, it's something in the paper I've come to ask you about. In an old issue that I found. I thought you could help me." I pulled out the old 1942 *Gazette* and placed it on the table before him.

"Say, now, that's in good condition. Where did you find it?"

"We were cleaning out the storefront where Bergen and Bohm's used to be," I said. "It was in the bottom of one of the display cases."

"Bergen and Bohm's Men's Wear," Herbert said, looking off into the distance. "I remember it well. I got my first suit there. Too bad it went out of business. But then they all do, eventually."

"Some faster than others," I said. "Now, here, do you remember this man?" I turned to Silas Gootch's obituary.

"Well, I knew of him, of course. Important man. He was involved in the making of this town, back in the 1870s. Was the mayor in, well, it says right here—1902, turn of the century. Now, he was the fellow who got Laingford electrified, you know."

"Did you ever meet him?" I asked. Herbert gave me a look with his one eagle eye.

"Just how old d'you think I am, Missy?" he said.

"Well, er…"

Bark, bark, bark. "I was born in 1917, so he was quite an old man when I was just a lad. Nope, never met him. But he was kind of a local hero. I remember when he died. I was twenty-five or so then, just married. Didn't go to the funeral, though. That was for the society people. I was just a lowly ink-rat, then." Herbert had worked in the print shop of the *Laingford Gazette* all his life, until the paper finally ditched its old presses and started sending the paper down to Orillia, where the big machines were.

"Did you know his daughters, Kate and Selma?"

"Well, I never knew Kate. She died before I was born. Hers is a sad story, really."

"I'd like to hear it."

"All right then. Let me think." Herbert had the histories of most of Laingford's families tucked away in his brain somewhere. I'd discovered this by accident, long ago, when I was doing my own family tree for a high school assignment. Herbert and I had become friends then, back in the seventies. He was like an oracle or something. A walking, talking history machine. Watching him, with his good eye closed and a kind of humming coming out of his long nose, I realized with a little twinge that I loved this old guy, almost as much as I loved George. Then, suddenly, with an exhalation like a steam train, Herbert opened his eye.

"Okay. I think I've got it," he said.

"Shoot," I said.

"Kate committed suicide in 1914, Polly. She was twenty-five years old. Her mother, Edna, was a McGillicuddy, and the McGillicuddys were from way up north somewhere— Timmins, I think. Anyway, Edna died having Kate, they say.

183

Edna was just a slip of a thing, according to what I've read. Just a child. So Silas Gootch was left with this newborn daughter and nobody to look after her. But he managed with nannies and housekeepers, I guess. Gootch had plenty of money. He came from England, son of a Duke or something. Kate was devoted to her father. Then, when Kate was a young lady, Silas started courting Rachel Bohm, the daughter of Ira Bohm, who ran the menswear store. She was only a couple of years older than Kate herself. They were married when Kate was twenty-five, and they say that's what made her do it. Kill herself, I mean. She jumped into the Kuskawa river in the middle of winter, a few months after her father married Rachel."

"Oh, how sad."

"Yes, it was. Of course, it was hard finding out the facts of that one. Back then, if somebody took their own life, the details were not reported in the papers. I figured it out through the death notices, diaries and so forth."

"So Silas married again when his daughter was twenty-five. A May/December thing."

"Yes. Silas was sixty-two when he married Rachel, who was twenty-seven. That was in 1914. It was a scandal, I guess, but he was a powerful man by that point. People accepted it eventually."

"So Selma was Rachel's daughter."

"That's right. She was born in 1914, the year that her parents married, so there's of course some question of how hurried the marriage might have been. That also could have had some bearing on Kate's suicide. We'll never know, of course."

"No, we won't."

"Now, Selma was a wild one. Silas wanted her to marry up, if you know what I mean. Into Laingford society, whatever that was. Instead, she ended up marrying the local grocer,

Gregory Watson. Nearly killed her father. He hardly spoke to her after that, they say."

"So that was the Watson of Watson's General Store," I said. Aha. I knew it!

"Correct. One of the few old businesses that's still going strong."

"And Archie Watson is Selma's and Gregory's son."

"Well, technically. Selma and Gregory had one son, that would be Victor. I heard he died a couple of days ago. Too bad. He seemed like a good fellow. Anyway, Victor was their natural son, born in 1938, I remember. Difficult birth. That's when I turned twenty-one—my coming of age announcement was in the paper right next to Vic's birth announcement."

"And Archie?"

"Selma and Gregory adopted Archie much later, in 1950. Selma couldn't have any more children after Vic. They were both very busy with their grocery business at that time. I heard a rumour that Archie was the illegitimate son of one of their grocery girls. Anyway, Archie was what you'd call a late child, in terms of his parents' ages. Some say they adopted Archie to work in the store when he got older. By that time, Vic was coming into his teens, and I guess he never showed any interest in taking on the family business."

"Did you know Selma?"

"She was three years older than me, but I knew her, yes. Had a crush on her for a while. She was a real looker. And, as I said, wild. She was one of those original flappers, you know? Short hair, short skirts. Golly, but her father did hate that."

"Is Selma still alive?"

"No, she died in 1997. By then, of course, Archie had been running the grocery business for years. His father, Gregory, pegged out with cancer in the late seventies, when Archie was a young man. Selma hung in there, though, sitting up on a tall stool behind the counter like she always did, keeping watch."

Bark, bark.

"So, around February of last year, Archie and Vic would have been the only remaining descendants of Silas Gootch," I said.

Herbert barked again, very softly this time, like a seal on an ice floe miles and miles away. "I figured you were coming to that," he said.

"Surely dozens of people who knew the family must know that," I said. "How come there's all this secrecy about the parkland thing in the paper? How come Town Council is keeping its mouth shut about it? Anyone with half a brain could ask around and figure out, or remember that Vic and Archie are Silas Gootch's grandsons."

Herbert patted my hand. "Polly, dear," he said, "people don't have half a brain these days. They spend so much time watching the darned TV and listening to their techno-music, they've forgotten how to think. They don't know how to dig for information. They expect it to be fed to them, piece-by-piece, like they get it on the news."

"But there must be lots of people who knew Selma—who remember her sitting on that stool at Watson's. They must remember that she was a Gootch."

"Sure there are," Herbert said. "But the kind of people who remember those things aren't the kind of people who want to get involved with a messy business like this Kountry Pantree superstore your aunt is so fired up about. They would rather let sleeping dogs lie."

"But I'm not that kind of person," I said.

"I know, kid."

"So, who do you think knows that the Watsons effectively

own, or owned the KP property?"

"Well, Polly, it was Vic, you know, and not Archie, who would have got title to it last spring. He was the elder of the two, and there wasn't anybody else. You'll have to ask around to find out how much he got for it," Herbert said.

"But he's dead, Herbert. And, jeez, he was supposed to have been against the project from the beginning. He voted against it, or at least that's what I heard. So what's up with that?"

"If he voted against it, I'll eat my hat," Herbert said. "Dig a little, my dear. Use your half a brain. And you might want to talk to young Arly, Archie's girl. She was in here asking me the very same kind of questions about a week ago." Herbert seemed to decide that the interview was over. He flipped the 1942 *Gazette* over to the front page again, folded it carefully and handed it back to me. Then, winking at me with his good eye, he rolled his wheelchair back over to the microfiche machine and fired it up.

Twenty-Three

The Laingford Police Station was perkier on Thursday than it had been on Sunday. Lots of people in uniforms scurried around looking busy, the phone was ringing pretty steadily, and the young female person in charge of the reception area was working at full capacity. When I entered the front door, she gave me one of those once-overs that you get from a tired waitress. A quick up-and-down "can this person wait?" evaluation, followed by a rapid sideways slide of the eyes to indicate extreme, about-to-explode tension. Three people sat on the bench in the waiting area, and there was a burly cop standing just behind the receptionist with his arms crossed. I could only see him from the waist up, (the reception desk took up the whole wall), but I would bet he was tapping his foot. She was talking on the phone and saying "yes, sir" a lot to the person on the other end. It could have been her mother and she could have been faking it, but I don't think so.

I decided not to be the one to tip her over into the red zone, so I sat down on the end of the bench to wait until she had a free moment. I was looking for Becker.

I had left "call me" messages on his home phone and his cell phone, and I had called the station a couple of times and had probably talked to the woman I was looking at now, but the recurring message was "he's out". What Herbert had confirmed about the Gootch/Watson connection was important enough for the police to know, and it wasn't something I wanted to leave in a message.

"Yes, thank you, sir. Goodbye, sir," the receptionist said and immediately spun round to face the policeman standing behind her. "Listen, Rogers," she said, "those copies are in a file folder in your mail slot, and tapping your foot like that isn't going to make me type out your damned report one moment quicker, so get lost." Rogers, who may well have been playing the impatient police-guy for the benefit of those of us on the bench, went a little pale and backed away.

"Just checking, Helen. Sorry," he said and disappeared into the back somewhere. The man next to me snickered.

"Now, who's next? You," she said, pointing a finger across the room at me, "what can I do for you?"

"Um, I think these people were here first," I said, waving my hand at the bench.

"Think I don't know that?" she said. "Do I look stupid or something? I know what they want. What do you want?" I approached her desk warily.

"Er, well, I was wondering if Detective Constable Mark Becker is here, please," I said.

"You the one who's been leaving messages for him all day? Jeez. You must be his girlfriend or something. Poor you," Helen said.

"I did call a couple of times," I said.

"Becker has not called in for his messages, Miz..." she shuffled a sheaf of pink message slips. "Ms. Deacon, is it?" I nodded. "He's out at the hospital with Constable Lefevbre. Has been most of the day. Morrison's just going off shift, though. You go around the side, maybe you can catch him."

"The side door? Where the police cars are?"

"Yep. The escape hatch, we call it. Heh. Hey, wait, c'mere," she said, urgently, as I made a move to go.

"Yes?" Helen leaned in close to me over the desk and looked me straight in the eye. "You are the girlfriend, aren't you?"

"Well, I guess you could call..."

"You know his kid, Bryan?"

"Bryan? Yes, I..."

"Well, if you see Becker before I do, can you pass on a message to him? From the kid?"

"From Bryan? What? Is he okay?"

"Oh, the kid's fine. But he called a couple of times today, and I've been too busy to chase down Becker. It's not urgent, or the camp would have called. But Bryan's not happy about something, and he really wants to talk to his dad. So tell him, okay?"

"Okay, I will. You sure that's all it is?"

"Oh, yeah. I got an eight-year-old of my own. He's got the camper's blues, most likely. Lonely."

"Thanks, Helen. I appreciate you telling me."

"Well, somebody's gotta look out for the kid. Becker doesn't. Oh, jeez, I shouldn't have said that. Don't tell Becker, okay?"

"Not a word. Take it easy, eh?"

Helen leaned back to an upright position behind her

counter and snorted. "Take it easy? In here? You gotta be kidding. Now, you! Mr. Brown. Get up here."

Mr. Brown sprang up from the bench and scuttled over to Helen. I could hear her shouting at him all the way down the front steps of the building. Scary lady. She obviously ran the place.

I caught Morrison just as he was getting into his car, a big old sedan, wide as a pool table.

"Morrison! Hey!" I ran over, and he powered down the window.

"Polly. You've been avoiding me."

"Have not," I said.

"Have so. Just because you're going out with Becker doesn't mean you can't play a game of crib now and then. I'm over at the farm all the time seeing Eddie and your aunt. You never bother to come down and say hi, even."

"Oh, Earlie, I'm sorry. I didn't mean to, you know. It's just, I don't know. Things have been busy lately, and…"

"No sweat. Didn't mean to put you on the spot or anything. Just thought I'd play on your tender feelings a bit, that's all."

"Well, it worked. Now I feel like a total slime ball."

"Listen, Goat-girl, you're not a slime ball. Hey, what'sa matter?" To my shock, I found I was getting weepy. This was not like me at all. Normally, I only cry when I'm really angry, but at that moment, there wasn't anything to be mad about.

"Fer heaven's sakes, I didn't mean to make you cry," Morrison said.

"It's not that, dammit, Morrison. I'm just feeling a bit fragile, that's all. Must be coming up to that time of the month."

"Thanks for sharing that with me," Morrison said. "You

191

know how I just love the girlie stuff. Now, was there something you wanted me for? Take a message to your fella, maybe? Well, I can't. I'm off shift and I'm going home."

"I know you're off. Helen told me. I wondered if we could talk."

"What about?"

"The Watson thing. I have some stuff I just found out that you guys need to know."

"What makes you think I'm still on the Watson thing?" Morrison said.

"You're…what? You're not on it any more?"

Morrison set his lips in a thin line and stared straight ahead. "Becker went and spoke to the sergeant yesterday. It's been coming a long time, Polly. Me and him don't see eye to eye on most things. Me and Becker, I mean."

"I thought you guys made a great team. Good cop, bad cop. That kind of stuff."

"And who would you be casting as the good cop?"

"Well, er, you know. The way you guys worked it."

"We didn't work it, Polly. I ended up being the 'bad cop' just about all the time, because Becker really hates it if people don't like him. So I got the shit jobs and he got the glory, that's all."

"Oh, boy."

"I'll say, oh boy. Anyway, like I said, it's been coming a long time. Becker told the sarge I wasn't letting him in on the Watson case, which was true, I guess. He was on vacation and I didn't want to waste my time trying to hunt him down and fill him in. So, next thing I know, the sarge yanks me off the case, puts Becker back in there with Lefevbre, of all people, and sticks me with Rogers."

"Lefevbre? That's Becker's new partner? That girl?"

"Say that to her face and you'd be on the ground holding

192

onto your gut, Polly."

"She'd what? Slut me to death?"

"Polly Deacon!" He sounded shocked, but there was a grin splitting his face in two.

"I thought you had a little crush on her, anyway. The way she was hanging off the end of the desk like a piece of ripe fruit, waving her chest in your face. You certainly looked smitten on Sunday, big guy."

"Maybe she was coming on to me a little. But I wasn't interested."

"Huh. Does she do this a lot—come on to the people she's working with?"

"That's the only reason you can think of for her coming on to me, you mean?" Morrison said, bristling.

"Of course that's not what I mean." Except it was. Morrison wasn't exactly beefcake material. There was plenty that was attractive about him, but I didn't think the pretty little constable would spot that right away.

"Listen, Polly," Morrison said, "if you have stuff about the Watson case, you should be telling Becker, not me. I'm now officially working on a rash of cottage break-ins at Black Lake." He shifted in his seat and turned the ignition key to start his car. I grabbed on to the driver's door and leaned in a bit to make sure he wasn't going anywhere.

"I'd rather tell you," I said. "Anyway, Becker's still at the hospital with Lefevbre. What's her first name, by the way? Mary?"

"Marie. You could go out there and find him."

"Yeah, and have Becker and Miss Marie Lefevbre think I was doing the hysterical girlfriend bit. No thank you."

"You trust him, don't you?"

The fact that I didn't answer right away made me feel hot

all over. Didn't I trust Becker? If not, why the hell had I been contemplating marrying him? What was I doing being involved with him in the first place? I made a mental note to think about that later, when I was alone.

"Of course I trust him," I said. "But if he's in the middle of interviewing people or whatever at the hospital, I can't just barge in there and demand to speak to him. Although I do have a message for him from Bryan, now that I come to think of it."

"Bryan. He's out at that camp, isn't he?"

"Yeah. Kind of parked there, I think."

"So what's the message, in case I see Becker first?"

"The kid's lonely, that's all. Wants to talk to his dad. At least that's what your receptionist said. She's one brutal lady, isn't she?"

"Helen? You bet. She's my cousin, eh?"

"I should have guessed. Same blunt way of putting things. So, Earlie, what do you say? Can I bend your ear about this Watson stuff? Run it past you, anyway, and you can tell me if it's worth passing on to Becker?"

Morrison thought for a moment and rubbed a hand over his forehead. Then he let out a big, exasperated sigh. "You've never been to my place, have you?" he said.

"I've never been invited," I said, doing a little Marie Lefevbre wiggle on the car door.

"Cut that out. You driving?"

"I've got George's truck," I said.

"Okay, so follow me out to my place and I'll give you a beer and you can talk my ear off for one hour. Then I got a baseball game to watch."

"You're on. I'll be right behind you," I said.

I felt curiously happy driving along behind Morrison's oversized monster car. It would be great to sit down with him and lay out all the details that had kept me tossing and turning the night before. I remembered the first time we'd done that together—hashed over the "facts in the case"—back in the fall of the previous year, when my best friend Francy Travers had been a suspect in her husband's murder. I'd hardly known Morrison then, and he was definitely playing the "bad cop" at the time. But when I had come to him with a bunch of stuff I'd written down, stuff that I couldn't pass on to Becker for some reason that I can't remember now, Morrison had been wonderful. We'd met at Tim Hortons, had a coffee and just, well, talked it over. He ended up coming with me to find Becker at the local biker bar. It was good having him beside me, then. Morrison was safe, like having a friendly bear as backup.

Morrison's place was, as they say, in the boonies, on a gravel road that met the highway just past the turn-off for the Oxblood Falls. It was beautiful country. We passed a couple of original homestead farms, just clearings in the bush, really, with timber frame or log houses surrounded by the usual collection of dead cars that served as Kuskawa lawn ornaments. The forest was a mixture of old-growth pine and mature hardwood, soaring up to the sky and creating a canopy which cast a tender green light below. If you look deeply into those kind of woods, you can see for miles, because the undergrowth is rarely more than knee-high. I wondered how the trees had been allowed to get so big. Most of the old-growth forest in Kuskawa had been mown down by the lumber companies long ago. Still, the Oxblood area was right next to the Kuskawa Provincial Park, so perhaps it was protected.

I was peering off into the forest, thinking I'd seen a deer when I suddenly remembered I was driving. I looked up and almost slammed into the back of Morrison's car, which had slowed down and was indicating a right turn. I could see Morrison's eyes in his rearview for a moment. He was laughing.

The driveway was marked by two tall reflectors on steel posts (a common thing on rural roads where there are no streetlights) and a rusted and dented steel mailbox with "W.E. Morrison" painted on the side.

I followed Morrison's car another kilometre or so through the bush and then caught my breath as we came into a clearing. There was a gorgeous meadow, thick with wildflowers, a large pond with a small rowboat pulled up on its bank, and a half-finished squared-log house beside it. Piled next to the house were dozens of massive logs, some squared off, some on trestles waiting to be worked on. The house, when it was done, would be a big one. Next to it, like a calf next to its mother, was a trailer. Morrison parked beside the trailer and got out.

"You're supposed to keep your eyes on the road, ma'am," he called as I pulled in beside him.

"I thought I saw a deer," I said. "Sorry about that. Earlie, this is beautiful."

He grinned in a shy kind of way. "It is, isn't it?" he said. "I grew up here."

"In the trailer?" I said.

"Naw. That's temporary. Look over there." He pointed to a spot beyond the log construction where a few blackened timbers could be seen, silhouetted against the sky. Beyond that was an old barn, small, but sturdy.

"Had a fire here a few years back. Family home burnt to the ground. Nobody was hurt, luckily. My Dad's in a retirement complex now."

"Was he living here when the fire happened?" I said.

"Yep. We both were. Mom died back in the eighties. Me and Dad got along fine, but he was getting forgetful, I guess. Let the woodstove get too hot one night while I was out on duty, and the whole place went up like a woodpile." Morrison paused, and we both stared at the blackened remains. I imagined a dark winter's night, flames shooting up, the roar of it, and the terror.

"If you have a fire out here, you pretty well have to write everything off," Morrison said. "A neighbour a couple of clicks away saw the glow and called the fire department, but it was all gone by the time they got here. Dad was sitting in his truck with a bottle of whisky he'd grabbed before getting out, watching it go. First thing he says when I get there is 'Got any marshmallows, son?'"

"Sounds like a funny guy," I said.

"He is," Morrison said. "You'd like him. After that, Dad swore it was time for him to go live in a condo, and off he went."

"So you're rebuilding. That's great."

"Well, it's slow work. We didn't have any kind of insurance, and Dad's at that senior's apartment place on the river, so that took care of the nest egg, but that's okay. I'm doing it a little bit at a time."

"It looks like it's going to be amazing."

"Yep. One day. In the meantime, the trailer's home. Come on in."

While we had been talking, and indeed from the moment we had stopped in the driveway, a dog had been barking like a mad thing inside the trailer. Morrison turned to me just before he opened the door.

"She's a little excitable, but harmless. Her name's Alice." He opened the door and Alice broke free and started running excited circles around us both, yarping like the fluffy little poodle-thing she was. After performing the usual office that indoor dogs must perform when let out, she ran directly at Morrison, launched herself heroically and landed in his arms.

"I just have that effect on some females," he said and led the way in.

Twenty-Four

When you're shopping, the kids and dogs are hopping! At Kountry Pantree, you can get your groceries done in peace if you use our Kid and Pet Sitting Service. Located next to the KP beach play area, you'll find "Pups 'n Tots" will keep your little ones amused, two-legged and four-legged alike! (10% off if you present your KP grocery receipt when it's home-time!)

    —An announcement in the Kountry
    Pantree weekly specials flyer

The interior of Morrison's trailer was cramped, as you might expect. A tiny kitchenette took up one end, with a small propane stove and fridge, a doll-sized sink and a set of cupboards above and below. Directly opposite the door was a fold-down table surrounded by a padded bench seat. Books and newspapers crowded every flat surface, and a vase on the table was stuffed with pens, pencils and, interestingly, watercolour brushes. Beyond the table was a folding door, which presumably led into the bedroom and bathroom area. It was smaller than my cabin, but not by much. Morrison deposited the little dog onto the bench and reached into the fridge for a couple of beers.

"It's not exactly the Royal York," he said, "but it does me fine for now. I'm looking forward to having a little more space, though." He squeezed into one of the seats at the table and motioned for me to join him. Alice sat on his lap and peered over the table at me.

"Now," Morrison said, "talk."

"First, tell me if you've had a chance to read the *Gazette* yet," I said.

"Only glanced at it, but I heard about Tuesday's council meeting. It was nice of your aunt not to press charges against that Berry woman. Heard she drew blood."

"Yes. The town clerk should have her nails registered as dangerous weapons," I said. "Susan's got a nice scratch down the side of her face, but otherwise she's okay. I guess she realized that not filing a complaint against Frances Berry would give her the upper hand."

"So what was she so upset about?"

"Well, Susan's group, the League for Social Justice, found out a couple of things and wanted to make them public," I said. I explained about the irregularities concerning the MNR regulations about fish habitat, and the allegations that the clerk had used taxpayer's money to pay off the ministry.

"Funny she reacted like that," Morrison said. "She was just doing what she was told, wasn't she?"

"You'd have thought so. But there's more." I told him about the closed council meeting I'd overheard, and about stumbling across the mayor shredding documents.

"That's pretty strong stuff, although it's just your word against hers, you know. You had no right to be there, and she could just have been cleaning out her filing system or something."

"I know, although it was an odd time to be doing office housekeeping," I said. "Just before that, in the public meeting, Susan had questioned another procedure thing—when the mayor declared a conflict of interest in the Kountry Pantree issue."

"That's interesting. You mean, she's working for them?"

"She said she is now, on an 'unrelated matter', but wasn't when the deal first came up."

"Huh."

"Exactly. I think she was shredding evidence that she was in on it from the beginning."

"Well, Polly, this is all fascinating, but you know, municipal backroom deal-making happens all the time. It's not the first and it won't be the last. And it's almost impossible to prove. What's it got to do with Vic Watson?"

I gave him the short version of Herbert's Gootch/Watson family tree. "So you see, if Vic Watson was the one who owned the Kountry Pantree property after the Town gave it up, then it's not likely that he was against the project at all, even though he pretended to be. And he was a councillor, so how could he fool the others on council? Wouldn't they be in on it, too?"

"I guess he pretended to be against it to keep on the good side with his constituents—sort of being a fake knight in shining armour."

"But if that's true, then there's no reason for Watson and Kane to be the deadly enemies they pretended to be, is there? So how come all the rumours are flying around that Kane was trying to get revenge on Watson?"

"You mean that stuff Becker told me about someone maybe pushing Watson off the cliff at the falls, and trying to push him off the lookout tower?"

"Oh, he told you about that, did he? I wondered if he would."

"Well, it was after Marie talked to the kid. She thought he was holding something back."

"I thought so, too. So what happened at the hospital,

201

Morrison? Was Vic 'helped' into the next world?"

"I don't know, Polly. The nurse who called Becker wasn't all that sure, and it certainly seemed like a simple heart attack. That's what Becker and Marie are doing at the hospital today, interviewing the staff and so on."

"Did Becker mention that Serena Elliot was there visiting Vic Watson at the hospital the night he died? Her and a whole bunch of other people, she said."

"Yeah, he mentioned it. They'll have to do some more interviews, I guess."

"I still don't see why you're off the case, Earlie. You were in at the beginning, after all."

Morrison stood up and went to the fridge. "You haven't touched your beer," he said.

"I know. Beer's not agreeing with me, these days," I said.

"Want something else? I got some rye somewhere."

"No, thanks. I'm fine," I said. "So maybe this whole thing isn't a murder at all. Maybe Vic just died of natural causes, and this is a bunch of fuss over nothing. Except for the weird stuff about the land deal."

"And that's municipal politics—stuff we can't touch without a pretty damn good reason."

"Nobody's going to follow up the allegations about the mayor being in conflict and the fish habitat issue?"

"Only if someone can convince the Municipal Board to look into it."

"That's what Susan's trying to do," I said.

"Good luck to her," Morrison said. He was already halfway through his second beer.

A phone rang, a muffled sound, and Morrison dug through the papers on the table to get to it.

"Yeah?" he said, picking it up. He waited, his face impassive.

"You have gotta be kidding," he said. When someone takes a private phone call, it is only polite to move out of earshot, which I would have done if there had been room to move, but I was kind of limited. Instead, I snapped my fingers at Alice, who was snuffling around on the floor, and she obligingly jumped into my lap. She was very soft, with bright, intelligent eyes and a fetching little goatee.

"You're asking one hell of a lot, considering everything," Morrison said. "Yeah, I know. I like him, too." There was another long pause as he listened to his caller. I risked a quick look at his face and looked away again. He was getting red.

"When will you be back?" Morrison said. Pause. "You better be. And he knows I'm coming, eh? You cleared it with the administration?" After a few more belligerent grunts, Morrison put the phone down.

"I don't freakin' believe it," he said.

"What?" I said.

"That was my ex-partner, Becker," he said. "He said Bryan's miserable at camp and is threatening to run away unless somebody comes to get him. Becker's got to go to Toronto tonight, so he wants me to go spring the kid and have him over here for a sleepover."

"Wow."

"Bryan's been out here before, eh, but Becker should'a asked somebody else."

"I guess he could have asked me," I said.

"He said he tried calling you, but couldn't get you. You don't have a phone, Polly. He left messages at the farm for you to call him, but he needed someone right away."

"I've been calling him all day."

"Well, it looks like I get to be the babysitter this time," Morrison said. "So you're off the hook."

"You could have said no," I said. Morrison glared at me.

"And leave the kid high and dry? He's a great kid, Polly," he said.

"I know he is, but what if you hadn't been here? What if you were going out tonight or something?"

"I never go out," Morrison said. "Anyway, it's just overnight. Becker said he'd pick him up first thing in the morning." He looked sadly at the remains of his beer then set it aside.

"What's he going to Toronto for? Something to do with the case?"

"He didn't say. Just said he and Lefevbre had an errand in the city is all."

"He's spending the night in Toronto with her? Was he planning to let me know?" I had turned into a green-eyed gorgon in less than a second, and this remark may have been delivered a trifle shrilly. Morrison patted the air in a calming motion.

"Hey, relax, Polly Deacon. You can't expect him to live like a monk. He has to work. He has to spend time with other members of the female species occasionally. Jeez. You're scaring me."

"I'm scaring myself," I said. "You know he asked me to marry him?" It just blurted out by itself. I wasn't planning on it. Morrison flinched, as if I'd smacked him, then his face smoothed out so it was almost completely blank. I couldn't tell what he was thinking.

"Did he now?" he said.

"I haven't given him an answer, yet," I said.

"Well, congratulations."

"Congratulations are hardly in order at this point," I said.

"No, congratulations for getting under his skin enough to

have him ask you. That's something."

"You think I should say yes?"

"Oh, for Chrissake, Polly, don't ask me. I'm not exactly the person to give you an unbiased opinion, you know." Of course he wasn't. He and Becker had a complicated relationship, that was obvious. He could be mad as hell at his partner (well, ex-partner as it was) and still agree to look after the man's son at next-to-no notice. He was Becker's friend, in spite of the fact that they quarreled like teenage brothers. And he was my friend, too. Asking him if he thought I should marry Becker was unfair, and I should have kept my mouth shut.

"Sorry," I said. "You're right. Dumb question."

"Look, Polly. I have to get going and pick up Bryan before he does a jail break. You want to come?"

"I don't think I'd better," I said. "I think I need to go away and think some more. Bryan's kind of tiring to be around."

"Kids are."

"Of course, their parents can be a bit of a trial sometimes, too. Thanks for the talk, Earlie. I guess there's no point passing on this stuff about Vic Watson probably being the guy who sold the property to David Kane, eh?"

"Oh, you never know. I'll tell Becker tomorrow if you want."

"That would be good. I'll call him when I get back, just in case he hasn't left yet, but it won't hurt if we both mention it."

"Safe drive home. No looking for deer, okay?"

"I promise, officer. Eyes on the road the whole way." He stood in the doorway of the trailer, Alice tucked under one arm like a pillow, and waved as I headed out. I felt like a slacker for begging off the Bryan-thing. Morrison probably would have appreciated me being there, for a little while at least, and it might even have been fun. Morrison's place would be heaven for an eight-year-old, with the pond, the boat, the meadow and the dog. But I was in the clutches of what I figured must be PMS—my moods swinging wildly, my temper on a hair-trigger, and it hardly seemed fair to subject either Morrison or Bryan to its dangers. At least, that was the excuse I gave myself. Besides, Eddie was supposed to be coming over in the early evening to model Kountry Kow for me, and I still had a few adjustments to make.

As I drove, I tried to get my mind back on track, back on the work at hand, but it was skittering all over the place like a squirrel on ice. Whether or not anybody ever found out if Mayor Lunenburg was involved in easing the way for the Kountry Pantree development, wasn't there something they had talked about in the closed meeting, something about votes that they were trying to cover up? I needed to know about that, even if there was diddly squat I could do about it. I also had to decide how much to tell Susan. I hadn't had the chance to talk to her on Tuesday after the meeting, and on Wednesday morning, she had gone off to Queen's Park in Toronto to talk to our Provincial Member of Parliament, the mayor's brother, Ken Rivers. Maybe that's where Becker was headed, too. I gripped the steering wheel of the truck a little bit harder and eased up on the accelerator. I was going too fast, transferring my tension to the road. Bad idea.

Becker. I needed to clear my mind around him, too. Why was I so freaked out about his being partnered with Constable Marie Lefevbre? I had said some awful things about her, and I hardly knew her. Why had I turned into such a jealous idiot? Why, oh why, didn't I seem to trust Mark Becker?

And another thing. Even though I'd suggested to Morrison that maybe Vic's death was totally natural, and all this was a tempest in a teacup, I didn't really believe it, did I? No freakin' way, as Morrison would say. I was frustrated that I didn't know more. The last time I'd been peripherally involved in one of these messes, I'd gone to a lot of trouble to snoop around and get the story myself. I prided myself, in fact, on having been instrumental, both times, in finding out the missing link that solved the case. What Becker and Morrison both called my "Nancy Drew stuff". I felt I was deliberately being shut out of this one. Morrison, after all, hadn't told me a thing I didn't already know, although I had spilled all my beans.

I wanted to know who had visited Vic the night he died, for one thing. And I knew just how to get that information. I resolved to call Serena Elliot as soon as possible.

These thoughts kept me occupied all the way back to Cedar Falls, and by the time I parked the truck in George's driveway, I was feeling more normal. The engine pinged and clunked a little as it cooled off—I'd been driving the poor old thing rather harder than it was used to, and I felt my brain sort of pinging and fizzing, too. Everything on the farm was serene. There were no vehicles parked outside the farmhouse, which meant Susan wasn't back from the city yet. I saw George's figure off in the distance, heading for the barn with the milking pails, my dogs trotting by his side. They were too far off to hear the truck arrive, I guess, unless the prospect of a squirt or two of goat's milk was more interesting than I was. It was the perfect opportunity to slip inside and call Serena.

Next to the phone, there were a couple of messages for me, written in George's careful script.

"Mark Becker called at 2 p.m.," one said and gave Becker's cell phone number. "Mark called again at 3:30 p.m.— Urgent!" another said. The time was five o'clock, and it had taken me about an hour to get back from Morrison's place, so I guessed that Becker must have called Morrison soon after leaving the last message. If I had gone straight home after the library instead of trying to find Becker at the police station, I would have received his message, and I'd be gearing up for a sleepover party with Bryan. I didn't feel guilty that I wasn't, though. I was sure Morrison would manage better than I would have. All I felt was relief. Prime stepmother material, that's me.

There was a message for Susan, too. I read it because I am a bad person.

"Susan—Brent Miller will be at Rico Amato's at 5 p.m., and he has something to tell you." Brent Miller. The clerk who was in hot water over something at Town Hall. This would be good. I looked out the window and checked the driveway. No sign of Susan's car. Had she come back already and was at Rico's, or would she return from the city too late to meet Brent?

I heard thumping on the stairs and turned around, my heart sinking. She was back, after all, and there was no way she'd let me come with her. She'd tell me it was in my best interests to stay out of it. Just like everybody always said. But it wasn't Susan, it was Eddie, dressed in his barn overalls. "Hi, Polly," he said. "I didn't hear you come in. We still on for tonight?"

"You bet," I said. "It may be a bit later than I said, though. I have to go out again for a while. Is Susan back yet?"

"No. She called a few minutes ago from a gas station in Orillia. She had a flat tire, so it slowed her down some. She said she'd be home by six-thirty. Are you staying for dinner?"

"Nobody asked me, but I'd love to. I have a lot to tell Susan."

"She'll have a lot to tell us, too, judging from what she said on the phone. She was pretty excited."

"Good. You off to help with the milking?"

"Yep. Coming down?"

"I can't, Eddie. I have to go somewhere. Could you tell George I was here, got the messages, and I'll be back for dinner?"

"Sure. I'll feed Luggy and Rosie." There was a big bag of kibble in the porch of the farm house for "guest dinners". Actually, my dogs had spent more time with George, Eddie and Susan than they had with me, lately. I suddenly had a little pang of sympathy for Becker. A reliable babysitter was a beautiful thing. And when you took advantage of it, you felt as guilty as hell. I thanked Eddie profusely, which seemed to surprise him, and ran back out to the truck. Brent Miller wasn't going to get Susan Kennedy, president of the League of Social Justice. He was going to get me, which was almost as good.

Twenty-Five

Rico Amato's Antique shop, called "The Tiquery", was tucked into a little strip mall by the highway leading into Cedar Falls. He did a brisk trade in Canadian pine furniture and bric-a-brac, haunting the flea markets and estate auctions in the area and occasionally (I happen to know this) buying pre-owned-and-sadly-missed goods without asking too many questions. If Morrison was investigating a bunch of break-ins in the Black Lake area, he might perhaps have been wise to drop in to Rico's place, where a gorgeous Georgian oak tea table I hadn't seen before sported a price tag of $165.

"Rico…" I said, spotting the table at once.

"What? A nice boy from Sikwan brought it in yesterday. He let me have it really cheap, and just look at the finish."

"French polish," I said. "Very nice. A hundred and sixty-five bucks?"

"You have to move your stock, you know."

"This is worth three times that, Rico. You get the kid's name?"

"He was wearing a very big hat. And he had a cold…"

"So he was wearing a scarf or something, right?"

"I thought he was sweet being so careful not to spread germs."

I sighed. The Black Lake district was full of monster cottages owned by city folk with a lot of disposable income. They stuffed their usually vacant summer palaces full of antiques, top-end stereo equipment and booze and then squealed like stuck pigs when their cottages got stripped like clockwork every summer.

"You better move this one fast, Rico, honey—Morrison's on the case," I said.

"Morrison? Oh, hell. I like Morrison. And he knows his stuff."

"I know he does. You don't want to get fined again, do you?"

"Well, what could I do? The boy would just have gone over to that wretched Peter Teal in Sikwan, and I'd be the loser. How come the police never check out his stock?"

"The meek shall inherit the earth, Rico," I said.

"Goodness. Where did that come from?" he said, his eyes wide.

"Dunno. Let's go upstairs. Susan can't come. Delayed by a flat tire. I'm her deputy."

"Brent's taking a bath. He's awfully upset." I followed him up the narrow staircase to the apartment above the shop.

Rico's cat, Oscar, greeted us at the door, purring and winding himself around my legs. He wasn't the smartest of cats, as T.S. Eliot would put it, but he made up in size for what he lacked in grey matter. He was as big as Morrison's poodle.

"Oh, stop, Oscar," Rico said, shooing him away. "You've been fed twice already. Brent? You pruney yet?"

A sloshing noise emanated from the bathroom. "Almost," Brent said. "Is that Susan?" Rico went to the bathroom door and talked through it. I could smell a lovely perfume, jasmine, I think, and the air was comfortably moist, as if Brent had been bathing with the door open.

"Susan is stuck on the highway," Rico said. "Polly's here instead. Susan's niece. She's okay. You can talk to her."

There came that big sploosh that's made when someone who has been lying in very deep bath water stands up. "I'll be right out," Brent said.

Rico rapidly put together some tea things and set them out on a low coffee table in the middle of the room. There were china cups (Royal Doulton, I checked), a silver tea service and nice little cucumber and smoked salmon sandwiches, cut in triangles.

"We all need a little civilization these days," Rico said. "Lemon or milk?" Brent emerged in a cloud of vapour, wearing a plaid bathrobe. "I won't be a minute," he said and disappeared into the bedroom.

I leaned back in the soft, overstuffed sofa, sipped my cup of sweet, milky tea, and allowed Oscar to give me a massage on my left thigh.

"Jeez, Rico. You should rent your cat out. He's phenomenal," I said.

"He is, isn't he? Although he hogs the bed something awful," Rico said. "Now, quick, before Brent comes back, let me fill you in on the details."

"You and Brent are seeing each other, I take it," I said.

"Well, duh," Rico said, smiling in a pleased kind of way. "We met just after that nasty little episode at that theatre you were working for in the spring. He works in the town office, or he worked there, I should say. He was canned after the council meeting."

"I have some inside information about that," I said. "Susan doesn't even know it yet."

"Well, Brent has inside information too, of course. And he's pissed off enough to want to go public with it, at least as far as talking to the League of Social Justice is concerned." He paused and looked sharply at me out of the corner of his eye. "You are a member, are you?"

"Well, not as such," I said, "but I'm interested in this land-deal thing, Rico, and I promise on my honour that I won't tell anyone other than Susan whatever Brent has to say."

"No pillow talk?"

"Becker will not hear it from me," I said. Which was a safe statement, as the police didn't seem to be interested in the Kountry Pantree land deal anyway. If Brent's information had any bearing on Vic Watson's death, I could ask Susan to tell Morrison or Becker, and thereby stay pure as the driven...er, soot.

Brent emerged finally, with his hair slicked back, wearing a shirt I'd given Rico for Christmas the year before. I stood to shake hands, which annoyed Oscar, who was just starting in on the muscles around my knees.

"Brent, Polly. Polly, Brent," Rico said.

"Pleased to meet you," Brent said. He was in his late twenties, with dark, close-cropped hair and a lanky build. He had slightly protruding teeth and his cheekbones were dusted with freckles. Cute. Very.

"If you're in on this, you probably know that I was the one who passed along those documents Susan Kennedy referred to in the meeting on Tuesday," Brent said. I nodded, having figured as much.

"They fired me on Wednesday morning. I was expecting it, of course. After all, we all have to sign a confidentiality agreement when we start working for the Town, and, well, I suppose I blew that one sky high."

"Well, if you were aware of wrongdoing, you could hardly keep quiet about it," I said.

"That's what I told him," Rico said.

"But still, the interesting thing is, they weren't concerned so much with the memos from the ministry as they were about the voting record, which didn't even come up."

"Voting record?" I said.

"Yes. The record of who voted yes or no to the Kountry Pantree development in the first place, back in May. It was a secret ballot."

"Meaning what?" I asked.

"Well, if there's an issue which the council has to vote on, but they don't want their votes on the public record, they have a secret ballot. The clerk oversees it, so it's all legal, but it lets the councillors vote on a motion without letting the people attending the meeting know who voted for what."

"It sounds South American," I said.

"Nope. Pure North," Brent said. "So the motion on the table last May 12 was whether or not to approve the initial Kountry Pantree proposal for the Superstore. Of course, it was really early on, before the Ministry of Natural Resources got involved, and not a lot of people knew about it. We'd had planning meetings and so on, and this was like the first big go-ahead. There were plenty of people present who knew enough about it to care who supported it."

"Like who?" I said.

"Like David Kane, for example. And Duke Pitblado. Archie Watson was there, as well. He'd heard about it, I guess, through his brother Vic. He was a real pain at that meeting, shouting and saying the store would ruin him. The mayor threatened to have him removed a couple of times."

"So it was a secret ballot, but you knew who voted for what?" I said.

"Well, nobody was supposed to know, of course. But the idea was that Vic Watson would vote against it and everybody else would vote for it. So it wouldn't matter. Four to one, right, because the mayor only votes if there's a tie and there are five councillors."

"So what happened?"

"The vote came out officially, when Mrs. Berry read the ballots aloud, with two in favour of the development, two against and one abstention. So the mayor had to publicly vote in favour of it, which decided the motion. She wanted to remain impartial. She was livid. I don't think I've ever seen her so angry. You see, it was all set up so that there would only be one vote against. Everybody would know that the against vote was Watson's, and it wouldn't make any difference, except in principle."

"So what's the big deal? Two of the councillors, apart from Watson, thought the development wasn't a good idea. So what?"

"Well, it wasn't just two of the councillors. It was three of them. I saw the ballots afterwards. The council went into private session after the vote, and there was so much shouting the paint practically peeled off the walls. The ballot box was sitting right there and everybody had gone, so I just, you know, took a look at them."

"And what? It wasn't a tie?"

"There was only one vote in favour of the development, three against, and one person wrote 'I abstain'. Even with the mayor's vote it would have been defeated. Mrs. Berry deliberately lied in open council. I was flabbergasted."

"Holy cow."

"Well, yeah. That's what I thought," Brent said. He had become agitated while telling his story. His cheeks were flushed and his dark hair was all over the place, from his having run a frantic hand through it. He was really a very theatrical raconteur.

"What did you do?" I asked.

"The only thing I could do," Brent said. "I gathered up those ballots and took them home with me. I had to think."

"Do you still have them?" I said.

"Of course I do," he said. "And when they told me I was being let go yesterday, I could tell that they knew I had them, because Mrs. Berry was flexing her nails and looking bullets at me."

"What are you planning to do with them?"

"Well, I suppose council would deny that they were genuine, if it came to an inquiry, but you never know. Handwriting experts, and all that. But for me, that was reason enough to be comfortable about handing over those other documents about the MNR to Ms. Kennedy. I was working for a bunch of crooks, and I wanted out."

"What I want to know is who voted for what, and how come nobody complained at the meeting when the votes were read out wrong?" Rico said.

"Well, let's say that the three of us were going to do a secret ballot," Brent said. "I vote no, and you two vote yes, okay?"

"Okay," Rico said.

"So, I personally know who voted no, but neither of you two do. You'd suspect each other, right? Or me."

"Right," I said. This was too much like math, but I was with him so far.

"Okay, so now say there are five of us," Brent said. "We all know that one of us is definitely going to vote no, right?"

"Right. Vic Watson. He'll vote no."

"And the rest of us are planning to vote yes, okay?"

"Okay." Rico grabbed a sheet of paper, ripped it quickly into five pieces, and put one in front of me, one for Brent, one for himself, one for Oscar and one for the teapot.

"Great," Brent said. "The Teapot is Vic. So, what we're expecting is four Yeses to one No. Got that?" We nodded.

"Now, when it gets down to the moment of voting, three of us have a crisis of conscience. We know we've been told to vote yes, but two of us decide to vote no instead, and one of us decides to abstain, so we do it. All right?" Brent marked a big "N" on Vic the Teapot's ballot, a "N" on Oscar's, an "A" on Rico's, a "Y" on his own and an "N" on mine.

"Hooray for the good guys. Yes, I'm with you," I said.

"I abstain," Rico said, loftily.

"Now, when Mrs. Berry reads them out loud, she's honest until the last one," Brent said and flipped all the ballots over. He took a red marker and marked a big "N" on the Vic the Teapot's ballot (which had an "N" on the other side), an "N" on Oscar's (which also had an "N" on the other side), an "A" on Rico's (which truly had an "A" on the other side), a "Y" on his own ballot (which had a real "Y" on the other side), and then after gasping theatrically and looking right and left like a vaudeville villain, writing a "Y" on mine (which was really marked "N" on the other side).

"She was on the ball," Rico said. "She knew, when she got to that last ballot, that it was a deciding vote."

"You got it," Brent said. "So, when the votes are counted aloud, you, as a councillor, hear that there are two no votes. Vic Watson's, which was expected, and your own. You hear there's an abstention and it's either your own or someone else's, so you feel better, knowing someone else had a change of heart."

"Oh, I see," Rico said. "Because it was secret, you wouldn't know that three people had changed their minds. You'd think it was just you and one other person."

"Exactly! So it wasn't until they went back into closed session, after the public meeting was over, that they realized that the real, true vote defeated the Kountry Pantree motion. It was only then that they knew Mrs. Berry had lied, when she admitted it, and by then it was too late. They couldn't go back on it, or they'd bring the whole integrity of council under scrutiny. There would be a scandal."

"So who voted no and who abstained?" I asked.

"Well, that's the funny part. Although Mrs. Berry and the mayor didn't think it was very funny," Brent said. "After I grabbed the ballots, I listened on the other side of the door where they were meeting."

"I've done that," I said.

"All the councillors, with the exception of Vic Watson, swore black and blue they had voted yes. Every one of them. And all but one of them was lying. But there was no way to tell who was telling the truth. It was great! That was when Mrs. Berry screeched that she'd get the ballots and do a handwriting test. There was a lot of yelling. I ran for the exit."

"Good idea," I said.

"And now, I guess, they're all implicated in an unbelievable piece of municipal fraud," Rico said.

"Which is why they were so eager to keep the lid on it on Tuesday night," I said, and told them about the closed session I'd overheard. Brent thought it was hilarious, especially the part about demoting him to the bylaw department.

"I would have gone for that in a big way," he said, turning

to Rico. "A uniform, Rico. My very own uniform!"

"It's time I was on my way," I said. "You want me to pass this along to Susan, I guess, Brent?"

"If you would. Tell her I've still got the ballots, if she wants them. I'll testify, too, if there's ever an inquest."

"I'll let her know. Thanks for the tea, Rico."

"My pleasure, dear. I'll see you to the door."

At the bottom of the stairs, Rico touched my arm. "Polly," he said, "about the tea table..."

"Rico, if it's gone tomorrow I won't say a word about it," I said. "Sometimes, if it's a question of ethics, we just have to abstain from voting."

Twenty-Six

There's nothing like fresh baked goodies for brightening up your day! Right now, at the Kountry Pantree bakery, our master bakers are working to bring you that old-fashioned flavour of home baked bread, cakes, pastries and cookies. Drop in and sample a free cookie, hot from the oven— all day, every day, we're cookin' at Kountry Pantree!

—An ad, spoken with up-tempo fiddle music
in the background, on MEGA FM radio

There are times when you realize, after wasting a great deal of energy fretting, that what you expected would be awful turns out to be wonderful. This never happens when you're in the middle of the fretting part.

Dinner at George and Susan's was lovely. I was expecting Susan to be mad that I went to Rico's to talk to Brent in her stead. She wasn't. She was grateful and told me so. I was expecting to be late for dinner and have people pissed off at me. I wasn't. I was right on time. I was expecting to hate the fish dish that George had made because I was in that kind of mood, and he said he'd never tried making it before. I didn't. It was delicious. I spent the whole meal being delighted by how pleasant everything was, as if I were wrapped in a cocoon of goodwill, but expecting that at any moment it would all be ripped away, and I'd have my worst suspicions confirmed.

"Am I cynical?" I asked George, as we were doing the dishes together afterwards. Susan and Eddie were in the living room playing boogie-woogie duets on the piano.

"Cynical? You mean in the philosophical sense?"

"What's the philosophical sense?"

"Let me see. A cynic is an ancient Greek philosopher who has contempt for pleasure, and does not believe in human sincerity and goodness," George said.

"Do you carry a dictionary around in your head, George?"

"No. But I have studied the philosophers a little. Why do you ask this?"

I tried to explain my feeling that everything was sort of dusty and worn out and that it felt like just about everybody was lying all the time, including me.

"I just seem to be expecting the worst these days, and when it doesn't happen, it surprises the hell out of me," I said.

"You don't sound cynical, Polly. You sound depressed. Have you been eating and sleeping properly?"

"I guess so," I said. "I mean, you know. I've been feeding myself. Well, when I remember. And I might go to bed late, but at least I'm up bright and early and ready to rock."

"And you are not drinking too much or smoking too much of that plant you smoke?"

"No more than usual," I said, beginning to feel uncomfortable. Jeez. It was just an idle question.

"Hmmph. I do not think you are a cynic," he said. "I think you are working too hard, and you are worried about your future. That is all. It will pass." He passed me a large platter that wouldn't fit in the draining board.

"Thank you, Doctor Hoito," I said, taking it with a bow.

"Well, you did ask," George said.

Earlier, I'd called Serena Elliot and arranged to meet up with her the next afternoon. Becker hadn't called her, she said, but she was clearly eager to discuss her theories about who might have bumped off Vic Watson. I would have to be very careful with her, I decided. It would be easy to slip into that gossip-mode and let her know more than she needed to. She invited me to join her for a drink at the Mooseview lounge after lunch.

Susan's trip to Toronto had been fruitful, but not as exciting as Eddie had made out. She hadn't been able to meet face-to-face with Ken Rivers, which wasn't all that surprising. His sister, our mayor, had probably called to warn him. However, she had managed to get a personal interview with a fairly senior official at the Municipal Board and had passed along photocopies of the MNR memos and a verbal synopsis of the Tuesday night council meeting. The official had been very interested, she said.

"I told him all we really wanted at the moment was a stop work order on the project so that there was a chance for a full inquiry," she said.

"If they put a stop work order in place, the Kountry Pantree doesn't open, right?" I said.

"Not any time soon," Susan said.

"Isn't it more likely that they'll just launch an investigation of council procedure and maybe levy a few fines?"

"Of course, that's the most likely scenario," she said, "but you have to aim high with these people, or the whole thing will sink. Ideally, they'd do an investigation, decide the whole thing was rotten from top to bottom, ban the whole scheme and make them take the building down and replace every rock and every blade of grass."

"And dismantle the GST while they're at it?" I said.

"Yep, and resurrect David Lewis and Tommy Douglas."

"Hee, hee. And set up universal day care." We started

dancing around. George joined in.

"And abolish milk quotas," he said.

"And abolish NAFTA," Susan said.

"And bring back music programs in the schools," Eddie piped in.

"And stop taxing books!"

"And support the arts!"

"And stop privatizing utilities! Save our health care! Save our trees! Save the children…"

We stopped suddenly and looked at each other. We'd been shouting.

"But at least they could investigate and issue a reprimand to council," Susan said quietly.

"Come on, Eddie," I said. "You have a cow costume to try on." We headed on up to the cabin.

I had finished the head of Kountry Kow and most of the body as well, though I wanted to make sure it was roomy enough to adjust for whoever was wearing, or "animating" it. Mascot costumes are rarely animated by one person exclusively. This is because it's exhausting work, and you usually can't last more than an hour or two inside a costume before you're drenched in sweat and desperate for some fresh air. If the mascot is booked to appear at an all-day function, as they often are, the organizers have to schedule a few animators, working in shifts. Groups and organizations who commission people like me to make mascots, usually need to be warned about this the first time after taking possession of their giant dragon, or bird, or whatever. Some ignore the advice, but they usually only do that once.

"Oh, Kenny says he'd love to be our Bizzy Bee, and he's very strong, you know," they'll say. And Kenny will suit up and wade into the crowd, and two hours later they'll be calling

911 because Bizzy Bee has collapsed on top of a three-year-old who was hugging his fuzzy belly just before he passed out.

To give yourself some idea of what it's like to be a mascot, (lock your door first), get the heaviest blanket you can find and wrap it around yourself from head to toe. Put a heavy pair of gloves on your hands and socks over your shoes. Now get a sweater and a wicker wastebasket, pull the sweater over the basket and put the whole thing on your head, adjusting it so that you can see out the neck part. Now take some time moving around your home. Dance a little jig or two. If you have small children (who will, by now, have decided that you've gone right round the twist), encourage them to attack you, hug you and try to climb up your arms and legs. After only a few minutes, you will have had enough, I guarantee it. If you do try this, drop me a line. I'd love to hear how it went.

I'd suggested that Eddie might want to change into shorts and a T-shirt for the fitting, so he wouldn't get too hot. Experienced mascot animators often wear nothing but a bathing suit under their rigs.

First, there was the cow body, which was made of black and white synthetic fun fur. The cow's belly was padded extensively so that it stood out a good twelve inches from the body of the person inside it, and (I couldn't resist) there was a big fuzzy pink udder hanging down between the baggy white legs. I figured that the Kountry Pantree people would take one look at the udder and demand its removal, so it was attached with velcro. Maybe they could save it and bring it out for use at staff parties. I'd hidden the squeaker from one of Lug-nut's chew toys inside one of the teats, so that if you tried to milk the cow, it let out a mewing shriek, like an injured mouse. The cow's bum was shaped with foam rubber padding, resembling a rooftop on its side, so that two bumps protruded like the hip bones on your classic cartoon cow. The tail hung down between the bumps and was stiffened with wire so that it had some life to it.

"This feels like a winter coat," Eddie said.

"It'll even be hotter in the sun," I said. "I don't envy the poor person who has to wear it for the Bath Tub Bash on Saturday. It'll be pure torture." Eddie just grunted. I made some minor tucks and adjustments with pins, then helped Eddie into the big fuzzy cow gloves. I'd considered making huge, hoof-like things for the hands, but seeing as the animator was expected to operate a motorized Bath Tub while wearing the costume, I'd compromised. The gloves were black, and divided in two so that they were half mitten, half glove, allowing some finger movement. The pinky and ring fingers went into one side, the middle and forefinger into the other. The thumb had its own separate hole. The gloves attached to the cow arms with velcro.

The feet were sort of like gaiters, fuzzy, black, elasticized things that would fit over a pair of running shoes and give the impression of hooves without completely crippling the animator. Eddie was beginning to perspire already.

"Man," he said. "Could you maybe put a built-in fan in here?"

"If you get too hot, there is an escape route," I said, and showed him the tear-away strips attaching the belly to the main body of the costume. "I always put an emergency escape hatch into these things, although the idea is only to use it if you think you're about to keel over. If it gets used too much, the Velcro loses its strength."

Finally, we were ready for the head. It was about the size of a large pumpkin, built around a light wire frame. The neck-piece, like a short collar or cape, fell down over the shoulders to hide the join and was fixed in place with snaps and, once again, good old Velcro. Eddie was an extremely tall young man, about six-three, and with the Kountry Kow head in place, he was monstrous. I stepped back to view the effect. Kountry Kow was truly magnificent, if I do say so myself.

Rosencrantz and Lug-nut, who had been ignoring most of what was going on, because they knew Eddie as well as they knew me, suddenly looked up. The effect on them was startling. They backed up, tails down, and immediately started growling.

"Hey, you guys! Take it easy. It's okay!" I said. "It's Eddie. It's okay!" Luggy started barking and Rosie joined in.

"Luggy! Rosie, it's me!" Eddie said, his voice muffled. He crouched down to reassure them, but both dogs obviously thought that meant the monster was getting ready to charge. Rosie yelped and ran under the table and Luggy, my hero, scuttled around behind me, still barking.

As soon as I unsnapped the headpiece and removed it, the dogs settled down.

"Jeez. It's only me," Eddie said.

"I'm glad neither of them is trained to attack," I said thoughtfully. I shouldn't have said it. Eddie was looking a little pale. "Here," I said, pulling up a stool. "Sit down for a sec."

"So what do I do if that happens on Saturday?" Eddie said. "What do you do?"

"I guess I didn't tell you, eh?" he said, but he wasn't fooling me. He hadn't been planning to tell me at all, I could tell.

"You're going to be wearing this thing and racing in the Bath Tub Bash?" I said. "For Kountry Pantree? Does Susan know?"

Eddie rolled his eyes. "What do you think?" he said, ladling on the sarcasm as only a teenager can.

"Holy cow," I said. "And what about your job at Watson's? Archie will go absolutely berzerk when he finds out."

"Well, I was going to give him my notice anyway, this weekend," Eddie said.

"You were going to quit before you were fired, you mean. What's the matter? I thought you liked working at Watson's."

"I do, Polly. It's just that Mr. Kane, well, he's going to give me a job in his new store."

"Mr. Kane is? I see. You've been headhunted."

"Headhunted? Like cannibals in the jungle? Huh?"

"Sort of like that. Here. Let's get you out of this thing and then we'll talk," I said. I put the Kountry Kow head down carefully on the worktable and made Eddie turn around so I could undo him. "By the way, if you're going to be risking your life in one of those stupid Bath Tubs wearing this thing, you'd better be sure you can see okay. How was it in there?"

"It was fine, Polly. Stuffy, but I could see fine. You made the eyeholes really big." I had. After I'd tried the head on myself, I'd cut the eyeholes bigger and screened them with see-through mesh. From the outside, the eyes were just big black holes and you couldn't see the person inside.

Eddie took off the gloves and gaiters and stepped out of the body suit.

"Whew," he said. "I need a shower now."

"You'll have to wait for that one, I'm afraid, unless you want me to haul out the zinc bath tub."

"Maybe I should get dressed up again and sit in the zinc tub for a while to get the feel of it," Eddie said with a grin.

"That might be an idea. Now, you want a coke or something? A beer, maybe?"

"A beer would be great," he said. I grabbed a cold one from the icebox and cracked it for him, then made myself a brown cow.

"Given up beer?" Eddie said. "I noticed you were drinking water at dinner."

"Just for the time being," I said. "I think I've developed an allergy to it."

"Poor you," he said and took a sip of his own.

Now, please don't shoot me for giving a kid a beer. I know Eddie was underage, and what I was doing was strictly illegal and Becker, if he had been there, would have said something disapproving. So be it. I knew Eddie had an occasional beer with George and Susan, and our collective theory is; better they learn to drink like a grown-up, in the company of grown-ups, than to sneak out on some back road with a twelve-pack and end up puking on their shoes or driving into a tree. So there.

"Now, Eddie. Tell me how you met David Kane," I said.

"Oh, he came to our culinary arts class at school," Eddie said. The local high school had a great hospitality program attached to its cafeteria, so that kids could learn cooking, restaurant business stuff and serving skills. The kids ran a pretty impressive restaurant, open to teachers and staff only, planned the menus themselves, cooked and served the food. Eddie, who had been in the program since Grade Nine, was a pretty good chef and a first-class baker. That's how he had got his job in the bakery at Watson's.

"He came to your class?"

"Yeah. My teacher invited him, I guess," Eddie said. "He gave a presentation about the Kountry Pantree store and all the great jobs they had available, and he gave out applications. I filled one in and had an interview a couple of weeks ago. Mr. Kane is offering me twice what Mr. Watson pays, and I'd have a lot more responsibility."

"Including playing Kountry Kow, apparently."

"Well, that was an extra. He said I'd still have the bakery job, even if I didn't want to do it, but there's a bonus if I do."

"A big bonus?"

"Enough for a down payment on my first car," he said with some pride. "But now that I've tried on the costume, I'm thinking it should be bigger," he added.

"Hah! Go for it, Eddie. Has anyone else at Watson's been lured away with promises of big bucks?"

"A couple, maybe. Maybe even Arly Watson, though I don't know for sure. I thought I saw her getting into Mr. Kane's car the other day."

"Really? That's interesting."

"Robin said Arly wasn't driving around with Mr. Kane for employment reasons, though, if you know what I mean. But then Robin's got a dirty mind."

"Does she have any idea what that will do to her father?" I said, feeling suddenly enormously sorry for Archie Watson.

"Robin says that's probably why she's doing it."

"Oh, my."

"Are we done here, Polly? Robin's coming over later, and we're going to do some astronomy in the hayfield."

"Astronomy? I've never heard it called that before," I said.

"Polly! And don't you dare say what I know you're about to say. I got it covered."

"Well, keep it covered," I said and followed Eddie out the door. As I stood on the porch, looking up at the stars, which were very bright (a fine excuse for Eddie and Robin), I heard Eddie's voice come back at me out of the dark.

"Polly?"

"Mmmm?"

"Don't tell Susan about the Kountry Kow thing, okay? I'll tell her after it's over, maybe. I don't want to hurt her feelings."

"Archie will tell her if you quit," I said.

"I know. I'll tell her that part. But not the cow, okay?"

"Okay, Eddie. Goodnight." I sighed and went back inside.

I really hate keeping secrets.

It wasn't until a couple of hours later that I realized I hadn't returned Becker's phone calls. I wondered why I had blocked on it, and whether it would be okay to wait until the next day. I could say that an emergency had come up—after all, he knew that I didn't have a phone at the cabin, so it wasn't easy for me to just punch in a number, the way normal people do. I could say I had suddenly been taken ill and was running a fever. I could say that George's phone was out of order. I went through a few of these scenarios before admitting to myself that I was looking for a good lie. The truth was that I forgot, which was not very flattering to either of us.

After realizing that I was making excuses for forgetting, I noticed another emotion building up inside myself. I was getting angry. (This navel gazing is unpleasant. I wouldn't recommend it. Far nicer to be deceitful and oblivious.) Becker had not returned my phone calls earlier in the day, had he? In the messages he left with George, he hadn't said "Tell her I'm sorry for not getting back to her sooner," or anything like that. So what if I didn't call him back? Wasn't he doing the same thing to me? Where was the message saying he was going to Toronto? Wasn't he there right now with another woman?

In a matter of minutes, I had turned a mild feeling of guilt over a forgotten phone call into an indignant, self-righteous rage. Clever stuff.

I got myself into such a state that even a joint didn't calm me down. In fact, I took one puff, felt my stomach heave and put the wretched thing out. Then I made myself some warm milk and went to bed, sticking my tongue out at Kountry Kow on my way.

Twenty-Seven

Cheer on the newest addition to the Laingford Bath Tub Bash lineup—it's the Kountry Pantree Scrub-a-Tub-a-Doo! We're proud to be part of this fine cottage country tradition, and in addition to running a tub in the race (driven by our own Kountry Kow!), we're giving away free hot dogs at the grill down by the first aid tent. Come on by and get your free lunch, and don't forget to cheer for Kountry Kow!

—One of the largest advertisements in the
    "Bath Tub Bash" programme, printed and
    distributed by the *Laingford Gazette*

Vic Watson and I are enjoying a quiet picnic at the top of Oxblood Falls. There is French bread, brie, caviar and champagne, and I am utterly happy. Vic is telling me about a house he is building on the shores of Lake Kimowan and says I must come and visit him and fish for pike.

Suddenly, out from behind a low bush, Arly Watson and David Kane appear, heading straight for us, their faces full of menace. They are both dressed from head to foot in red, and Arly's fingernails are long and deadly. Kane whips out a camera and shouts "Smile!" at us as Arly lifts her foot, grown suddenly very big in its huge, red sneaker, and kicks us both over the falls. I scream as I go down, knowing there is a herd of killer cows waiting for me at the bottom.

I just love bad dreams. Who needs an alarm clock when a nice, well-timed nightmare can wake you up at the crack of dawn, covered in sweat, hyperventilating and ready to start the day? The early start wasn't such a bad thing, so I didn't bother trying to go back to sleep. Anyway, I wasn't in any hurry to meet the killer cows at the bottom of the falls.

Over coffee and a slice of toast, I made a quick list of the day's errands. I had a whacking great headache and dry toast was about all I could handle.

1. Get big Audrey puppet from barn and load puppets etc. in truck for show.

2. Call Becker.

3. Tell Becker about the Watson thing and show him Sophie's photo. (The picture was still in my jacket pocket and had been there since Monday. I know when a dream is trying to tell me something.)

4. Drop off puppets at show space.

5. Meet Serena Elliot at 1 p.m.

6. Call David Kane re: Kountry Kow costume. (Now that I knew Eddie was going to wear it, I figured I could bring both of them into town together on Saturday morning.)

7. Set up art show with others. (2 p.m.)

8. Get blow up of newspaper picture from Calvin for show. (A colour copy would do it.)

9. Eat something.

10. Go to bed early.

I got tired just looking at it. Still, having it written down helped me get motivated. I slugged back a second cup of coffee and loaded up a cardboard box with some smaller puppets for the show. Then, just as I was stepping off the porch, there was a great rumble of thunder, a flash of lightning, and the heavens, as they say, opened.

"Shit!" I said. Now, I don't often swear, at least not unless I am heartily provoked, but in this case, I was. Kountry Kow may have been designed to be waterproof, but the majority of my puppets weren't. Before any loading could be done, I'd have to get someone to help me put the cap on George's truck, and everything that I was planning to carry down from the cabin and up from the barn would have to be covered in plastic first. I went back inside and cranked up my clockwork radio to see if I could get a weather report. At least, I realized, that explained the headache. I had been worried that I might be coming down with something, but thundery weather often makes me feel sick.

The CBC, our beloved public radio service, is very obliging when it comes to weather reports. Although they broadcast out of Toronto, they do their best to cover their whole listening area. Unfortunately, they put Kuskawa at the very end of the list. I don't know why this is, but they do. I sat and listened to rain and thunderstorms forecast in every city and town from Hamilton to North Bay until finally they got to Kuskawa. Not surprisingly, the nice CBC lady told me that steady thunderstorms and showers would be the order of the day, and very possibly might continue into the next. Great. The Bath Tub Bash would be just charming in the rain. I felt a twinge of sadness for the organizers of the event. All that planning. All that advertising, all that hype, for one single day of the year. The Bath Tub Bash traditionally took place rain or shine. It was part of their mandate. But I had seen it wet, and it was depressing as hell.

I put my box back inside, threw on a yellow rain slicker and headed down to the farmhouse to see if I could find Eddie.

If he wanted me to keep his Kountry Kow secret from Susan, he was going to have to pay for it in hard labour. Blackmail? Well, yes. So what's your point?

After the loading had been done (Eddie was extremely obliging and I didn't have to threaten him more than once), I used George's phone to call Becker at home. It was only seven in the morning, but I figured I could catch him before he went to pick up Bryan at Morrison's. He answered after about six rings. "Yeah?"

"Why do all policemen answer their phones with 'yeah'?" I said.

"We learn it in cop school," Becker said. "Where were you yesterday?"

"I was going to ask you the same question," I said. "I guess we were just doing the phone tag thing."

"What was it that you wanted to talk to me about?" he said.

"I had some new stuff about Vic Watson that I thought you might want to hear," I said.

"Yeah, well. I'm sorry I didn't get back to you. I had to go to the city."

"I heard. Did you get what you wanted?"

"What's that supposed to mean?"

"Sorry?"

"Oh. Oh, nothing. Just still asleep, I guess." There was a pause and a rustle, as if he was getting up and moving into another room. "Look, if you're not busy this afternoon, why don't we meet for a coffee and we can talk, okay?"

"That sounds good. I have a full plate, but you probably do, too. Is four o'clock too late?"

"Four is fine, but I can't go too far from the station. Tim Hortons?"

"Tim Hortons it is. See you there."

"Okay. See you." Just before he hung up, I would absolutely swear I heard a high-pitched voice asking a question in the background.

"What's the matter, Polly?" Susan said. She and George had just come in from the barn and caught me gazing off into the middle distance. I hadn't even heard them come in.

"Of course," I said out loud. "He got back early enough last night to go pick up Bryan at Morrison's, that's all. That was Bryan."

"Was that Mark Becker?" Susan asked. "He called very late last night, Polly, wondering if you were here."

"Was he calling from home?" I said.

"It sounded like he was calling from a bar," she said. "I think he might have been a little tight, actually. He said 'they' were wondering if you'd like to come out for a drink. Whoever 'they' are."

"He didn't say, I take it."

"No. I told him you were probably in bed. I hope you don't mind, love. It was after midnight."

"No, Susan. I don't mind a bit. I apologize on his behalf. That was a bad move." A bad move in more ways than one, I thought. My mind was already going down a very predictable road, and I had to shut it down, immediately. Work was the key. At least until four o'clock. Work.

Eddie came with me to the show space to help me unload. He was booked to work at Watson's that afternoon, so it fitted in very nicely with his schedule. We didn't talk much during the drive into town. I think he was off in the land of astronomy, judging from the dreamy smile on his face, and if he was thinking about the stars, it might be said that I was thinking about the big, deep void beyond them.

The rain had let up by the time we pulled up outside the storefront. There were more showers lurking in the sky, but perhaps someone up there took pity on us, or at least on my poor puppets. We got the smaller boxes in quickly but had an awful time with Audrey. Audrey the man-eating pitcher plant is seven feet tall and about three feet wide. Each of her nine tentacles are six feet long. Although her foam rubber construction allows her to be squeezed a fair bit, the box she lives in would not fit through the door.

"We'll have to take her out of the box," I said.

"What if it starts raining again?" Eddie said.

"Then we're screwed. Actually, if it does, be ready to grab the tarp from the truck and cover her. If she gets wet, her paint will run and she'll get mouldy."

"I don't know if the two of us can keep the whole thing up off the ground, once we've unpacked her," Eddie said.

"Good point." I scanned the street. Up near the Town Hall, a group of about nine boys and girls were skateboarding off the front steps. This is a no-no, according to the Town bylaw department, and there was supposed to be a fifty dollar fine attached to the crime, as well as confiscation of the skateboard. The problem with the bylaw, though, is that you had to catch them first. I had a sudden mental image of Brent Miller, in a brand new bylaw officer's uniform, leaping along the street in pursuit of some delinquent ten-year-old.

"Guard the fort, Eddie. I'll be right back," I said and ran up the street to the Town Hall steps.

"Hey guys," I said. The kids immediately picked up their skateboards and looked for an escape route. "Oh, please," I said, "do I look like a bylaw officer?"

"Nope," one boy said, "you look like a marine." I looked

down at myself and realized that I did, indeed. I was wearing army fatigues, one of my favourite schlepping-around outfits. The kids giggled. My young friend was wearing a pair of pants that were a zillion sizes too big for him (the crotch was at his knees), an oversized T-shirt that said NO FEAR on it and a black baseball cap on backwards. Very trendy.

"And you," I said, "look like someone who can help me."

"Oh, yeah?" he said.

"Yeah. I'm trying to smuggle a top secret government alien into that store down the street, and I can't do it alone. You guys want to give me a hand?" It was a hokey line, and they were way too old to believe me, but it was a Friday morning at the end of a long, boring summer.

"Yeah, sure," he said and gave a little flick of his head to his companions, like the general that he was. They all hopped back on their skateboards and arrived down at the truck long before I did.

With six kids in charge of a tentacle apiece, Eddie at the top end and me at the bottom, we managed to get Audrey through the door without letting her touch the wet pavement. While we were struggling in the doorway, Calvin Grigsby showed up (always on the ball, that Calvin) and snapped a couple of photos, and I got the chance to ask him if he could do me a blow-up of the council meeting "attack photo" for the show.

"I'll have to ask Hans if that's okay," he said. "He already took a whole lot of flack from the Kountry Pantree people about it."

"Why? It was news, wasn't it?"

"Yeah. But the KP people are already big advertisers."

"Of course. I get it," I said. Calvin said he would see what he could do, though. I said I'd drop in on him later on in the afternoon. I promised him a photo credit and "Courtesy of the Laingford Gazette" written large, if Hans okayed it.

Everybody helped get Audrey set up in the middle of the room, where she dominated the space like the man-eater she was.

"That is so cool," the kids said, after I explained what she was. I let the little general climb inside and work the mouth mechanism, which was almost too heavy for him, but it looked like it was worth it to him. Then I gave them each a ticket to the show (a buck admission, to be donated to the food bank) and thanked them for their time.

Eddie went off to do Eddie-things, and I was left with an hour to kill before my meeting with Serena, so I wandered down to the river, where they were setting up for the Bath Tub Bash.

The race course is set up for fun, more than as a test of speed and skill, as the fibreglass Bath Tub boats with their nine horsepower motors can't go more than a couple of knots at most. There were buoys set up to mark the course, and according to a big billboard displayed near the spectator stands, the "tubbers" had to go around each buoy, pick up a hula hoop, throw it over top of one of the buoys, pick up a rubber ducky with a net and so on, all the while racing to get to the finish line. As I watched a group of people down at the dock taking the tubs out for test runs, I saw that it obviously took some considerable skill to keep the boats upright, never mind the rubber ducky and hula hoop nonsense.

Each tub, about four feet long and a couple of feet wide, was set up on pontoons. The motor at the back was run by twisting the handle, like the accelerator on a motorcycle. The problem was that the tubs were extremely lightweight, and an average human adult, once aboard, made it extremely top-heavy. The idea seemed to be to hunker down low in the boat, grab onto the front of the thing with one hand and the handle of the motor with the other and try to stay upright.

I went up to one young woman who was being towed back

to shore by a Sea-Doo after dumping her tub.

"What happened?" I said. Her tub had the "Emma's Posies are Bloomin' Lovely" slogan on the side and was painted bright purple. I recognized her as one of Emma's shop clerks.

"Oh, hi, Ms. Deacon," she said. She was soaked and shivering in the cool breeze. If it didn't clear up for Saturday, there were going to be plenty of people buying cold remedies at the Downtown Drug Store on Sunday.

"I was going okay there," the flower shop girl said, "until I tried to go too fast. If you twist the handle, it, like, goes real fast, eh? That brings the front up like you're doing a wheelie. Well, I did a wheelie right into the drink!" She laughed delightedly.

"It looks like fun," I said, meaning to be sarcastic.

"Oh, it's a riot. I'm glad I had this chance to practice, though. I really want to win the trophy for Emma. The winner gets a month of free advertising in the *Gazette*, you know."

Whoop-de-doo, I thought to myself, and wondered if Eddie knew that the contestants were allowed to come down to the river and have a practice run.

Then my jaw dropped, because the next person to get into a tub for a practice run was David Kane himself, dressed in a wetsuit, looking very much like a politician staging a photo-op. Sure enough, Calvin Grigsby was right behind him, his camera flashing like a strobe light in a dance club. The Kountry Pantree tub was painted fluorescent orange, sleek and sort of streamlined, if a tub can be that way.

"Wow," the flower shop girl said. "That's Mr. Kane, isn't it? He came to our school. He must be pretty fit to be doing the tub race, eh? I don't know anyone who's like, that old, who's going in it."

"I heard something about him coming to your school," I said. "I guess you filled in an application, too, did you?"

Emma's young employee gave me a very sharp look and muttered that she had to go and dry off. "See ya," she said. Another one down, I said to myself. The predictions of the League of Social Justice seemed to be coming true at a most alarming rate.

David Kane certainly was fit, or at least he knew how to handle the treacherous little watercraft he was racing around in. He didn't tip it once but flew around the course, tossing hoops and rubber duckies like a pro. I waited for him on the dock and accosted him after he shook a couple of hands and slapped Calvin Grigsby on the back.

"Er, David?"

"Polly! Great to see you. You going in this thing, too?"

"God, no. I'd sink like a stone. But I thought Eddie Schreier was racing in the cow suit for Kountry Pantree tomorrow." Kane's face changed in a flash from genial bonhomie to guy-who-holds-the-purse-strings. He grabbed my arm and pulled me to one side.

"Shhhh!" he said. "Nobody's supposed to know that. I'll kill that kid if he's been blabbing it."

"You hardly need to do that," I said. "Eddie's a friend of mine, and my aunt's ward. I don't think he's told anybody but me. But why the big secret?"

Kane sneered and gave a laugh I didn't quite like. "You think I'd race in that tub wearing a cow costume?" he said. "I'd risk a lot for this project, but I'm not crazy."

"But you'd send a kid in there to take the risk for you," I said.

"Hey, it's not dangerous. I just mean, you know, reputation and so on," he said, backtracking much too fast.

"Uh-huh," I said. "And if Eddie wins the race? You collect the trophy, right?"

"Of course. Why'd you think I was down here getting my

picture taken? Hell, Polly, you have to play the media, you know."

"That sounds like a big fraud to me," I said, shaking off his hand, which was still clutching my arm.

"You sound just like your aunt," he said. "You're taking this way too seriously for your own good."

"That sounds like a threat, Mr. Kane," I said.

"It sure does, doesn't it?" he said. "So, here's the deal, Ms. Deacon. I am paying young Eddie a lot of money to run this race for me, and if one word gets out about it, Eddie's gonna lose the down payment on his car, and I'll tell him why. Got that? Think about it. Think how that's going to make him feel." He started to walk away, then turned back. "And you can tell your aunt that she better watch her step. I got lawyers that cost more than her whole pension plan." He folded his neoprene encased body neatly into his sleek black Mercedes, gunned the engine and tore away in a dirty spray of water and mud.

Twenty-Eight

Forget to make a shopping list? Never mind. It happens to all of us. Pick up your free Kountry Pantree checklist and pencil at the courtesy counter to make your shopping experience a breeze!
—A sign over the grocery carts at the Kountry Pantree

Serena Elliot was waiting for me in the piano lounge of the Mooseview Resort, toying with what looked like a martini.

"Hello…dear. I'm so glad you called me. I've been hoping that someone would follow up on that little remark I made the other night, but nobody has."

"I thought Detective Becker called you," I said. Hadn't Becker mentioned it to Morrison? It could be that he'd forgotten, or maybe he just didn't think it was important.

"Believe me, I would remember if he had," she said. "Still, I don't suppose he'd normally pay much attention to an old broad like me. He's obviously more interested in, er, the young outdoorsy type." She had given my army fatigues a thorough appraisal as I approached. Seeing as they were Canadian Forces Made and not Linda Lundstrom, I guess the remark was reasonably accurate.

"You're hardly an old broad, Serena. You look terrific," I said. Smarm, smarm. Sometimes I sicken myself.

"Well, thank you. Not that I didn't fish like a lunatic for

that one, I might add." A glint appeared in her eye, and I remembered her few, well-chosen comments the week before, at Duke Pitblado's office. Serena Elliot was no fool and had a sense of humour to boot. I was inclined to like her, though she felt distinctly dangerous, as if she were a bundle of razor blades, wrapped in designer silk.

"You mentioned, er, the other night, that you were at the hospital on Saturday, the day Vic Watson died," I said. We were interrupted by the bartender, whom I knew slightly, who came over and asked me what I would like. I almost ordered a beer, then remembered and asked for a brown cow instead. "One brown cow coming up, Polly," he said, and went off to mix it.

"Polly! Polly!" Serena said. Was she making fun of my name? It was hard to tell.

"Yes?" I said.

"Well, Polly, Vic and I go way back, you know. He was my date for the high school prom."

"Old friends," I said.

"That's right. So, although he disapproved of our little grocery store project, I couldn't let that stand in the way of an established friendship, now could I? So I took him a big bunch of roses after I heard about his little accident."

"Was that before or after our meeting at the real estate office?" I said. There was a pause, and she examined my face carefully before she replied.

"Before, I think," she said. "Why?"

"Well, it's just that I was there, you know, when he had his little accident, as you call it. That was in the early afternoon. And our meeting was at six. So the word must have got around pretty fast that he was in hospital, that's all."

"David Kane called me and told me, actually. He was there

243

at the accident scene, too, you will remember."

"Yes, I remember. So why did he call you?"

"Why, because he knew we were friends, of course. It was our little joke, that my old beau was the Kountry Pantree's biggest enemy."

"Except he wasn't, was he?"

"Excuse me?"

"Vic Watson may have pretended he was against the project, but of course you and the rest of your 'numbered corporation' knew perfectly well that Vic was the one who sold you the land you're building on."

"What?" Serena Elliot was either an unbelievably good actress, or she was truly shocked by what I'd just said. You can act surprised, but you can't force your pupils to dilate, and hers did.

"Surely you knew this," I said.

"I certainly did not," she snapped. "You mean all that bluster was faked? Hah! Just wait till I tell Winston. He'll poop in his pants!" Then she went off into a peal of laughter that made the people at the other end of the bar look over to see what the joke was.

"None of you knew?"

Serena sobered up, fast. "Well, now. That's a question. Duke brokered the deal, so he might have known. We certainly didn't. We were just told that the land was being sold by a person who wished to remain anonymous, some distant relative of the original owner. When we signed the papers, well, I never read that stuff anyway, Winston takes care of it usually, there was just a number, just like ours, where it said 'vendor'."

"What about David Kane?"

"Well, he can't have known, can he? David was the one who kept saying all those terrible things about Vic in the papers after Vic voted against the proposal in council. He certainly seemed to dislike the man, and it didn't come across as faking to me. But now that…wait a sec." Serena rooted in her purse and came up with a bar napkin, folded carefully in half. She handed it to me.

"I wrote down the names of the people that were waiting to see Vic after I came out. I wasn't with him long, just a few minutes, and he truly did look awful. I wasn't kidding about that, you know." I unfolded the napkin and looked at Serena's list.

"Archie Watson," I read. "Well, you'd expect that, seeing as he's his brother and all. And Arly Watson. That's his niece. She was there at the falls that day, too."

"Yes, so David said. She looked terribly upset. I saw her in the hallway, crying."

"Where was Archie?"

"Just waiting outside the door. He went in as soon as I came out."

"And your list says that Sophie Durette was there, too. That was his girlfriend, I think."

"Yes. She was trying to console young Arly, but Arly was sort of shrugging her off, the way young girls do."

"You're very observant," I said.

"It comes of being in the resort business," Serena said. "It pays to keep an eye on things."

"Serena, why is it you made a list? There are only three names on it."

Serena avoided my eyes and took a large swallow of her martini. "Insurance," she said.

"Insurance? Against what?"

"I may be observant, Polly, but I also have this little tiny problem with my memory. Nothing major. I just…sometimes forget things, or worse, I forget people's names."

"Oh," I said.

"I forgot your name completely and had no clue what it was until the bartender called you by name just now," she said. That explained the "Polly! Polly!" thing, I guess.

"Yikes," I said. "Have you had this checked out?"

"You mean by a doctor, or a shrink?" she said and gave a laugh with no humour in it. "Both. It's early-onset Alzheimer's, dear, but I have my little ways of coping." She finished her martini and signalled the bartender for another.

"Oh, Serena, I'm so sorry," I said.

"Not half as sorry as I am," Serena said. "Anyway, that's the reason for the list. I probably would have remembered, but you never know. But there was something else I was going to tell you…" She screwed her eyes shut for a moment and clenched the tip of her tongue between her teeth. I held my breath in sympathy. "Damn! It's gone," she said after a moment.

"Well, if you remember it, can you call me? It may be important," I said. "I have to go back into town, but you can leave a message at this number." I scribbled down George's number on another bar napkin and passed it over to her. "Can I keep this one?" I said, holding up her list.

"What? Can't remember three little names?" she said. "Hey, it was a joke, Polly. Lighten up." I tried to pay for my brown cow, but she wouldn't hear of it.

"I'm looking forward to seeing the real thing tomorrow," she said. "The Kountry Kow, I mean."

I wondered if she knew about the cowardly switcheroo David Kane was planning and decided that she probably didn't. I wasn't about to tell her. She had enough to worry about.

"Let's pray for no rain," I said. "Or else the Kountry Kow will be more like drowned rat."

"I never pray," Serena said and reached for her fresh martini. I left her to it.

When I got back to the storefront, Yolanda and Dimmy were already there, busily unpacking and hanging their work. Arly Watson arrived shortly after I did, carrying a large, colourful sculpture in her arms. It was the found-object figure with the Christmas ornament naughty bits. Right behind her was Archie, carrying another human-shaped form, this one female, with full ashtrays for breasts. Weird stuff, for sure.

"Hi, everybody," Arly said. "This is my Dad—well, I guess you know that. We've got the rest of my stuff in the van out front. Hey, thanks for letting me in on this. I am soooo excited!"

"Afternoon, Archie," I said.

"Hello, Polly," he said and smiled pleasantly. I guess, now that I was more or less publicly associated with the LSJ, I was in his good books. He looked very sweet when he smiled.

He grunted as he placed his burden on top of one of the display cases. "It'll be good to get some of this stuff out of the garage. Maybe have room for the van again."

"Dad!" Arly said, swatting him as she walked past.

"Actually, I'm so proud of her I could bust, but it wouldn't be good to show her," he said quietly to me as Arly went back outside.

"Why not?" I said. "She'd probably love to hear it." And probably won't for some time to come, I thought dismally, remembering what Eddie had told me about Arly's defection to the Kountry Pantree camp. Obviously, the girl had not told her father about her job change yet. Maybe she was waiting until she didn't need his help moving her artwork around. I wasn't very impressed with young Arly Watson right then, actually. Her artwork was terrific, but I was mad at her for her dad's sake.

Calvin Grigsby came in then, obviously dragooned by Arly,

247

with a tall coatrack thing hung with coat-like objects made from what looked like human skin. He set it down, stared at it for a moment, then shook his head.

"I like what it says," he said, "but it makes me feel like taking a bath."

"That's exactly my point," Arly said, coming in behind him. There was a bulky object cradled very carefully in her arms, covered with a blanket. She put it gently down on the display case and let out a breath.

"Whew," she said. "That's a relief."

Yolanda came over to have a look. "What's this one, Arly? I thought you said you were only bringing three?"

"This one is new," she said. "I hope you don't mind. I think it has a profound effect on the viewer." She whisked away the blanket. It was a large glass jar on a pedestal, painted with black and silver skulls and cross-bones. Inside the jar, about a dozen live hornets flew around angrily, trying to get out. It certainly affected this viewer profoundly. I backed away immediately.

"Jeez, Arly," I said.

She grinned. "Weird enough for ya?" she said.

Yolanda shuddered. "That jar's sealed up really, really tight, right, Arly?"

"You bet," Arly said. "Don't forget I'm allergic. These suckers may be scary to you—they're deadly to me."

"How on earth did you get them in there?" I asked. Arly put her finger beside her nose in the exact gesture I'd seen her father make a few days before. "My secret," she said. Yolanda and I looked at each other, frowning. It was like somebody had brought in a bomb.

"I'm glad you didn't make me carry that one," Calvin said. "Oh, here, Polly. Hans said it was okay, as long as the *Gazette* got a credit somewhere." He handed me a rolled up, poster-sized picture—the "attack photo".

Archie crowed with laughter when he saw it. "Oh, perfect," he said. "Now that's what I'd call weird. That Berry woman looks like one of those hornets, all right." He put an arm around his daughter. "Gotta go, sweet pea," he said. "Polly here says I ought to tell you what I think, so I will. I may not understand this art stuff you do, but I'm damned proud of you." He gave her a kiss on the cheek and was gone. Arly, plainly taken by surprise, stared after him and put her hand to her face. I suddenly seemed to have something in my eye.

"We should hang that photo right where it belongs," Arly said. "Right next to the Jar of Death."

"Your title for the piece, I presume?" Yolanda said.

"Fitting, don't you think?" Arly said.

"Oh, yes," Yolanda said. "How long can those things survive in there?"

"Well, there are air holes, small ones, Polly, it's okay, they can't get out—and I put some honey at the bottom, so they should last a couple of days, if they don't get too hot."

"You've experimented?" I said.

"Oh, quite a lot," said Arly. "I like to consider them a kind of medium, like clay or metal. Only alive."

"No hornets were harmed in the making of this art," I intoned. "Well, you're a brave lady, Arly. It's like you're experimenting with using poison ivy as toilet paper."

"Well, that's enough for me," Calvin said. "I'll come back tomorrow and take some pictures after the Bath Tub Bash, if that's okay."

"That would be great, Cal. We'd appreciate the publicity," I said.

"And that photo of the Audrey puppet with you and all those kids is amazing, Polly," Arly said. "Front page material, except they'll probably have to put a stupid Bath Tub Bash thing in next week to please the advertisers."

"Oh—you've developed that one already, Cal?"

"Yeah, it's downstairs in the darkroom at the paper," Cal said. "Arly helps out down there, and gets to use the darkroom for her own stuff in exchange. She also gets to see the newspaper photos before anybody else, right, Arly?"

"And I get to see the outtakes. It's amazing how much film you waste, Cal," she said. Cal took a good-natured swipe at her with the rolled up picture, and I quickly rescued it before it could get damaged.

"Thanks again for this, Cal," I said as he left.

"So," Dimmy said, emerging from the back, where she had been fussing with some lighting effects. "I'm all done. You need some help, Polly?" I hadn't even begun to unpack my own work, but with everybody pitching in, we soon had the space looking very Toronto-galleryesque. Audrey was lit from above by a single beam from a halogen light Dimmy had brought for the purpose, and I told the others that Eddie had agreed to work the huge puppet for us for a couple of hours before the Bath Tub race. I'd warned him to take it easy, so he wouldn't be tuckered out before the Big Event.

"Are we going to close up the show tomorrow while the race is on?" Arly said.

"We should, I think," Yolanda said. "After all, we're sort of stealing their audience, so we should, you know, be supportive."

"My Dad's determined to win it this year," Arly said.

"Archie? In a tub?" I said. "Has he done it before?" I would have thought he was a bit, well, mature, to be a "tubber", but I didn't say so.

"Oh, yeah," Arly said. "He's done it for years. He's really good."

"Well, I hope he wins," I said.

"So do I. It'll be great when he beats that creep David Kane," she said. I stared at her. That creep? Wasn't Arly rumoured to be involved with him? Wasn't she supposed to be planning to ditch her father's business? I was awfully confused. Maybe this "anti-Kane" stuff was just a blind to convince people that she didn't like him. Who knew? The teenage mind was a mystery.

I glanced at my watch. "Oh, hell, it's almost four o'clock," I said. "I have to go. I'm meeting Becker—listen, I'll see you guys at nine tomorrow morning, all right? Have I forgotten anything?"

"Just your head, girl," Dimmy said. "We were supposed to be going out to dinner after we set up, don't you remember?"

"We were?"

"True love, must be," Yolanda said. "All her buddies get ditched for the boy. How sad."

"It's not like that, Yolanda. I have to talk to him about... about some stuff," I said.

"Like white dresses and bouquets, I suppose," Yolanda said.

"What's this?" Dimmy said.

"Oops. Sorry, Polly. Cat's out of the bag. Girls," she said, turning to look sternly at Dimmy and Arly, "not a word, you hear?"

The other two were preparing to do that girl-gossip thing. I could see it coming. That "Ohmigod, are you serious?" stuff that makes my teeth ache. I fled before it could start.

Twenty-Nine

I'm in a pot now, but plant me in a warm place and I'll flourish in your garden for years!
—A little tag on a Bleeding Heart plant
at the Kountry Pantree garden shop

When you're late for something, you almost always end up driving behind one of those cars that's going ten kilometres per hour. Susan has a theory about the drivers of these cars. She announces, whenever we're together and stuck behind one, that the driver is an "old flat cap".

Sure enough, if we get a chance to have a look at him, either by overtaking, or if his car goes off the road and comes to a gentle stop in a ditch, the guy driving is invariably an extremely old man, wearing a flat cap. I don't know why this is.

I ended up behind an excruciatingly slow driver on my way to meet Becker, and he stayed in front of me right into the Tim Hortons' driveway. When he pulled into a parking spot, I risked a quick look at him. A really old guy. Wearing a flat cap.

I scurried to the door, flung it wide and dashed inside, but Becker wasn't there. It was only five minutes past four, so I was sure I couldn't have missed him. Immediately, and quite irrationally, I might add, my first thought was "Dammit, he's late." I bought myself a coffee and a sour cream cinnamon donut and chose a corner table, away from the general Tim

Hortons hubbub. Becker arrived five minutes later, doing the same dash-and-fling that I had done, though with more decorum, because he was a policeman in uniform and had appearances to keep up. I lifted my hand slightly as he surveyed the room, and he came straight over.

"I'm sorry, Polly. I couldn't get away—" he began.

"No. It's okay. I was late, too," I said. "Go get a coffee. There's no rush."

"Actually, I'm kind of coffeed out," he said. "It's been that kind of day."

"Okay. Get a juice, then. A tea. Something to do with your hands."

"I'll just sit here and twitch, thanks," he said and sat down opposite me. "So," he said, and went no further.

"So," I said. Pause. "You said we needed to talk. Or I did. One of us did."

"Well, you did. But I agree we need to," he said. We both just sat there. I sighed. This was slow going.

"Why don't we do this," I said. "It appears that there are two distinct kinds of conversations we need to have. One of them is personal. Why don't we tackle that one first and get it over with, and then we can move on to the information sharing part of the deal, where I tell you stuff and you tell me stuff and we solve the Watson case together."

"Sounds reasonable," he said. He took a quick look around to see if there was anyone sitting near us. There wasn't. His eyes were all over the place. Mine probably were, too.

"Becker, can I ask you a couple of questions?" I said.

"Is this the personal part or the information part?"

"Personal."

"Yeah, Polly," he said. "Go ahead. I know what it is."

"You do?"

253

"But I'm not going to play any guessing games with you, so you might as well just go ahead and ask your question." His arms were crossed and his voice had tightened up like an over-tuned guitar string. Man do I hate this bad cop stuff.

"When I called you this morning, and woke you up, you got out of bed and went into the living room, right?"

"Right."

"Were you alone in bed?" There. I'd said it. Becker exhaled and put his chin on his chest. He stayed like that for a good while.

"Nothing happened," he said, speaking to the knot in his tie.

"Spare me, please," I said. Now that I knew, I wished I hadn't asked. I guess it's always like that. Like when you wake up from an accident and you know damn well your arm is missing, but you still have to ask the doctor about the empty sleeve.

"Second question," I said. "Becker, why on earth did you ask me to marry you?"

"I thought, if you wanted to, it would be a good thing," he said, looking up, finally. "But I knew on Monday that you didn't and that it was a stupid idea. Sorry I asked."

"Oh, I'm not sorry," I said. "I've been thinking about it non-stop ever since. It's been very clarifying. But jeez, Becker…" The rest of the sentence had something to do with him at least waiting until I'd had a chance to say "no thank you" before boffing Lefevbre, but I didn't get the chance.

"I know. Call me names, now, okay?" he said. "Make a scene or something. I know you want to."

"You want a scene? Really? Then how would I tell you about all this stuff I found out about Watson?" I do the jokey thing really well, sometimes. He smiled and relaxed a bit. I felt like throwing up.

For the next hour, I told Becker everything I knew or suspected about the Kountry Pantree project. I told him about Vic Watson's ancestry and how he was the only possible vendor of Lot 6, Concession 4—the land that the developers were using for the superstore. I told him that maybe only Duke Pitblado and possibly David Kane knew this. I reminded him that Vic had publicly been against the project.

I filled him in on all the details of the Town Council's faking the vote on the initial proposal, the mayor's current conflict of interest and possible earlier involvement, and the fish habitat thing, which it seemed Becker hadn't quite grasped at the Tuesday night meeting. I told him what I'd heard in the secret session, and that I'd seen the mayor shredding documents. I suggested that taken together, there might be enough evidence to stop the Kountry Pantree project, at least for a while. There was certainly enough to prompt some sort of inquiry.

I shared my disgust at David Kane's headhunting practices and what it would eventually mean to Archie Watson, Emma Tempest and God knew who else. (I did not share the rumours I'd heard about Arly and Kane, or tell him about Kane's Bath Tub/costume deal with Eddie. Kane was a creep—that was enough.)

Finally, I gave him the bar napkin with Serena Elliot's three-person hospital visitor list on it, explaining why she had written them down. Whether or not the names were significant depended on whether or not there was anything funny about Vic Watson's death, I said.

"Okay, so that's my information," I said. "Do you think you might feel up to reciprocating?"

Becker put the napkin away in his notebook, in which he had been scribbling—not a lot, but a little. Presumably some of what I had said, he knew already.

"Polly, I am a police officer conducting an investigation," he said. "I can't just blab about the case to someone who isn't authorized."

"You said a while ago that you wanted a scene," I said. "This is going a long way towards getting one, Becker."

"If you made a scene, I would know you were faking it," he said. "It's too late for that now."

"Don't you bet on it,' I said. "I have been keeping my emotions under very tight control, and I could blow at any moment."

"What do you want to know?" he said. "The sergeant is right over there, dammit."

"Oh, goody. An audience," I said. And that really was very fortunate. There was no leverage in making a scene unless there was someone important in the cheap seats. "Please can you tell me why you went to Toronto?"

"We took tissue samples to the forensic lab at Metro," he said.

"Vic's?"

"Yes."

"And?"

"He died of a heart attack, brought on by a massive rush of adrenaline," he said.

"What, he was excited to death?"

"In a way. There's a name for it, but I don't have it off the top of my head. Adrenaline is what the lab guy told me, in layman's terms."

"Well, that's weird, isn't it?"

"Not if someone said something to him that made him so upset that he had a heart attack," Becker said. "I have to wait until our guys can sort of explain the results."

"But saying something to somebody isn't murder," I said.

"Not in our books," Becker said. I didn't ask him how come he had to take Constable Marie Lefevbre down to the city with him. Maybe it's a rule that partners have to do field trips together. I decided to believe that, for the sake of my own adrenaline.

"I guess that means there isn't a case, then, as far as Watson is concerned."

"I guess not. At least, not unless something else comes up."

"Hey, Becker. Where's Bryan?"

"What?"

"Your son? Bryan?"

"Oh," he said, looking surprised. "He's back with his mother, of course. I thought you knew that."

"Why would I know that?"

"She came back early from Calgary yesterday and picked him up from Morrison's place."

"Your wife?"

"Catherine, yeah. She had someone housesitting at her place and didn't want to kick them out, so she took Bryan over to my apartment. They were waiting for me when I got back."

"But…"

"Well, she was bagged and wanted to go to sleep and I was wired from the Toronto trip, so I called up Morrison and we went out for a couple of beers at the Slug and Lettuce."

"And you called me…"

"Way too late. Sorry about that. My apologies to your aunt. We thought you might like to come out and party a little bit."

"I probably would have."

"You really have to get a phone, Polly."

"So you went drinking with Morrison…"

"...who stayed at a friend's place, and I took a cab home. Catherine was asleep in my bed and, well, you know how deadly that couch is, Polly, and I'd been driving all day, so I just crawled in beside her. But I swear nothing happened. Neither of us would have been interested."

"And Lefevbre?"

"Who? Lefevbre? Constable Lefevbre? I dropped her off at the station when we got in from Toronto. How come—oh. Wait. I get it. You asked 'was I alone in bed this morning', right?" He was gazing at me with a shocked expression, which quickly turned into contempt. I was frozen in my seat, a horror of my own washing over my body so that I couldn't have moved if you'd set fire to me. There was a long, cold silence. He just stared into my face. Finally, he spoke, very slowly and quietly. "When I asked you to marry me—what was it? Last Saturday?—I thought I knew you pretty well, and I thought you knew me. Enough, anyway, to give us a good start. But Jesus Christ, Polly. You don't know me at all, do you? You must think I'm some kind of, I don't know...animal. To believe for even one second that I would...after I..."

"Mark," I said.

"No," he said, "spare me." He stood up and picked up his hat. Then he left.

I got up from the table, went into the ladies' room and threw up again and again and again.

Thirty

Serena Elliot may not have been doing any praying for good weather, but a lot of other people must have, because Saturday dawned with a perfect blue sky and a big, happy, yellow smiley-faced sun that was completely at odds with the way I was feeling.

First of all, I didn't sleep much at all on Friday night. After I got home from Tim Hortons, I went straight to bed and lay there, staring at the ceiling, tears leaking out of my face and turning my pillow into a disgusting, slimy mess. I wasn't feeling sorry for myself. I was, in fact, hating myself pretty thoroughly. Hating what I had done to Mark Becker and picking apart the threads of the rope I'd used to hang myself. I played his last words to myself on a continuous loop: "You must think I'm some kind of, I don't know...animal." Well, yeah. I guess I had thought that. I had assumed that he had no integrity, and in doing so, had proved that I didn't have a scrap of it myself. The dogs thought I'd gone crazy. Eventually they gave up whining and licking my face and just curled up beside me on the bed, heaving great melancholy sighs until they fell asleep. I continued to stare at the ceiling.

I must have slept a bit, because I did wake up, or at least come to. And I was still in a wretched state. I threw up again.

I did make it to the Art Show on time, though, with the Kountry Kow costume and Eddie beside me. Eddie had taken one look at my face and said "You sick?" It was easiest just to say yes. "Well, don't give it to me," he said and stayed at his end of the truck cab. The only way I could give it to you, my lad, is to teach you an instinctive mistrust of the opposite sex that goes so bone-deep you don't even know you're doing it. Maybe it is something you can pick up from somewhere. Maybe it's something you can blame on your parents or your genes. Maybe it comes to you in the form of experience. The night before, I had walked through every sexual and/or romantic relationship I had ever had. There were dozens of them. Some made me hot with shame to remember. Some made me sad. Some angry. None of those memories gave me any indication that I'd ever trusted the men I was trying to love. I was completely empty long before I'd emptied my insides in the ferns next to the woodpile.

"Morninggg!" Yolanda called as we came in, moving towards us, wreathed in smiles. "Arly was here first and brought food! Jesus, Polly, what happened to you?"

"She's sick. Don't get too close to her," Eddie said, and headed for the back, where Arly's pastries and a pot of coffee were set up.

"That right?" she said, taking my chin in her hand and turning my head towards the light from the window. "You look like you've been beat up."

"Nothing I didn't do to myself, Yolanda," I said. "Drop it,

okay? I can't talk about it right now, and we have to get through this day." Perversely, I had put Becker's ring on its chain back around my neck. I don't think it was for comfort. I'm not sure what it was for.

Arly breezed in with a stack of Bath Tub Bash programmes, which weren't available to the general public yet, she said. She'd gone out to the *Gazette* office and scrounged them. Then Dimmy arrived, and I was able to snap out of my daze, or at least appear to. I drank a cup of coffee and nibbled a cherry danish and chatted, saying whatever came into my mind, and apparently passing for an intelligent, fully functional human being.

At twenty after nine, Eddie finished his fourth danish and climbed inside Audrey, ready to give our visitors a bit of a scare by making her move and occasionally try to bite people. At nine-thirty we opened the doors. The streets were already starting to fill with people—the Bath Tub Bash attracts thousands. The Race wasn't scheduled until noon, so we had a bit of time, and the Art Show was a pleasant novelty for those who had already walked the downtown strip a couple of times.

We had decided to put prices on most of the work on exhibit, although we didn't expect to sell more than one or two pieces. The point of the show was to offer something different, to suggest to the solid citizens of Laingford that art in Kuskawa wasn't all pastel puppies and canoes on lakes. Maybe we hit the right idea at the right time—who knows? But by eleven thirty, there were little red "sold" dots on three of Dimmy's photos, two of Yolanda's big (and expensive) paintings and two of my marionettes. Arly was over the moon, having found a home for the ashtray breasted lady, and I had turned down a thousand-dollar offer from an American who wanted to take Audrey home with him. Eddie was a big hit, especially when there were little kids in the place.

The only low point was at about ten-thirty, after Eddie had been snapping Audrey's mouth and waving her tentacles at a pair of middle-aged sisters who giggled like children and swatted at the foam rubber with their handbags. Suddenly there was an almighty yell from inside the puppet, and Eddie burst out of it, waving his arms over his head.

The sisters shrieked and then burst out laughing, thinking it was part of the act, but Eddie was obviously in pain.

"What on earth?" I said, moving in to provide comfort if I could. Had one of Audrey's springs come loose and stabbed him?

"I just got stung!" Eddie said, outraged, pointing to a nasty red weal that was rising on his forearm. "I felt it buzzing in there and then it stung me. Jeez, Arly! I thought you said they couldn't get out." The sisters looked over at where Eddie was pointing—to the Jar of Death, where Arly's angry hornets buzzed and butted at the glass. The women beat a hasty retreat.

"Shit," Yolanda said. "They were about to ask about the blue canvas, I'm sure of it."

"Eddie, you're not going to have a reaction, are you?" I said. "You're not allergic?"

"Oh, no. I've been stung before. But man, it hurts." Arly, full of apologies and insisting that the insect that stung Eddie couldn't have been from her jar, went out to get ice and some baking soda, which she said was the best remedy.

"Did you kill it, whatever it was?" Dimmy said. "Or is it still buzzing around in there?"

"Oh, I squished it, I'm pretty sure," Eddie said. Cautiously, he went back to the giant puppet and checked inside it. "Yeah. You can see bug parts on the floor. I got it okay."

"Yolanda, I know Arly said those things can't get out, but I'm not so sure," I said.

"Me neither," she said.

"And if Arly got stung, it could be dangerous." I remembered the epi-pen thing that she'd displayed at the Oxblood Falls the week before. I hoped fervently she had it with her, just in case. We didn't need any more death.

"Why don't we put the jar into that closet at the back?" Dimmy said. "I'm sure Arly won't mind, once she sees how concerned we are. The closet's got a good tight door. I know I'd feel better."

"Me, too," Eddie said. "In fact, I'm not getting back in there until the jar's out of here." That clinched it. We entombed the jar in the closet and everyone inspected the inside of Audrey in case there was another lurking hornet. It was too bad, because the Jar of Death had been a popular exhibit—Arly had managed to instill the piece with a kind of evil that went far beyond the buzzing creatures in the jar. However, we were all palpably relieved with it out of the way. Arly, when she came back, was perfectly understanding, and continued to apologize to Eddie as she bathed his wound. Eddie went back inside Audrey for another half an hour, and all was well.

At eleven, Eddie emerged and went into the washroom to splash cold water on his hot face, then he and I headed for a room at the back, where Kountry Kow was ready and waiting.

"Is David Kane coming up here to put the costume on?" Arly said.

"Oh, no, Arly. Eddie's doing it, but you mustn't tell anybody. He's getting big bucks to be Kane's stunt double," Yolanda said. Eddie and I had stressed the need for secrecy, explaining that Eddie wouldn't get paid if the secret became known.

"Eddie? He's wearing the Kow thing?" Arly said. She seemed to be horrified.

"Hey, chill, Arly. It's not as if I'm, you know, joining the Nazis, eh?" Eddie said.

"No, it's just, wait…" she said and dashed into the room where the costume was, slamming the door behind her.

"What's with her?" Eddie said, then he chuckled and whispered in my ear. "She probably left a mooshy little love note pinned inside or something."

"Yeah," I whispered back, "or taped a 'Kick Me' sign to the back of it."

"Huh?"

"Never mind. Come on. We haven't got a lot of time." Arly came out, blushing and stammering, but Eddie only patted her arm. "We understand, Arly. We won't mention it." She gave him a peculiar look and went back to the front of the show room.

It didn't take us long to suit Eddie up and velcro and snap him into costume. Yolanda pulled a curtain across the front window of the storefront to mask the interior from prying eyes, and I led Eddie out into the room.

"Brava, brava, Polly," Dimmy and Yolanda shouted, applauding. "It's a beautiful mascot," Yolanda said. "I love the udder!" She gave one of the teats a squeeze and it squeaked at her. Even Arly laughed when Eddie, who was a natural animator, backed off and grabbed the teat as if he'd been pinched.

"Now, the trick to pulling this off, Eddie, apart from staying afloat, is to stay silent. One word from the mascot and the illusion is gone, as well as your secret identity."

Kountry Kow nodded majestically. Eddie had picked up the trick of nodding using his whole head and his neck muscles. Just nodding normally wouldn't do more than make the mascot head jiggle a bit.

There was a knock at the back door, and I opened it furtively. There stood a young man in a Bath Tub Bash T-shirt and a walkie talkie.

"I was told to come and get Mr. Kane," he said. "Is that him?"

"It's Kountry Kow, yes," I said, determined not to lie outright for the sake of the developer's ego. "He won't say anything because he's in character," I added.

"Cool," the young man said and grinned. "I'm supposed to guide him back here, too, after the race. You'll be here?"

"Sure. Keep him safe. He can see quite well, but he might tend to trip over his feet."

We watched from the back window as the Bath Tub Bash official led Kountry Kow slowly to the docking area, which was teeming with contestants, officials, spectators and media.

"I see they've got two TV stations this year," Dimmy said. "Nice coup for the organizers."

"Nice gig for the media," I said. "A day up in Kuskawa, soaking up the sun and having a bunch of starstruck northerners treating you like a god." It was true. I saw one fairly well-known video journalist from the Barrie station being positively mobbed by scantily clad teenage girls. "Tough job," I muttered. "Well, we might as well lock up and go down there. I'll make sure I'm back to let Eddie back in."

"I'll be here, too," Arly said.

"We all will," Yolanda said. "To congratulate the winner, maybe."

"He'll be lucky if he makes it through the race without half drowning," I muttered. Through the window, I could see that Kountry Kow had been noticed already. The TV cameras were moving in on him, and there were several little children trying to catch hold of his tail. Saying a little "Please keep him safe" prayer to whomever might be listening, I let the others precede me out the back door, locked it firmly behind me, and waded into the crowd.

The contestants were lined up in a row along the side of the public dock, each bobbing tub held in place by an official, lying on his or her tummy and holding on with both hands. There were about twenty tubs, and already, one contestant had dumped theirs. Dumping meant disqualification. Over a powerful public address system, a radio voice announced each tub sponsor one-by-one, and the corresponding rider lifted a hand and acknowledged the crowd as it roared its approval. The mascot gimmick had worked, big time. When the Kountry Pantree tub was named and Kountry Kow raised its fuzzy arm, the crowd went nuts. Two tubs over from the Kow, Archie Watson, dressed in an old fashioned grocer's apron and a top hat, glared malevolently at his rival.

"This is a grudge match," Arly muttered in my ear. She was standing beside me, looking pale. "My dad wants this so much he can taste it." What do *you* want, I wanted to ask, but I just nodded. Archie Watson did look like this meant more than just a silly race in a bunch of fibreglass Bath Tubs.

The starter's pistol fired, and the tubs were off, with a buzzing of tiny engines, like a swarm of electric shavers. Then the noise of the tubs was overwhelmed by the noise of the crowd and the blaring of the loudspeaker. The beginning of the race was not as spectacular as an Indy heat—you have to remember that the tubs were moving at a slower pace than you or I can run, but it was exciting, nonetheless. The pack of tubs thinned out very quickly as the less experienced tubbers bumped into each other, got tangled and sank. The rescue team, a very decorative clutch of buffed and tanned muscle boys from one of the resorts, rode in on Sea-Doos and picked the fallen from the river, towing the waterlogged tubs back to the dock.

Maybe it was the added weight of the costume, or maybe Eddie was being guided by a higher power, but he was somehow in the lead. The announcer started providing colour commentary.

"It's Kountry Kow in the lead, and Emma's Posies right up his butt," the announcer said, to appreciative laughter from the crowd. "Sports Cave third and right behind him, Watson's General Store!" Archie, in his shiny black Watson's tub, was gaining every moment, his face grim.

"Now it's the first turn and the hoop pick-up. Can they do it?" the announcer asked. Kountry Kow reached out to a Sea-Doo rider, whose job it was to distribute the hula hoops. He grabbed the hoop in his black hoofed hand and went on.

"This is the hard part," Arly said. The Kountry Pantree tub raced for the marker buoy marked with a big red flag with Emma's Posies hot on its tail. The Kow tossed, and a roar went up as the hula hoop ringed the buoy neatly. "Horseshoes," I muttered. "Eddie's a great horseshoe player."

"So's my dad," Arly said, and sure enough, Archie's hoop went over the buoy first time, too.

"That's two hoops and Kountry Kow's in the lead, with Watson's getting the jump on Emma's Posies," the announcer said. "Emma's Posies is having a little trouble with this one, folks. Get the pointy thing into the round thing, dear!" the announcer shouted. I only hoped the tubbers couldn't hear him. The crowd thought it was hilarious. The Posy girl took two tries before she ringed the buoy, but the Sports Cave guy ringed it easily and aimed for the leaders.

"Atta boy," the announcer said. "He knows where to put it, folks."

"Jeez," I said to Arly, "I thought this was a family event."

"Oh, it's always like this," she said. "The announcer's Dick Dolly from MEGA FM. He's a little crude."

"No kidding."

Kountry Kow was still in the lead, and now Emma's Posies was back up with the pack. "Hey, there, the little lady plays dirty!" the announcer cried, as Emma's girl got hold of the back of the Sports Cave tub with her free hand and started trying to tip it.

"Is that allowed?" I said.

"Anything's allowed, short of shooting your opponents," Arly said. "Oh, he's down." And he was. Even above the roar of the crowd, I could hear the Sports Cave guy shouting at Emma's rider. He was calling her a bitch, and his face was contorted with rage.

Now Archie was trying to pull the same move on Kountry Kow. Both tubbers had small fishing nets inside their boats for the purpose of catching a rubber ducky, and Kountry Kow grabbed his net and whacked Archie's hand with it.

"Ouch, that smarts," the announcer said, but the crowd was loving it.

"This reminds me of roller derby," I said.

"What's that?" Arly said.

"Think World Wrestling Foundation on roller skates," I said.

"Cool. Oh, poor Dad," she said. Archie had dropped his net in the water. He had to circle around to pick it up again and lost valuable ground. The Emma girl was upon him, screaming like a maniac. Behind them, the rest of the pack was catching up.

"Uh-oh. Kountry Kow's in trouble," the announcer said. And he was. The rubber duckies, which contestants were supposed to scoop up in the nets, were small, and Kountry Kow's net was tangled. He was having trouble snagging one, and Archie and Emma's girl were gaining on him.

The crowd roared louder as both tubs slammed into the Kountry Pantree tub from each side. Somehow, the Kow's tub stayed upright, and the sudden stability allowed the mascot to scoop up the coveted ducky. He dropped the net in his tub, pushed the pirates away and headed for the home stretch. Archie scooped up a ducky quickly and then reached out to give the Emma girl's tub a vicious yank. She went over at once, and a big "awwww" went up from the spectators.

"Never mind, dear. Your prince has come," the announcer said, as one of the Sea-Doo beefcakes rode in like a white knight.

The race would soon be neck and neck. Something seemed to be wrong with Kountry Kow's engine, and the KP tub was slowing down. Archie got closer and closer, shouting something at his rival that I couldn't make out.

"What's he saying?" I asked Arly.

"I don't think it's printable," Arly said. "Shit, I hope he doesn't keel over. I've never seen him this crazy."

A hush had settled on the crowd as Archie's tub got within touching distance of Kountry Kow. I could hear Archie now, yelling obscenities. He had picked up his net and was getting ready to take a swipe with it. He looked like it wasn't fun any more. He looked like he was preparing to do murder.

Suddenly, as if it had been very carefully timed, the Kountry Pantree tub roared into life and jumped ahead, only just staying out of reach of Archie's net. The announcer starting yelling incoherently, and the crowd was on its feet.

"Wow!" I said. "I think he did that on purpose—let him get close."

"Yup. Good thing, too. Dad's out of control, I think." There was a curious light in Arly's eyes. She looked almost proud.

Kountry Kow made it over the finish line about a foot in front of the Watson's tub. The spectators were roaring and clapping and stamping their feet and the noise was deafening.

"...never before in the history of the race," the announcer was shouting. "By a hair. By a nose. Well, hey folks, by a cow's head, eh?" Maybe most of the crowd was too excited to notice what happened next. I almost missed it myself, because the announcer, still practically hysterical, was directing the crowd's attention to the awards stage at the other end of the docks, where the winners would receive their prizes. Although the race was over, and Kountry Kow was put-putting slowly back to the dock, Archie was still in pursuit. The water was crowded with tubs—all the second, third and fourth runners up gathering for the ride back to shore. In the midst of the tub scrum, Archie finally got within striking distance of the Kountry Pantree tub. Then he picked up the net again, reared back with tremendous force and whacked Kountry Kow heavily between the shoulder blades with the metal edge of the net. The mascot fell forward slightly, and the tub started to tip. Immediately, the Sea-Doo guys were there. Maybe they had suspected, maybe they had seen it. Whatever the case, Eddie did not go over. They steadied the KP tub and escorted him back to shore. Archie, his rage apparently spent, followed.

I hurried down to the dock and was there to help Eddie ashore. Even after all that, he was determined to stay in character. When I asked urgently if he was okay, the big fuzzy head just nodded. With the help of the young Bath Tub Bash official, we got him through the jubilant crowds (who all wanted to pat his back and shake his hoof), and into the back door of the Art Show space. I thanked the official and closed the door, then quickly removed the Kountry Kow head.

"Eddie, are you sure you're okay? He hit you awfully hard," I said. Eddie's face was radiant.

"I'm fine. I'll have a bruise, that's all. Man, that was a blast!"

"You were amazing," I said.

"Did you see how I tricked him? Let him think he was going to win?"

"I saw, Eddie."

"Man, Mr. Watson was crazy! You should'a heard the things he was calling me."

"I heard some of them. He thought he was talking to David Kane, you know."

"Oh, I know. That's why it didn't bug me. It was like I was in someone else's skin, you know?"

"Hah. You've just discovered the joy of acting, my boy. You'll be doing amateur theatre, next."

"You got any water? I'm like dying in here," he said. Just then, there was a hurried tap on the door. I expected it to be Dimmy and Yolanda, but it wasn't. It was David Kane, dressed in a baseball cap and dark glasses. He slipped in quickly and took off his hat.

"Did you see it, Mr. Kane? Pretty good, eh?"

"Better than good, Eddie. You were magnificent. Now quick, get out of that thing and let me put it on."

"What?" I said.

"Part of the deal, Polly," Kane said, brushing me aside and grabbing at the costume as if he wanted to tear if off Eddie.

"Well, let me get…"

"Quickly, dammit!" Kane said. "There's TV cameras out there."

"Jeez, Mr. Kane."

"Jeez is right, David. Have you no shame?" I said.

Kane turned his face toward me, his eyes masked by the dark glasses. "Shame? Bullshit." Eddie turned around so I could undo the velcro. Kane stripped off his sweatshirt and put his glasses in a pocket. "Hurry, hurry," he said. I looked into his eyes. They were unbelievably red.

It only took a second to suit him up. Kane grabbed the mascot head but refused to wear it. "I want them to see me," he said. Then he was out the door and wading into the crowd, shaking hands and posing for the cameras.

I turned to look at Eddie. His radiance was gone, replaced by a kind of pathetic disappointment that made him look six years old.

"Oh, man," he said.

Thirty-One

Neither Eddie nor I had the heart to go watch the awards ceremony. We heard it, though. You could hardly help it, as the announcements were still being made at a volume cranked to top a roaring crowd. The crowd wasn't roaring now, although they responded dutifully as Dick Dolly of MEGA FM thanked the participants, the sponsors, the organizers and the media people. It was too hot to close the rear window, which let a cool breeze in from the river.

Eddie was obviously exhausted, and probably dehydrated as well. After Kane left, he drank down a whole litre of Kuskawa Springs water in less than a minute. Then just sat there in a chair with his eyes shut.

"Third runner up, and the award for most sportsmanlike, goes to Rodney Cooper of the Sports Cave!" Loud cheers, and some whistles.

"That was the guy who called the Emma's Posies girl a bitch," I said. "A real gentleman."

"I go to school with him," Eddie said. "He's a football

273

jock." As if that explained it.

"You should eat something, buddy," I said. "You want me to go get you a slice of pizza?"

"In a minute, that would be great, Polly," he said. "But let's hear the awards, first."

"We could still go down and watch, if you want."

"Nah. Hearing's better." He was still sitting with his eyes shut. It occurred to me that he just wanted some company, so I said nothing. It must have been hard, having performed so well, to have his glory torn away so brutally. Not that he had been unprepared—after all, Kane had made it clear that Eddie was to be a secret stunt double, but the greedy way in which the developer had barged in and grabbed the Kountry Kow identity had been unsettling, to say the least. I wondered if Eddie were picturing his long desired car, the one he could now afford a down payment for, behind his closed eyelids.

I wandered over to the window and looked out, but the crowds were still thick, and although I could see the top of the awards tent, I couldn't see what was going on.

"The second runner-up is the feisty Ashley Bernard, of Emma's Posies. C'mon up here, dear, and gimme a kiss." More applause. Some "woo-hoo" noises that indicated Ashley's compliance. I wondered how long it would be before Laingford entered the twentieth century, never mind the twenty-first.

"And the first runner-up, last year's winner and the senior participant this year, Mr. Archie Watson!" Loud cheers, which tapered off. "Archie? Anyone seen Archie? Wait…" A pause. "Well, folks, I guess our fallen champion has retired to the Slug and Lettuce, or maybe Kelso's, eh?" Laughter. "What's that? Oh, sure, dear. C'mon up." A murmur. "Ladies and gents, on behalf of Archie, here's his daughter Arly, to collect his prize." Some applause and cheering. Then Arly's voice,

274

clear and defiant. "My dad doesn't drink, Dick," she said.

"Heh, heh. Well, maybe he just started, eh? Beaten by a cow?" Loud laughter and some applause. "And now, the moment we've all been waiting for, our grand prize winner, and the finest tub racer we've seen in ten years of the Bath Tub Bash, Mr. David Kane, or, as he likes to be known, Kountry Kow!" The crowd cheered, whistled, stamped and laughed, presumably as Kane joked around on stage with Dick Dolly. Then Kane took the mike and started thanking people, and I didn't want to listen any more, so I closed the window, breeze or no breeze.

"It didn't sound like we missed much," I said and turned around. Eddie was fast asleep. I tiptoed around for a while until the back door opened and Yolanda and Dimmy piled in. Eddie woke up immediately and was soon grinning and looking more like himself again as my friends praised him. I left them talking over every detail of the race, like a bunch of guys at the horsetrack, and zipped out to buy Eddie a big slice of pizza.

While I was standing in line at Pete Holicky's Pizza Madness, I felt a light tap on my shoulder. It was Serena Elliot, dressed casually in blue jeans and a silk tank top.

"What an exciting race, didn't you think?"

"The mascot was terrific, wasn't he?" I said.

"The mascot was, yes," Serena said. "David talked too long at the awards, though." I raised an eyebrow at her. "Oh, yes, dear. I figured it out right away."

"You did?"

"Of course. The person in the costume during the race was at least six foot two, probably taller. David Kane is five-eight on tiptoe." She laughed, tilting her head back and making people, as usual, turn to look at her. "What a silly little man he is," she added.

"Shh, Serena. If the secret gets out, Eddie doesn't get paid." We were at the front of the line by that point, and we each ordered two slices of the deluxe with everything.

"Well, you tell Eddie, whoever he is, that he did a fine job," Serena said while we waited.

"I will," I said. "You observant woman, you. I wonder if anybody else noticed that."

"I doubt it," she said. "Actually, I'm glad I ran into you." We were served our pizza slices, paid and moved towards the door. "Do you have a moment?" Serena pulled me aside, and we leaned against the wall of the store. The smell of the pizza was making my stomach rumble. "I remembered what it was I forgot when we talked yesterday," Serena said, picking a single mushroom off one of her her slices and nibbling it. I did the same, then thought to hell with it and took a big bite.

"Mmm-hmm?" I said.

"In the hospital. The thing I meant to tell you, and seeing that man take credit that wasn't his reminded me."

"Kane, you mean."

"Yes, David Kane. He was there at the end of the hall in the ward where Vic was. He said the strangest thing to me after I came out of Vic's room. I was a little bit tearful, you see."

"What was that?" I had swallowed my bite of pizza and had forgotten the rest.

"He said 'it's no fun making little girls cry'. Then he went down the stairs, and I didn't see him again until the meeting at the Real Estate office."

"So he was there at the hospital. Hah. He said he was at the construction site, remember? He lied. Did you think he was talking about you? About your tears?"

"Well, I hardly knew. Then I thought maybe he'd said something unpleasant to young Arly Watson—she was crying too, you know."

"Wow," I said. So Kane had been there. Had he dropped in to see Vic? Before Serena had? Before Archie and Arly? Or afterwards? Maybe he said something to Vic after everyone else had left—something so awful it stopped the older man's heart. But he had been there. That was important, wasn't it?

"I'm glad you remembered, Serena," I said.

"So am I. I didn't put David Kane on my list, you see, because he wasn't waiting to go in, like the others seemed to be. My mind must have filed it away in a different place."

"Glad the file came up, anyway. I should go get this other slice to Eddie. See you around, I guess, Serena." She gave me a little wave and picked off another mushroom.

On the way back to the Art Show space, I wondered if David Kane had, in fact, said something to Arly to make her cry. Who knows what? When I'd seen Arly and Vic Watson exchange greetings at the Oxblood Falls the week before, after Vic's near-drowning, Arly hadn't seemed to like her uncle very much at all. So I found it hard to believe that she was weeping in distress at Vic's being ill in hospital. On the other hand, if Kane had said something unkind to her regarding what might, according to rumour, have been their relationship (they did share a picnic together at the falls), wouldn't that have upset her? It would also explain why she seemed to have turned against Kane later. At the Art Show space, she wasn't secretive about her contempt for him. That must be it. An older man seduces a young girl and then dumps her. Old story, and none of my business, except to confirm that Kane was a decidedly yucky guy.

When I got to the Weird Kuskawa Art Show, Eddie was gone.

"Arly came in just about twenty minutes ago with David

Kane, and they took Eddie away with them," Yolanda said. "Arly said she needed him to help set up this photograph she was going to do of Kane at Watson's."

"At Watson's? Is she nuts? Her father won't let Kane in there," I said.

"The store's closed today, Polly," Dimmy said. "And whatever Arly said at the awards about her father not being a drinker, I certainly saw Archie in the Slug and Lettuce, drowning his sorrows. It sure looked like beer to me."

"Arly said the photo was going to make Cal's shot at the council meeting look like amateur night," Yolanda said. "Kane was all for it. I think he might be on something, you know. Very manic guy."

"I thought Arly couldn't stand Kane," I said, thoroughly confused.

"Sure didn't look like that to me," Yolanda said. "They were all over each other."

"Yuck. And Eddie went, just like that? I have a slice of pizza for him."

"He said he'd be back in a few minutes," Yolanda said. "He said something about getting a cheque."

"Oh, yeah. He has to hang around, I guess, to make sure Kane pays him. I wonder if it was worth it."

"Maybe next year he can race without being anonymous," Yolanda said. "And he seems excited about the car."

"I guess." I suddenly thought about Susan, and how on earth Eddie was planning to explain his sudden increase in wealth. A lottery win, maybe? Then all thoughts of Eddie were crowded out of my brain, because Detective Constable Mark Becker walked in, followed by Constable Marie Lefevbre.

They were both in uniform, and they looked pretty serious. I found I was having a hard time looking at Becker, so I shifted my gaze to Lefevbre instead. She smiled pleasantly at me and nodded. We had, after all, met before. I don't know where I'd got the impression that she was so drop-dead gorgeous. She was actually rather plain and looked like a nice person.

"Is David Kane here?" Becker said. "We were told he came in the back door here a while back."

"They came in about half an hour ago," I said. "Why?"

"Who's they?" Becker said.

"David Kane and Arly Watson," I said. Becker exchanged a significant glance with his partner.

"Do you know where they went?"

"Maybe. Why are you looking for him?" I said. Yolanda and Dimmy had retreated towards the back of the store, perhaps sensing that I wanted to deal with this alone.

"Polly," Becker said, a warning note in his voice.

"No, it's a fair question," Lefevbre said. "She knows what's going on, doesn't she?"

"Jeez, Marie, will you let me handle this?" Becker said.

"You seem to be antagonizing the witness, actually," she said, lightly.

"Witness?" I said.

"Whatever," Lefevbre said. "Listen, Ms. Deacon. The lab report that we got on Vic Watson indicates that he had a heart attack following a massive rush of adrenaline—you know that, right?"

"I heard. So you think David Kane, who was seen at the hospital, said something to him to upset him enough to kill him, right?"

"You have proof he was there?" Becker said.

"Yes, I do, Becker. So, constable?" I said to Lefevbre.

"So, it wasn't just adrenaline. It was epinephrine. The active ingredient in a thing called an epi-pen, used for people who

279

have anaphylactic reactions to things they're allergic to."

"Oh, my God," I said. "An epi-pen. David Kane is allergic to wasp and bee stings. He carried one everywhere."

"That's what we wanted," Lefevbre said, turning in triumph to Becker. "I told you she'd know."

"You have a reputation as a snoop and a know-it-all," she said to me. "No offence, but Morrison said to tell you about it. He said you'd connect it with something."

Becker was getting red in the face. "Hello," he said. "Remember me? Your partner? Your fellow police officer?"

"What?" Lefevbre said. "Oh, go ahead, then."

"Polly, where the hell did they go?" he said.

"Oh, Lord," I said, suddenly remembering Kane's red eyes. "He's got Arly and Eddie. He's high on something, and if he injected Vic Watson with epi-whatchamacallit, he's capable of anything. They both know things he doesn't want people to know. We've got to go to Watson's right NOW!"

Thirty-Two

"*I never met a pickle I didn't like.*" —*Mae West*
Itching for a gherkin? Don't be shy. Check out our Pickles 'n Preserves section, with more international brands than you can shake a...pickle at!
—An ad in the *Laingford Gazette*

Watson's General Store was dark inside when we got there. David Kane's Mercedes was the only car in the small parking lot to the side. I had jumped in the back of the cruiser, against Becker's wishes, but with Lefevbre's blessing. Becker had torn up Main Street with the lights flashing and the siren going, which would have been fun if I had been thinking about that. But all I could think of was David Kane with his hands around Eddie's throat, or Arly's.

By the time we were out of the cruiser, the teeming Bath Tub Bash crowds were starting to converge on the store, attracted by the flashing lights, gawking like they were watching a film shoot.

"Okay now, Polly, you stay here," Becker said.

"As if," I said and sprinted for the front door. It was locked, and I peered through the front window into the gloom. Someone was sitting motionless on the stool at the cash register. Further inside, I could just see a pair of black and white, fuzzy-fur legs, poking out from one of the aisles.

281

"Oh my God. Eddie!" I said.

"That the boy you said was with them?" Lefevbre said. "Those legs on the floor?"

"I don't know. Oh, please, get the door open. Hurry!" Lefevbre banged on the door, trying to get the attention of the figure on the stool. The figure remained motionless.

"Jesus," she whispered. "It looks just like Selma Watson, come back to life."

"Who?"

"Selma Watson. The old lady who used to run this place when I was a kid. She always sat behind the counter, just like that. Gave us free gumballs. Hey!" she shouted suddenly. "Hey, open up!"

Around the back, we heard a cracking of wood. Becker, I presumed, doing the unlawful-police-entry thing. There was a pause, then we heard the thump of rapidly approaching feet. He let us in, twisting the old-fashioned lock on the heavy glass-and-brass door, and then turning back to the figure on the stool. It was Arly, and she still hadn't moved.

I didn't care about Arly. "Eddie!" I yelled and ran to the figure in the cow costume sprawled in the grocery aisle. I slipped and fell almost at once. There were broken jars everywhere, pickles and artichokes, I think. I put my hand down on some glass, felt a sharp pain in the ball of my thumb and caught a whiff of vinegar. I had to get to Kountry Kow, motionless among the wreckage. What the hell had happened here?

"Polly, I'm here," a voice said. In a corner, beyond the still figure of Kountry Kow, Eddie Schreier sat huddled on the ground, his arms around his knees. "I'm okay, Polly." I stood carefully and made my way over to him. As I passed the mascot, I smelled the sour, unmistakable odour of shit. At the end of the aisle, set up on a tripod, was a camera, aimed down towards the cash register.

"Kane?" I said, gesturing to the mascot. Eddie nodded.

"He died so fast," Eddie said. "It was like in fast motion. And Arly was grabbing on to me so I couldn't get to him in time, and he was thrashing around and sort of whimpering, and I swear I could hear his throat closing up."

"Do you know how he died?" Lefevbre said. She was standing behind us, listening. I was on the ground, now, hugging Eddie. He nodded, trying not to cry.

"He was stung. You know, like I was this afternoon, Polly. That was what she called a trial run. A hornet in the puppet head. Arly told me. She was whispering in my ear the whole time. Her voice was sort of sticky. It was awful."

"She set this thing up?" I said. "The photo op at David Kane's rival's store. He'd go for something like that. Convinced him to put the head on for the shot, right?"

"I helped put the head on," Eddie said. "Does that make me guilty, too?"

"No, Eddie. Don't worry about it," Lefevbre said. "Come on, now, let's get you out of here."

Becker was sitting next to Arly, writing down everything she was telling him. She was talking in a dull, sing-song voice, as if reciting a poem, or a piece of history.

"I saw David Kane push Uncle Vic over the falls, but he wouldn't tell me why he did that. I pretended to like him, because it was the only way to get close enough to find out. Then at the hospital, he told me that Uncle Vic was a partner in the Kountry Pantree, but he wanted more money because of some voting thing. I knew about the property from some guy at the library. You see, Uncle Vic was a traitor. I was so mad I cried. Uncle Vic was going to ruin Dad's store. He betrayed us. So I spiked him with my epi. I knew it would work. I looked it up on the Net.

"I didn't want to kill that other traitor in here," Arly went on. "The river would have been better. In front of everybody. I had a hornet in the cow head, but then Eddie was going to be the cow so I had to change it. But I should have left it there, because Eddie won the race. Dad was so sad. So sad."

"You know what's the weirdest part?" she said, suddenly looking up and straight into my eyes. I froze.

"What?" I said.

"How easy it was to make David Kane believe that I was a traitor, too. He just accepted that I hated my dad and wanted to go work for his stupid big store. That I wanted to betray Dad and everything he's worked for all his life, just to get a few dollars more an hour. He just believed that I was a bad person, because he was one. That's what's weird."

EPILOGUE

The aftermath was curiously quiet. Because Arly was a young offender, her name never made it into the *Laingford Gazette*. She was charged with the murders, but she wasn't tried as an adult, in spite of the Toronto Kanes putting a heckuva lot of pressure on the Powers That Be. It was suggested that her uncle Victor Watson had molested her at some point, and that Kane had messed with her as well, which got the child abuse people on her side, although I never heard the details. She got sentenced to a couple of years in a juvenile detention centre, but she'll be out soon enough, and I heard she got pre-accepted at art school. *MacLean's* magazine did a feature on her a while ago—the "Incarcerated Artist" type-thing. They used a fake name and put one of those black-out things over her eyes in the pictures of her doing sculpture in her cell, but everyone knows who she is. Her stuff is fetching big bucks now. I bought the male figure with the Christmas ornament genitalia myself. It's a nice piece.

The Kountry Pantree opened on schedule, with a nice parade and a free community picnic. Kountry Kow, however, having been stained rather nastily by its final animator, was tossed. I did get paid for it, though. I gave the bucks to Eddie, to help pay for his new car.

You will not be surprised to learn that nothing ever came of the Ontario Municipal Board inquiry into Laingford Council wrongdoing. Mayor Lunenberg is, as far as I know, still acting on behalf of the numbered corporation that runs the place. The beachside playground at Kountry Pantree went ahead and the pike, as far as we know, are spawning elsewhere.

The League for Social Justice disbanded after numerous attempts to be heard. Susan was particularly devastated by Eddie's involvement with Kountry Pantree, though I don't think she ever actually confronted him about it. She never shops there, though. Eddie still works at Watson's and has become quite a close friend of Archie, who seems to let him run the place. Archie is said to be back at AA meetings again.

Brent Miller moved in with Rico, and they're both trying to get the local United Church to recognize their partnership by legally marrying them. More on that next time.

After Arly Watson said what she did, I got to thinking about betrayal. Everything she did, I believe, was based on a kind of skewed sense of loyalty. But at least she was loyal. A couple of days after the Bath Tub Bash, when I was clearing up my worktable, I came across those notebooks from the Secret Stealing Club, and all of a sudden I remembered, like Serena, what my mind had filed away safely in a box marked "Do Not Open."

Gaby and I had been operating our club for a month or two. I was helping my Mom bake bread one day when there was a knock at the door. My mother opened it, and Mr. Murchison, the school principal, was standing there. Gaby was standing beside him, as pale as candle wax. I knew immediately what was going on. Mr. Murchison said that Gaby had been caught shoplifting, and that she had confessed everything, told about the club, and about me. I was so mad I could hardly stand up. What did I do? I denied everything. I called Gaby a lying, dirty thief and, being a fine actress, pulled it off. At least I think I did. That was why Gaby's book stopped suddenly. I carried on for a while longer, out of defiance, probably, then hid the books at Emma Tempest's store. But I will never forget the look on Gaby's face when I betrayed her. Never.

I guess, if I am looking for a place or a time when I first became a person without integrity, I'll have to go back to before I was ten.

You might be wondering about the Becker thing. Hah. Me, too. His ex-wife, Catherine, came back early from Calgary because she was offered a job there and had come back to pack. The rumours about her and Duke Pitblado were just rumours, I guess. Who cares? Anyway, she took Bryan with her. I saw him briefly, just after the Watson case. He offered to do me a website again, and I declined. Then I showed him Sophie Durette's photograph, the red blur at the top of the falls.

"I tried to tell you in that picture I did at your place," Bryan said. "I saw a guy at the top of the falls, and, well, I mooned him. I never mooned anybody before. Then I looked and there were two of them, then the red guy pushed the other guy over." The "red guy"—Kane in a red sweatshirt—had threatened the kid at the picnic, just before taking Arly off for champagne and caviar. "He told me I could get arrested for what I did," Bryan said. "I was scared to tell Dad." No kidding. I would've been, too. Cop's kids don't moon people.

Becker now flies out occasionally to see him, and they exchange e-mail. Bryan often writes "Say hi to Polly," which is sweet of him.

I still have Becker's ring, and I still haven't given him an answer to his question. The day after David Kane's death, we had a long talk, and we agreed to work for a little longer with what we have. I did a lot of apologizing, and he did, too, although I think I had more to apologize for than he did.

My disinterest in beer did not go away, but my interest in Kahlua did, about a week after the Bath Tub Bash. Then one day I lit a cigarette, put it out, and dumped the whole thing, ashtray and all, into the garbage. Next it was dope. Then I developed a peculiar, unprecedented appetite for perogies and sauerkraut and had to admit that something was up. I pulled Robin's "second opinion" package off the bathroom shelf, did the test, and the stupid, wretched stick turned bright blue.

I haven't told Becker yet, but I'm going to have to mention it soon, because my army fatigues are starting to feel distinctly uncomfortable.

H. Mel Malton was born in England and emigrated with her family to Canada in the 1960s. Mel has worked as a government forms designer, actress, stage manager, newspaper reporter, waitress, receptionist, a clerk in a candy store, a singing teacher and a church secretary. None of these jobs has harmed her.

Mel's crime stories have appeared in the anthologies *Menopause is Murder* and *Fit to Die* (RendezVous Crime, 2001). Her first Polly Deacon mystery, *Down in the Dumps* (1998), was short-listed for an Arthur Ellis Award for Best First Crime Novel. The second, *Cue the Dead Guy*, was published in 1999. She currently lives in a log cabin in Huntsville, Ontario, on ten acres of swampland with her two dogs, Karma and Ego.

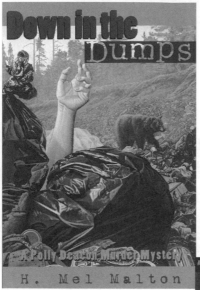